She's the unlikely wallflower of the extraordinary Shaw family. A woman who will never marry, but not for the reasons you might think . . .

Attacked on the streets of London, Lady Livia Shaw is relieved when a gentleman comes to her aid—and startled to discover her rescuer is Adrian, the Duke of Preston, a notorious rogue. But their association—and instant attraction—does not end there, much to the Shaws' distress. For Livia was robbed of a memento—one that is both her most precious possession and a reminder of a shameful secret. It is a secret she knows will cause her to lose Adrian forever, yet he is determined to track down the thief . . .

Adrian never wanted to be anyone's hero, but now he's finding the prospect as pleasing as he does Livia's company, and her beauty. Certainly he wants her in his bed, but what surprises him is how much she comes to mean to him. Which is why the revelation of her scandalous past is nearly his undoing. Arrogantly, he had assumed only he had the power to shock. But it is too late to turn back, and now Adrian may have to risk everything for Livia, even his heart . . .

Visit us at www.kensingtonbooks.com

Books by Lynne Connolly

The Shaw Series
Fearless
Sinless
Dauntless
Boundless

The Emperors of London Series
Rogue in Red Velvet
Temptation Has Green Eyes
Danger Wears White
Reckless In Pink
Dilemma in Yellow Silk
Veiled In Blue
Wild Lavender

Published by Kensington Publishing Corporation

Boundless

The Shaws

Lynne Connolly

LYRICAL PRESS
Kensington Publishing Corp.
www.kensingtonbooks.com

LYRICAL PRESS BOOKS are published by
Kensington Publishing Corp.
119 West 40th Street
New York, NY 10018

First Electronic Edition: December 2018
ISBN-13: 978-1-5161-0879-4
ISBN-10: 1-5161-0879-5

First Print Edition: December 2018
ISBN-13: 978-1-5161-0880-0
ISBN-10: 1-5161-0880-9

Printed in the United States of America

To my lovely daughter, Cat, who is finally old enough to read this!

Author's Foreword

So we come to the last story about the Shaw family. With Livia's book, I either have to leave them to their happy endings, or go on to the next generation. I doubt they'll disappear altogether though. I lift a glass to Marcus, Val, Darius, Drusilla, Claudia, and Livia. Thank you for all the fun I've had discovering your stories.

Chapter 1

Adrian slumped against the squabs of the hackney cab as it set off from his house in King Street. Correction—Ophelia's King Street house. He'd already had the deeds put in her name, but she'd generously given him another day to quit the premises.

In the shadows of the vehicle, he grinned. A house was a small price to pay to rid himself of the exquisite, grasping, tediously mundane person Ophelia d'Arblay had turned out to be. Every man in London wanted Ophelia for his mistress. Well, she was back on the market and they were all welcome to her.

With a groan, he stretched his limbs. After a tough all-night session in the House of Lords, he'd repaired here to find Ophelia entertaining one of the few peers not in Parliament that evening. Truly, he should have guessed she was seeing someone on the sly. But what had surprised him the most was his inability to care. Her subsequent spectacular tantrum merely bored him. It did not move him. She had broken his one and only rule, and she must suffer the consequences.

Exhausted, he looked forward to falling into his own bed and leaving the day behind.

A movement ahead caught his attention. A woman stood at the edge of the road, her gown a flash of bright blue, while children scurried like rats around her. One skinny youth had his mouth open, laughing, catching her attention while the other—Adrian spied trouble. And where trouble lurked, so did he.

Grabbing his cane, he rapped the roof of the carriage. "Stop! Stop now!"

Before the driver had managed to haul the nag to a halt, Adrian had opened the door and leaped into the street. Turning only to toss a shilling to the driver, who caught it deftly, pocketed it and gave his horse the office to continue in one smooth move, Adrian faced the trouble.

That blue silk belonged to a lady, although the gown had become sadly smeared with mud and torn in her efforts to escape her tormentors. Her face was obscured by the broad brim of her bergère hat, its pink ribbons askew and the jaunty bow on top crushed. For all that, this was a lady. The gown was good, the skirts too wide for this part of London, and her linen fine, the nearly sheer veil over her tantalizing bosom hinting at the pink flesh beneath. Despite his recent disappointment, Adrian's mouth watered.

All this he absorbed as he headed at speed for the unfortunate woman beset by street urchins. He kept his attention on her while he struck out with his cane, lashing right and left, ignoring the ensuing yelps and protests.

The woman whirled right into him, and Adrian found himself with an armful of warmth and silk. That made wielding his cane trickier. Rolling the woman to the left, he looped his arm around her waist and used his right hand to advantage. Battle heated his veins, sending a fire coursing around his body and rousing him from his ennui. He had not felt this alive for a long time. Although he was only one man against six urchins who had learned to fight on the streets, he made a good account of himself. The trouble was, they kept coming at him from different directions. Catching one importunate boy a crack across his shoulders appeared to deter them. All but one, who darted around the other side of the female before shrieking. A wordless yell meant to deflect, if Adrian knew anything about it.

The one in front crashed into her and a sickening crack rent the air. Not from him, but he couldn't stop to check her. He tightened his hold and dealt the boy a telling blow to the side of his head with his cane. The responding yelp warmed his heart.

"Let me go! You can't fight like this."

She was right. Her voluminous skirts and the cloak around her shoulders hampered him. He snapped, "Don't go out of my sight," before releasing her. He settled in to the rhythm of the fight. Fully awake now, all trace of tiredness gone, Adrian swung his cane, wielding it more like a club than a delicate fashion accessory. Sooner or later it would break, and then he'd have to resort to his fists.

He looked forward to it.

"Come on then, you cowards!" he yelled as one of the assailants ran off, screaming. Crouching into a fighting stance, he stood ready, his cane held before him, waiting for the next attack.

His maiden stood where he'd told her to, the bright blue of her gown a flag of fresh color in this grimy London street. She leaned to one side. Had that crack he'd heard a moment ago been one of her bones? And yet she didn't move and when she bade him release her, she'd sounded steady enough.

As if someone had waved a gun, the boys turned tail and ran, scattering into the alleys feeding the street, like the rats they were.

Adrian straightened up and shook his coat free of dust.

He flicked his gaze over the woman, scanning her disheveled appearance. Clearly she needed help. With the blood of war still thrumming through his veins, he drew a deep breath, savoring the sheer joy of being here, alive and healthy. Why would he not? His relentless pursuit of life led to that wonderful feeling, better than a case of wine, better than the finest French brandy. And for sure better than a night's gambling.

Better than spending a night in his mistress's bed? Perhaps. Not the one he had just discarded, but this one...he might have found his new interest. A well-dressed young woman in this part of London would hardly be the kind he'd meet in the ballrooms of Mayfair.

"They got my purse," she said then. Although her voice was soft, it still trembled. She was more shaken than she cared to tell him.

"Did they take much?"

She shrugged a delicate shoulder. "A few guineas, an ivory comb, a fine linen handkerchief—no, not much."

Aha. Any woman who considered that haul "not much" had recourse to more.

Gallantly, he offered his arm. "You are shaken, madam. May I offer you the hospitality of my house?" At least, it was his house until the morning when the new deeds came into effect. "You may tidy yourself up and recover from your ordeal."

From beneath the broken brim of her hat, she peered at him warily. "You speak like a gentleman."

"And you sound like a lady."

Without warning, she sagged, dipping forward, threatening to fall. Adrian caught her, curving his arm around her waist at the front and tilting her gently back to lean against his shoulder. "Can you walk?" he murmured, his mouth so close to her ear that her curls tickled his skin. She had blonde hair with a hint of red. He'd seen that shade before, but for the life of him he couldn't remember where.

She nodded, lowering her head to rest on his shoulder. If he had to, he'd carry her.

To his relief, when he took a small, slow pace, she came with him. Although her feet dragged, he detected no sign of a stumble, or anything that would indicate she was seriously hurt. If they took it at a snail's pace, they could manage the distance. "The house isn't far, at the end of King Street."

His hackney had almost reached Covent Garden. King Street abutted it. Since his mistress worked as an actress at Drury Lane, in fact was a star of the stage there, she liked the proximity. No doubt she would continue to do so.

"I should not," she murmured.

Shock, he assumed. Tilting up her chin, anticipating the credit his good deed would accomplish, he gazed into her face.

Damn and blast it. He recognized her. He would not be making this woman his mistress, sadly.

But what was Lady Livia Shaw doing in this part of London, and on her own too?

* * * *

She had not wanted to tell her savior, but Livia had suffered a wallop on the head before the man had appeared on the scene. She'd assumed her attacker meant to knock her out, but she had moved aside. Besides, her hat was new, and the stiffening in the straw hard. But he'd still caught her. The blow had made her ears ring and her head spin. Otherwise, she would not have gone anywhere with this stranger.

But he smelled good and he had a gentle touch that soothed her while it interested her. His body was as hard as any of her brothers', comforting to lean on, providing the reliable support she needed. More used to closeness with men than most young, single women, she did not find him inappropriate. She would deal with all that business later. When her head stopped spinning.

But coming here? Lord, what was she thinking?

He had taken her a short distance to a fine house fronting King Street. Respectable people lived here, but not her sort. Perhaps he was married, and he could have servants to help her. Servants gossiped.

Until he closed the door behind them and led her into a front parlor, full awareness had eluded her. However now, as she shook her head and lifted her hands to loosen the bow under her chin, the odd sensation of not-quite-there cleared, and appalled realization sliced through her.

"I cannot thank you enough for your help, sir," she said, trying to quell the tremor in her voice, "but if you would find me a hackney cab or a chair, I'll be on my way."

He stepped closer, taking her hat from her. The brim flopped over his dark hands, the sharp line of the break indicating its uselessness. Gently, he placed it on a nearby chair. He flicked open the clasp that fastened her cloak and let it fall where it would.

Livia turned her head to one side, strangely unwilling to meet his eyes. "Goodness!"

"I'm afraid these walls haven't seen much of that lately," he confessed. "But yes, it is—spectacular."

"You chose this scheme?" If that was the best way to describe her surroundings. Wallpaper red and gold silk vied with mahogany furnishings, their surfaces covered with porcelain figures, decorative plates and glittering candelabra.

"The lady who will own this house chose it. I considered the gift fair exchange for my peace of mind." He touched his lips, drawing her unwilling attention to their inviting fullness. "She has a larger reception room above this one, but I would not advise that you see it. Yesterday it rivalled this room, but now you need sturdy shoes to crunch across the floor."

"Oh! Was there an accident?"

"Only one caused by her fair hands after I presented her with her congé. I did not intend to drive her to cause such destruction. Perhaps the world can use fewer figurines." He picked up a porcelain monkey and turned it, handling the delicate piece so carefully. Livia could feel those fingers drifting across her skin, stroking her into doing his will. Heat spread over her, nothing to do with her recent altercation.

What on earth was she thinking? Her innate good manners came to her rescue. She must keep talking. She could not risk that enforced closeness again. Because she did not have the same response to this man as she did with her brothers. What had he said? Oh yes. "So you had to break bad news to the lady? Pray, where is she?"

"She is gone to the playhouse. She performs there tonight."

Livia's gasp bounced off the walls. "An actress?"

"The actress, as she would no doubt insist. Yes, my lady, Ophelia d'Arblay owns this house. Or will, after I have quit it." He gave Livia a broad smile. "And I could not be happier. By the way, her real name is Fanny Smethurst, but I presume she did not consider it good enough for the stage. I never asked."

The room spun, and she momentarily lost her footing, her knees sagging. He tucked a hand under her elbow, his touch sure, and helped her to a green upholstered chair, lowering her gently into it. Very fine, and also comfortable, but Livia would not have placed it in this room. That was none of her concern. She only needed to recover and leave with as much dignity as she could.

At least the giddiness had stopped, and the brim of her hat no longer drooped in her eyes. Livia tilted her head, surveying the mountain of a man standing before her. His sober clothes and easy demeanor had fooled her. He wasn't even wearing lace at his wrists or around his neck, just plain linen.

Her second gasp sounded just as loud as the last one. "You're the Duke of Preston."

She was eye to eye with the most scandalous peer in London. Olive-skinned, black-eyed, with gleaming black hair tied ruthlessly back from his sensually handsome face, there he was in person. Unmistakable now she could see him properly. He stared back boldly. According to rumor, he avoided respectable women like the plague and ran with the less respectable ones. That explained this house, and why she had not immediately recognized him. He rarely inhabited her part of society.

He bowed mockingly. "The last time I looked, yes. And you are Lady Livia Shaw. Since no one is here to do the honors, we must shift to manage the introductions for ourselves." He grinned.

That smile would make stronger women than Livia faint. It was reported to have done so, but she had always doubted the stories. Until now, that was. Perhaps the smile hadn't caused the hot wash of attraction that swept over her. The attack may have had more serious effects than she had first thought.

So here she was, sitting in the parlor of an actress with the woman's keeper. So scandalous that only a Shaw could survive it. Except Livia wasn't that kind of Shaw. "How did you know I wasn't my twin sister?"

"The possibility never crossed my mind," he said. "Why, are you Lady St. Just? Do I have to meet your husband at dawn?"

"No, though you might have to meet one of my brothers." She grimaced. "Although they should learn to mind their own concerns."

That grin returned. "Ah. I sense irritation."

Turning away, he crossed the room, his tread surprisingly soft for such a large man. Of course, the rugs under his feet would help to cushion the sound. Was there any part of this room not covered in decoration of some kind?

Without asking, he poured two tumblers of brandy and brought them back, placing one for her on the side table at her elbow. "Drink it," he advised. "It will help you to recover from the shock. Were you hurt at all?"

"A small knock to the side of my head," she confessed, still stunned by her discovery of his identity.

Immediately he was by her side, touching her head. "Hold still," he ordered. "And get rid of that linen cap."

She'd kept her clothing plain today, knowing where she was going, so her cap was the kind maids wore, enveloping most of her hair and with pin-tucking rather than expensive lace. The ribbon under her chin had tightened into a thin string, and the bow was no more. "It's in a knot. It needs cutting."

With a curse, he dived a hand into his pocket and came out with a small, but wicked-looking knife. "Hold still." His teeth flashed in a feral grin, but perhaps he meant it as reassuring. Letting a man she barely knew hold a knife anywhere near her throat was a new experience and not one she was keen to allow. But she had no choice.

Coming around to the front, he went down on one knee, a graceful gesture. Purely for practical purposes, of course. Livia swallowed. His eyes really were the most liquid she'd ever seen, such a dark brown they were close to black, but with little specks of gold near the center. That must be why they looked as if they were flashing when he turned his head. He had full lips, their coral pink a delightful contrast against his bronzed skin, which was so soft and velvety she wanted to touch it, to discover if the sheen on his skin was real or if she was imagining it. The brandy he'd just drunk added sweetness and a tang to his breath.

Lowering his heavily-lashed eyelids, he concentrated on his self-imposed task, as if his life depended on getting it exactly right. His chest moved with his breathing, regular and deep. Something glittered when he moved, a diamond pin stuck deep in the folds of his neckcloth. Not so plainly dressed, then.

The tiny snick when he slit the cord sounded loud in the quiet room. Despite the constant sounds of passing traffic and the tread and chat of passers-by outside, they seemed to be in a space of their own, untouchable and disregarded.

"There." He lifted his eyes and met her gaze.

Staring so deeply into the eyes of this meltingly attractive man was probably a bad idea, but Livia didn't care. When would she get the opportunity again? Despite his appalling reputation and the scorn he evinced for society and everyone in it, she caught sight of a vulnerability in the depths of his eyes. Not many people had ever seen that. He strode through ballrooms, on the few times he deigned to appear, with supreme arrogance and superior amusement. So many people wanted to bring him down that bets were laid in the coffeehouses on when it would happen.

His lids lowered again and he got to his feet. When he turned back to her, that vulnerability had gone. Perhaps she had imagined it. Well no, she hadn't, but he obviously didn't want her to mention it, so she wouldn't.

Livia had spent much of her life watching, warily waiting for the wrong approach or criticism, and she had grown adept at discovering changes of mood or hidden emotions in people.

The seductive expression was firmly back in place. A suspicion crossed Livia's mind. Did he use that to frighten people off? Obviously it wouldn't work with most men, but perhaps he used something else on them. Although she should not, a powerful urge to hunt out this man's secrets hit Livia. Usually content to let people live their own lives, in this case she wanted to know more.

He returned to her side in a couple of quick steps. "I must touch your head. Is that permitted?"

Too late, he already had, and her skin still bore the imprint of his soft touch. For a rake, he certainly had respect. Because of that, she nodded. "By all means. I don't want to bleed to death because you are too squeamish to look."

Gently he probed her scalp where she'd received the blow. "It's hot."

She flinched and let out a sharp expression of dismay when he hit a tender spot.

"Ah, I see it." He separated her hair at the place. Her neat hair arrangement must be a complete shambles by now. "I won't touch it again. It's a cut and a lump, fairly small, but you will bruise there. If you get a particularly bad headache, or you feel drowsy, let me know. Or anyone who happens to be with you."

Once her older brother Val had tumbled out of a tree in the grounds of their family home. The blow he'd received hadn't knocked him unconscious, but he was not himself again until the next day. Their mother had sat with him until she'd been certain the damage wasn't more serious. She would take heed of his strictures. "I will, I promise."

"Be sure you do. There is a little blood, but it's hardening now. Better leave it until you get home." He smoothed her hair back over the sore patch. The touch calmed her, but he left a trail of interest in his wake, as if her body was reluctant to let him go. "Drink your brandy."

The firm order had her reaching for her glass and swallowing some of the fiery liquid. She'd drunk enough brandy to know a good one when she tasted it. This glowed down her throat, heating and sliding. She took another sip. "Do you enjoy giving orders?"

"In certain circumstances." He walked behind her this time, closer because there was no table on this side. "Your hair is like silk." He said the last words as if giving her the time of day, or some other mundane comment. "It is the most glorious color. You should never hide it away."

He took a seat opposite her, closer than she felt comfortable with. To be honest, if he'd sat in another room he'd probably be too close for her liking. Considering her scarecrow appearance, he should not be looking at her as if she were a delectable morsel for him to consume.

He'd probably gobble her up and walk away, hardly noticing the snack.

"I don't usually, but the color brands me." For some reason his offhand compliment affected Livia far more than the more fulsome praise of society beaux. "I needed the cap and the hat in this area."

He frowned, his black eyebrows almost coming together. "What were you doing on your own in the street? Where is your maid, where are the footmen you no doubt have?"

She glanced away, not willing to tell him or anybody else why she'd shot out into the street. "I intended to stay at the orphanage, but I wanted some air, so I left early. Mama is sending the carriage for me."

"What orphanage?"

"The one on Brownlow Street."

"Wait here." He got to his feet and left the room. A moment later a door slammed somewhere below, and voices carried to her, one male, one female. The door banged again, and the sound of feet on stone stairs reached her. He returned. "I've sent the maid to let them know where you are. Otherwise I daresay they'll set up a hue and cry for you." Smiling grimly, he added, "Let's pray your servants are discreet."

"They'll tell my mother."

"Not your father?"

"Him as well." When she got home, there'd be hell to pay. Here she was, in the house of a mistress of a notorious rake. That was enough to have her denied access to every ballroom in London.

Retaking his seat, he propped his elbow on the arm of his chair and leaned his cheek on his hand, regarding her closely. Livia felt like a specimen in a jar, thoroughly inspected and found wanting. "Better they know where you are than they set up a search for you."

She shuddered, clutching her upper arms. "Yes indeed." As it was, she'd have to bribe the coachman heavily. Her maid she could trust. Finch had much to lose if Livia dismissed her, far more than the money a piece of gossip could acquire.

"What were you doing at the orphanage?"

She curled her fingers around her chair as she gave him a partial answer. "Trying to help. Since I'm destined to become an old maid, I might as well be a useful one." Last year she had faced that reality. He could accept that, surely. A spinster turned philanthropist. London contained many of those.

To her shock, he burst into laughter. "You? Why would you think that? Your dowry must be substantial, and your physical attractions are obvious." Lazily he let his gaze wander over her, not at all constrained by societal expectations.

Or hers. Nevertheless, warmth at his evident appreciation spread through her body, heightening her awareness of the parts of her she rarely considered, except to clean them and ensure they were well tucked away from view. She should be offended, affronted, but although she waited for it to happen, the emotion refused to arrive.

With his shot of laughter rocketing off the walls, she lifted her chin and lowered her eyelids, in a way guaranteed to quell the most importunate of her suitors. But he was a duke, and he was not a suitor. He met her expression with amusement. "You're rallying. Good. A perfectly scandalous situation is averted."

Her sharp laugh made him sit up, and his eyes widen. "You think my family members are strangers to scandal? Do you know nothing about the Shaws?"

Livia braced herself, ready for the prying questions. People always asked them things they wanted confirming. The truth about the Shaws was scandalous enough, and she had sketched the bare facts to him, but people loved to embroider on it, and invent even more outrageous stories. They generally ignored them loftily.

He shrugged. "Tell me. Let me see if I can overtop it."

A person could find affinity in the strangest of places. "Since you insist, I'll tell you. Scandal has followed my family like an unwanted guest. My brother Marcus married the daughter of our land steward. My brother Val was on the town for years. He fought duels, gambled a fortune away and won several more back. His twin, Darius, well, you probably know about him, although society has chosen to turn a blind eye to his passions." Notably the lawyer Andrew Graham, who Darius was sharing a house with. And a bed, although they tried to be discreet.

"My twin sister, Claudia, met her husband in a brothel that she owned. My other sister Drusilla wrote a book that lampooned most of the prominent members of society. Do you want more? My cousin Max, who married a woman from the City? My cousin Julius who is married to a lady who was once a governess and the daughter of a village vicar? Or my cousin Alex, who married a woman he met in one of the most notorious brothels in Covent Garden?" She glared at him, daring him to comment.

A chuckle began low in his throat, a rumble that spread before he suppressed it. Only then did she hang her head in shame. She had carelessly revealed secrets her family had worked hard to conceal. The bit about Alex, for instance. She wasn't even supposed to know that. And Claudia's exploits, her own twin. Of course, she could do what everyone in her family did, and blithely ignore any rumors, or counter them with others. Or lie. That worked too, though only as a last resort, because, as her brother Marcus said, holding the truth of a lie was very difficult. "Don't worry. I won't tell anyone a thing or reveal that you just confirmed what many people suspected already."

"Suspicion is one thing. If they grow bored, or if something even juicier comes along, they'll forget it."

He waved his hand carelessly. "I have scandals of my own."

Too late, she remembered his wife, for the duke was a widower. The late duchess had created her own share of scandal, but Livia had never paid much heed. "I'm sorry about your duchess."

"Oh, yes." He swallowed but showed no other signs of the grief he had displayed at her death. Probably he'd learned to control his emotions. At the time, five years ago, stories hurtled around the country that he had destroyed the contents of his house. Much, she assumed, as his mistress had destroyed the room upstairs. "She was astonishingly beautiful."

Livia nodded. "I saw her once. We did not move in the same circles." That sounded bad, but it was true. The Gradfields were country gentry, but their daughters had been lovely enough to outclass all the other girls who'd made their come-out that year. Anna had been a treasure, a beauty beyond compare. Deep bosomed, with a head of dark, gleaming hair, a pair of fine blue eyes, straight nose, and rosebud mouth.

The duke and Anna Gradfield were a perfect match, at least that was what people said at the time. Fast, scandalous, even worse than the Emperors, they had spent money as if it was going out of fashion. Society said she would ruin him before they were both thirty. Sadly, or fortunately, considering the way a person viewed these events, she died before she reached that age. And the Duke of Preston was still rich.

Society would have welcomed him for that alone. Except for one thing, the scandal of his birth, and the risk any woman took in marrying him.

His mouth twisted. "Indeed, you did not."

She glanced down at her hands, which had twisted themselves together. "They did hurt you," he said gravely. "I am sorry for that."

And yet society did not mark him as a man of chivalry. He had certainly acted as her savior. She wouldn't like to be at the wrong end of those fists. Or that cane. "You carry a sturdy weapon."

"The cane is probably beyond repair. But it was worth it." A thin smile curved his mouth.

Livia enjoyed that smile. She could spend time winning it from him, except, she reminded herself once more, she would never see him again. "You were my savior." Imitating the more demonstrative of her peers, she pressed a hand over her heart and fluttered her eyelashes. If she'd had a fan, she'd have wafted it, or hid behind it. But that had gone with her pocket.

In the mêlée, someone had lifted her skirts and cut the cord that she used to tie her pocket around her waist. The thought made her shudder, of someone she didn't know touching her so intimately, bearing a knife.

The duke waved his hand, curling it in an elegant circular gesture, reflecting her mocking gesture. "You are entirely welcome, my lady. So riddle me this. Why did you leave the orphanage early? Come, my dear, truth now."

Turning her head, she winced when the sore part caught the wing of the chair. "Because," she said steadily, not meeting his eyes, "the place appalled and frightened me in equal measure. Since it is likely that I will never have children of my own"—she swallowed, hiding the sorrow that always flooded her when she reminded herself—"I thought I would help those less fortunate than myself. I wanted to see what I could do. Some ladies take lessons at these places, help the girls in particular to read, write, and learn a skill other than the life many are headed for."

She glanced around. "Not many ascend to these heights." For his mistress was one such, had dragged herself up from the stinking streets. "But they clustered around me and they all spoke at once, and oh, you will think me a superficial fool, but they smelled. The whole place stank. Cabbage and sweat and damp, a noxious mixture. I suppose I could have accustomed myself to that, but not the children. So I left early. The carriage was to pick me up, and I asked the driver to give me two hours. But those thieves attacked me."

He didn't speak immediately, but his expression turned hard. His mouth flattened and his eyes became as sympathetic as hard, black pebbles caught in the backwash of a tide going out. "So the lady bountiful discovered that life is not all sweetness did she?"

Damn, she sounded like the worst kind of spoiled society miss. But she could not tell him the real reason she'd shot out of that place as if the hounds of hell were after her. She could still taste the panic and the sheer, pounding horror as she'd run her finger down the page of the admissions book and discovered—nothing.

Where was that blasted carriage?

As if she'd willed it into existence a shadow fell over the small parlor as the traveling carriage rattled over the cobbles and drew to a halt. Hastily, Livia got to her feet as the footman, thankfully not in livery but definitely one of her family's, rapped smartly on the door.

Preston was already on his feet, crossing to the door and opening it for her. As she passed through, a maid was gawping at her, mouth open. "Sir, I thought…"

"No," the duke said firmly. "And you did not see this lady, Jane."

The maid, a disheveled little thing that Livia's mother would not have allowed upstairs, bobbed a curtsy. "No, sir."

Livia did her best to ignore Preston's wink. "You may go now, Jane. I'll see to the lady."

"Yes, sir." The girl scuttled off downstairs and a door slammed far below.

"I'll keep her happy," he said, obviously meaning a few coins.

Before she could curb her tongue, Livia said, "I'm sure you will."

Oh no, oh damn and blast. She shouldn't have said that. London society considered this man dangerous and scandalous. The Shaws had earned their reputations. This man was a scandal all on his own. Riling him was not wise, from the stories she'd heard.

Still, what harm could one tart retort do? She would likely never see him again. He didn't frequent the same ballrooms, or any, come to that, or the same social circles.

When he opened the front door air and light flooded in, giving respite from the small, cramped house and all its contents.

Stepping outside, she smiled at the footmen, feeling on firmer ground for the first time in hours. She turned to face the duke with a smile. "Aren't you worried that people will gossip?"

"Why should I care?" Putting his hands on her shoulders, he swung her to face him.

Astonished, she stared up at him, eyes open wide, lips parted. He gazed back down at her, a wicked gleam in his black eyes. Since she'd entered the house he'd seemed like a sensible man but not now. The recklessness he was famed for came out to play and Livia tried to recoil. But he held her firm. She hadn't seen that expression before, as if something inside him had come to life. His personal devil, perhaps.

Livia's heart pounded double time and she had to take a deep breath merely to regain her balance. That fierce stare held her completely. Until he pulled her closer, dragging her against his chest, his arms clamping around her like iron bands.

His mouth came down on hers.

Livia had been kissed before, at least she'd thought she had. But never like this. Never with a ruthless efficiency she couldn't fight. His lips melded to hers until she forgot who she was, where she was. Nothing else mattered, nothing outside the circle of his arms.

He crushed her body against his, her breasts slammed against his chest, swelling above so she was in danger of popping out of her corset. If he touched her there, she'd be lost. But that didn't stop her wanting him to.

Heat poured through her, tingles attacked every part of her body, particularly her groin and thighs, but he held her tightly, so she wouldn't collapse like half a pound of melted butter at his feet.

When he thrust his tongue into her mouth she was no longer sure about the collapsing part. Maybe she was melting already; she had certainly heated to boiling point. Surely kissing shouldn't be like this.

She sucked him in, greedily claimed his tongue as he explored every part of her mouth, demanding everything she could give.

She did her best. Spearing her fingers into the hot silk of his hair, she found the soft, velvet ribbon confining it, and ruthlessly pulled it free. A curl of her own locks tumbled down and tickled her cheek. If she could have spoken, she'd have begged him to take her back inside and find a convenient surface.

With a muffled moan, he dragged his lips away from hers. Whimpering, she reached up, went on tiptoe to find that bliss once more, until her whirling thoughts slowed and she blinked.

"There she is," he murmured. "I see you now." A self-satisfied smile curled his reddened lips. She'd done that. She'd made that difference. No doubt her mouth was in the same state.

A shudder of horror froze her where she stood. He released her with one arm, using his freed hand to tuck the curl behind her ear with exaggerated care. Even his light touch sent sensual shivers down her spine.

This would not do at all.

"I am perfectly able to stand by myself." Her usual hauteur, the frigid politeness she used when she wanted to depress someone was gone, and her words came out in a breathless rush.

He unwound his arm from her waist, but crooked it and tucked her hand underneath, as if he were used to doing this every day. He leaned closer. Still her senses reached for him, even though she knew she could have sealed her own doom by responding in the way she had.

They were standing in the street now, curious passers-by blatantly staring as they passed. How much had they seen? Had they recognized her?

What in God's name had come over her?

His breath tickled her ear. "My lady, now you have been marked—by me. So how many of your friends and acquaintances will hear that you were standing in the street kissing the Blackamoor Duke? Think of that in your lonely bed tonight." He raised a brow. "You should know better than to leave a place early, however smelly or demanding the children are. Worse fates await you, as I have just demonstrated."

With an elegant gesture that had more force than it appeared, he handed her up the steps and into her carriage.

He touched his lips to the back of it. "I thank you for a pleasant hour, Lady Livia," he said in a voice loud enough to be heard in Mayfair. Or so it seemed to Livia, now sitting rigidly upright in the carriage, staring straight ahead, as near to the cut direct as she could manage in the circumstances. "Please call again whenever you wish."

The footman slammed the door and the coachman immediately whipped up the horses, obviously keen to be gone.

The Duke of Preston was a scandal. He didn't have to do anything. He was the product, society claimed, of his mother and her blackamoor page. Neither he nor his grandfather, the previous duke, had denied it, so by now society accepted it as fact. He was a walking scandal. If he had gone into the church and become a pattern-card of respectability, he'd have been a scandal. Not surprisingly he'd chosen to go the other way. But she could not afford to be seen with him, and he'd deliberately provoked gossip.

Only when she had nearly reached the sanctity of home did Livia realize her precious brooch was gone. Her stomach plummeted, and she felt sick. She couldn't have lost it.

She always wore it. In her chamber she'd asked her maid to help her to strip, then dismissed Finch and meticulously searched every garment. Nothing.

Livia sat on her bed, stark naked, in a sea of silk, lace and linen, staring into space. It was gone. The last link she had with the secret that had haunted her for ten years.

Perhaps losing the brooch had been nature's way of telling her to give up the search. That orphanage held no record of what she searched for, even though she'd asked to see the registers. She'd scoured them. Nothing.

Hardly able to bear the disappointment, Livia had reeled into the street— and a swarm of children had attacked her, looking for rich, easy pickings.

They'd found them. Not only taking her purse, which she didn't mind at all, but the brooch, which she cared about more than anything else.

Unless, by some miracle, she'd dropped it in the Duke of Preston's house. She'd seen the disgust in his eyes when he'd taken his revenge in that devastating kiss. Despite that, she would have to approach him, ask him if he'd found it.

Losing it didn't bear thinking about. It held her only memento of that terrible time. She had to get it back.

Chapter 2

"Whatever have you done?" Lady Strenshall demanded of her only unmarried daughter.

Livia started guiltily. "In what way, Mama?"

Livia and her parents sat at the sadly reduced breakfast table, its once considerable size shrunk from a majestic oval to a mere circle. The maid serving them had disppeared. Her mother always preferred breakfast that way. In the past that had given her an opportunity to talk frankly with her family and resolve problems. Now all her chickens had left the nest except for Livia, who consequently had the full force of her attention.

"Don't be disingenuous, child. What on earth got into you?"

The marquess shook his newspaper. "Preston very nearly did."

"John, I'll thank you not to make vulgar remarks at the breakfast table."

"Humph." Her father turned a page.

Reports were flying around town of Lady Livia Shaw being seen kissing his grace the Duke of Preston in the street. Unfortunately she was not wearing a hat, or even a cap, so that red-gold hair was on full display. Livia, correctly attired this morning, sighed. She flicked her lace elbow ruffles, more to avoid her mother's gaze than to adjust the way they fell.

Carefully, her father folded the journal over and met Livia's eyes, his gray gaze filled with compassion. He could be a tartar, but he had a heart of gold. Or rather, soft blancmange, if one approached him the right way. "I'm sure the altercation was of his making."

"Tell anyone you meet that we have no idea where they get their foolish ideas," her mother said. "Livia was nowhere near King Street yesterday."

"That won't work," the marquess said. "It's gone too far for that. What we need is a good, juicy scandal. A real one. Perhaps Princess Amelia can be persuaded to run away with her groom."

Livia thought of the horse-faced, middle-aged princess, and snorted. At least her father could still make her laugh. He chucked her under the chin on his way out. "Cheer up, puss. We've survived worse."

His wife watched him leave the room, a jaded expression gleaming in her eyes and turning down the corners of her mouth. "Maybe we have."

When the marquess had gone, she got to her feet and crossed to the door, ensuring it was securely closed. In this house, servants did not listen outside doors. She returned with a swish of pink silk skirts and gracefully sat next to her daughter. "Now," her ladyship said. She reached for Livia's hand. "You can have nothing to do with the Blackamoor Duke."

She flinched. "Don't call him that. The conditions of his birth are nothing to do with him." The Duke of Preston was supposed to be the son of his mother and her black page. Nobody in the family had denied it, and his darker than usual coloring was a vivid reminder of the story, it was mostly accepted as reality.

"He has done nothing to deny it and everything to perpetuate the scandalous reputation he was born with."

Livia could understand that. "If he'd entered the church and become a pattern-card of respectability people would still have talked."

"Indeed. And one cannot blame the duke. The current duke's grandfather defined the word tyrant. It's no wonder his son ran wild. He was married at sixteen. It's no wonder that when he insisted on an heir, they produced one. Even if the boy was not his father's son."

"Is that certain?"

Her mother shrugged. "They have not denied it. But that cannot matter to us, child. More important is the way this incipient scandal affects *you*. You know why you must avoid any whisper of scandal."

Nobody better. If her transgression became known, she could become a pariah overnight.

"If he'd stayed in the shadows and let you make the short trip to the carriage on your own, nobody would be any the wiser," her mother said.

She nodded sadly. "I know it. All I can assume is that I said something to annoy him, because I saw it in him, a change of mood. Maybe when I disparaged the orphanage and told him that they smelled. I think he was exacting revenge for a careless remark."

Livia bit her lip. "And I have to speak to him again, Mama." She raised her eyes to meet her mother's gaze. "I lost my brooch."

"Oh, my dear!" Lady Strenshall tightened her grip on Livia's hand. "I'm so sorry! Can you tell when you lost it?"

Livia shook her head. "Either the cutpurse took it, or I dropped it in the duke's house. I cannot understand it. It's a tawdry thing, not something a thief would normally go for."

Livia would have given all the jewels she owned for that small gold brooch. It had a transparent back meant to hold precious mementos. It did, and that was the trouble. "It's all I had left. I don't even have that anymore." She tried for a smile but failed miserably. That curl of baby hair set in the back of the brooch was the only memento she had of the son she had borne and lost too soon. Tears pricked her eyes, but she blinked them away.

"Perhaps, my dear, it's time you let go and moved on with your life. It is hard to say it, and harder for you to hear me, but this time—he's gone, my love."

Yes, he'd gone. Visiting the orphanage had been Livia's last attempt to trace her son. Receiving a faint, though promising hint that her nurse had put him there, Livia had rushed to the place and found nothing. For Nurse Sherwood had died before she could return to Derbyshire and tell Livia what she had done with her baby.

If he had died, perhaps she'd have found the task of putting her past behind her easier. But with no definitive answer, the memory of holding that tiny, mewling bundle in her arms for a few precious minutes had ruled the rest of her life since.

"We have been patient, my dear, but please try. For your own sake." Her mother had been a rock Livia could lean on when she most needed it. Even though she had never told her mother the entire truth.

She'd refused to tell anyone who had fathered her child.

If she had, the knowledge would only have caused trouble. If they'd known who had seduced her, her parents wouldn't have rested until they had destroyed the boy and his parents. What good would that have done?

Before she could tell him of her condition, he'd married someone else and run. She didn't entirely blame him. She'd have run too, given the chance.

Livia was still stinging from the celebrations of her nephew's birth three months ago. Having to celebrate it, loving the new baby but having to keep her secret had refreshed all the emotions she'd carefully locked away. After this first child, she would get used to it. She had to. Her mother was right. She couldn't spend all her life sobbing uncontrollably in the safety of her bedroom.

She would take control. Starting now.

"I'll talk to the duke and discover if I lost the brooch in his house."

Lady Strenshall nodded. "If you are seen with the duke in a socially acceptable place, the gossip will turn toward a possible courtship and not a clandestine affair. If we go all hugger-mugger about it, then gossip will multiply. You can ask him about your brooch, and then you may be seen to drop him. We're leaving for the country in a few weeks. Let gossip die a death over Christmas. We don't have to return to London for some time, after all."

She brightened, her blue eyes recovering their sparkle. "Yes, that tactic would work better. A short flirtation, cut off in public."

Leaning back, the marchioness surveyed the garden, watching as a gardener trundled a wheelbarrow across the green space. "We are, after all, an influential family with a reputation every bit as colorful as his. He is but one man. We are legion."

The unexpected quotation startled Livia into laughter.

Her mother patted her hand. "There, my dear. Things are never so bad as they seem."

Livia smiled automatically. But sometimes things were that bad. Sometimes they were worse.

* * * *

In the autumn balls happened less frequently than during the spring. Then Livia could count on at least one every night, frequently more. The pleasure gardens were closed, and not every family of note had chosen to return after the summer. Only the ones wishing to attend Parliament or bored by the country.

Adrian stood on the other side of the street, watching the guests arrive for Lady Crawford's ball, the flames from the torches in their holders that bracketed front door putting the house into a glow. Light blazed bravely from every window, and people swarmed into the hall, handing their heavy outer garments to the footmen.

Tonight the Duke of Preston had decided to attend the ball, but he was in no hurry to rush inside, even though he'd seen his quarry arrive with her parents twenty minutes ago.

He took a few minutes to steel himself and set his mind into the appropriate channels. Every now and again he tested the waters to see if he was acceptable to society, or more than before. He could go to any house in London, and he would find a group of coldly polite people, unwilling to give him the cold shoulder because of his rank, but equally unwilling to allow him into their exclusive club.

Adrian told himself he didn't care. For the most part it was true, but the injustice of the situation struck him from time to time and he would go, ostensibly to taunt, tease and behave badly. However tonight he was on a mission.

Ever since he'd kissed Lady Livia Shaw he'd been unable to shake the memory. He'd woken in the night rigid with desire, his hands already at work on an activity he rarely had to employ. During the day he'd thought of her, and he was mightily annoyed that he continued to do so. A woman he disliked to come up with something as ridiculous as a dislike of orphans because they smelled? He found that attitude hard to forgive.

But he would. On reflection, perhaps the sheer squalor of a place like that had shocked her enough to send her reeling into the street. Gently nurtured, spoiled even, reality would have hit her hard. His revenge, swiftly enacted, might have been a little too much. Or not, depending on what he found tonight. He might forgive her. He might even like her.

Perhaps.

He would brave society's constant opprobrium to discover it.

Striding across the street to the one house illuminated from top to bottom he allowed a smile to touch his lips. He would show them how much of a gentleman he could be, smile in their faces and behave perfectly. He was a man of influence, and worth a fortune, so what did he care?

Except, deep down in a place he barely acknowledged, he did. He was still that little boy trying to kick down the gates forever barred to him. Knowing that only made him more determined to force them to accept him, so that he could spit in their faces farther down the line. Lure them in, then reject them.

The last thing he would admit to was walking through those doors with his heart in his throat. He'd entered gambling dens, thieves' kitchens and coffeehouses thronged with political opponents with more bravery than he experienced now.

That would pass. It always did, the minute he drawled his first insult.

Walking inside and handing his cloak, hat and gloves to a waiting footman took nothing at all. He'd done that any number of times. Even the gasp from his left didn't surprise him, especially since he'd chosen his most flamboyant coat of scarlet figured velvet. He didn't want anyone to miss him. Nodding at the lady who had muted her surprise, he received a glacial acknowledgment.

He couldn't remember being here before, but the house was similar to many owned or leased by the great and the good. His own London residence had a similar arrangement. Stairs swept up to a hallway that led to the public rooms, more stairs up to the bedrooms and private ones, each staircase growing progressively less grand and more domestic. Rooms downstairs led to smaller reception rooms, offices and family rooms. All depressingly familiar. Even the portraits of ancestors ranked up the stairs had a look of jaded cynicism.

He recognized most of the people climbing those stairs too. This time of year, the younger aspirants to society were balanced by their older siblings and family members, a more comfortable mix. Especially for a widower with no children who must be searching for a new wife. Surely he was, they just knew it.

Some were desperate enough to approach him, a man with high rank and wealth, but a reputation few could equal, and none surpassed. That, plus the circumstances of his birth, kept most away. But not all.

Chin high, a supercilious smile firmly in place, he walked up the stairs and into the main room. People stared. A few gowns swished as their owners turned around to quit his presence. His hostess came forward, either to greet him or tell him to leave. Really, it could be either.

She curtseyed in return to his bow. "Welcome, your grace. It's a pleasure to see you."

He allowed one eyebrow to climb infinitesimally. "Thank you, my lady. I'm glad I dropped in." As if he'd plummeted down here from the heavens.

The lady appeared to smile, and the movement of her brow echoed his. He loved a woman with a sense of humor. "I'm happy you landed unharmed. Allow me to introduce you to my daughter, Lady Eliza. She will make her debut in next year's season, but she is currently in London to order her wardrobe and attend a few social events."

Appropriate revenge, to settle him with a girl fresh out of the schoolroom. He prayed Lady Eliza wouldn't giggle.

He was doomed to disappointment. As he bowed over the young lady's trembling hand, he distinctly heard it. Her parents smiled at them indulgently. Why were they welcoming him, even allowing such a demon close to their delicate flower?

Nothing came to mind. He had no choice but to try to converse until he recalled their circumstances. They could be desperate, bankrupt or merely naive.

"Will we see more of you in the season?" her ladyship asked. "We usually spend most of our time in the country, but with Eliza's debut imminent, we have come to town." She unfurled her fan slowly, a teasing gesture. Although she wore her hair powdered, glints of dark curls hinted at her true hair color. Her face paint wasn't too extreme, and she had large gray eyes. No doubt she was an accredited beauty from her grace and confidence.

No, he hadn't had her. He'd have known that gesture anywhere. "Possibly," he admitted. "I rarely think that far ahead."

The quartet of musicians in the corner struck up for a country dance and Adrian faced the inevitable.

He bowed to the young lady and asked her to make up a set with him. He would do the pretty and move on. The earl would probably pay him a visit tomorrow, but Adrian was too old a hand to allow anyone to trap him into marriage. And by then he'd have more details about the family and exactly why they greeted him so warmly.

Lady Eliza who, under her layers of silk and corset would be a waif of a child, placed her hand on his arm in exactly the correct manner and allowed him to lead her into the dance. Rather like a wolf guiding a lamb away from the flock.

Still, she danced prettily. The part arrived where they had to separate and move on to another partner. Adrian gave a sigh of relief, until he saw who was waiting for him.

He stiffened. Would she reject him? He wouldn't blame her. The last time he'd seen Lady Livia Shaw, she'd been glaring at him from the safety of her carriage as it drove away. Pasting a smile on his lips, he waited for her to turn and walk away.

She did not. "Charmed to see you," he said as they hopped from foot to foot in the dance like cats trying to avoid hot stones. Graceful cats, naturally.

"Yes." She didn't glare at him.

"I thought you were avoiding me." He wouldn't blame her. As usual when confronted with a scandal, he didn't confirm or deny it to anyone. He'd attended Parliament, he'd dropped in on Whites Club, and said nothing to any of the men who'd confronted him. That had only fanned the embers.

"I need to talk to you." She took his arm for the promenade to her next partner in the dance.

He raised a brow. "Can it be that you want a repeat of what happened? I am only too eager to oblige."

Her eyes glazed and her delectable mouth settled into a bland smile, but before that happened, he caught a glimmer of her unguarded expression. She wanted another kiss. He'd seen that particular expression too often to imagine it. "Outside in half an hour."

His short laugh told her what he thought of that notion. "In the gardens? My dear, it has been raining all day. The gardens will be a mud bath. I have no intention of ruining my appearance even if you do. Not that. Excuse yourself and head for the ladies' room. I'll find somewhere."

She shuddered and turned on one foot to greet her next partner but threw a parting remark over her shoulder. "If you like your meat young, by all means court Lady Eliza, but be warned, they'll make you settle the earl's debts. He's a devil for the horses."

Ah. "Thank you for that." They preferred the country, they'd said. Including, no doubt, steeplechase betting and buying ruinously expensive horses. Not his circuit, which was why they had not rung any bells with him.

"You're welcome." Suitable words to move on to.

Getting rid of Lady Eliza took more effort than Adrian had imagined. On the brink of telling her parents that selling their daughter was worse than any—well, most—of the things he'd done, they peered over his shoulder and spied someone else entering the ballroom.

Ivan Rowley, son of the Earl of Leverton and wealthy in his own right. Also, Livia's cousin, one of the so-called Emperors of London. The troops were, no doubt, gathering to protect one of their own. Adrian suspected that, above all, was the reason why the Emperors had become so predominant in every field they entered, and so powerful. They were close.

If Adrian pursued his attraction to Livia, unless he was careful he would find himself one of them. The prospect did not appeal. Adrian preferred the kind of club he could leave whenever he chose. He had lived his life alone and he was happy to continue to do so. His one incursion into intimacy had ended in total disaster.

Rowley offered him a cold nod. In return, Adrian smiled warmly enough to make his lordship widen his eyes. He ambled across the polished wooden floor, his dance partner leaning heavily on his arm and greeted him. Rowley's persistent expression of cynical amusement deepened when he saw who Adrian was escorting.

Adrian handed Lady Eliza off to him and tipped him a wink as he left. Rowley's muttered, "You're welcome," would be heard by nobody else. Adrian had done business with him in the past and, despite his family, liked the scoundrel, but had no compunction in handing him the poisoned chalice.

Even if Livia had not told him of Lady Eliza's family problems, he'd have extricated himself as soon as he could. The girl had no brains, and that giggle would drive him to Bedlam in a week.

Clashing with Livia again would come as a relief after spending half an hour with the child and her parents.

Adrian wandered aimlessly around the room, threading his way through the guests, exchanging the occasional word with people before slipping out through the as-yet thinly populated supper room.

The ladies would have a bedroom set aside for their use. Knowing how these houses worked, Adrian climbed the stairs and found a nearby powder room with little trouble. Better still, it had a jib-door of its own, a hidden servant's door where he could make his escape if he needed to, plus a door to the guest bedroom beyond. Better to have two exits than one—a strategy he'd learned the hard way.

When he heard the rustle of silk, he opened the outer door slightly, and peered through. Sliding the door open, he silently beckoned to her, crooking his finger like a demon tempting his victim into his den. Which, he had no doubt, she would be thinking.

Nevertheless, after a cautious glance over her shoulder she came to him.

The powder room barely held them, so she had to enter sideways because of the width of her skirts. Not as wide as the walking sofas of ten years ago, but still too large for comfort. He liked her in neater hoops. They would suit her more, echo the curve of her hips instead of distorting them unnaturally.

The lack of all light except that cast by the moon gave them an even deeper sense of intimacy. Of romance.

No, not romance. Flirtation with a little teasing, perhaps another kiss. A little dalliance and he'd be on his way. But he wanted to know why she wished to talk to him tonight when she should rightly be avoiding him.

Her scent overpowered him. His instincts told him to throw his head back and suck it in, feed off it like a hungry dog. His visceral response shook him, especially the wave of raw lust that swept through him before he quelled it ruthlessly.

"Thank you for meeting me," she said primly.

She made him smile. He spread his hands and murmured, "We should be fine as long as we keep our voices down. But if we're discovered, we'll have to do something about this meeting."

She sighed. "I know. That's why I didn't want to be seen in your company again."

His smile turned wry. "Thank you for that."

She touched her fan to her mouth. "Oh, I'm sorry, I didn't mean for it to sound like that. But you don't want a lasting arrangement any more than I do, do you?"

"No." Why would she not want a lasting arrangement? She was perhaps a little old in the tooth by society standards, but she hadn't seen thirty yet.

Besides, men would crawl over broken glass to belong to her family and
have control of her dowry. He didn't care about those, but he'd love an
hour in bed with her in some secluded place somewhere.

"You'd better tell me what this is all about before I ravish you
where you stand."

She glanced around doubtfully. The room held a long, low table, a
large pounce-box and brush, a wig stand and a single chair. Probably had
a chamber pot somewhere, but he didn't choose to search for it. He had
better things to look at. "You couldn't do it here."

Stifling his laugh took effort, but he managed. "Is that a bet? Because
I take all wagers where making love is concerned."

The delicate flush that rose to her cheeks looked good enough to eat.
"I would not know about such matters."

Something about what she said roused Adrian's interest. What exactly
did she know? Her response to his kiss had been eager and she had definitely
kissed a man before. "I could teach you."

"No, you could not." Ah, that intrigued him and again, he couldn't
quite put his finger on why. After all, a young unmarried lady would know
little of what he could get up to in cramped powder rooms. She tapped his
knuckles with her fan. "Never mind about that now."

The slight sting roused him, sending his desire for her higher. Never one
to reject a challenge, Adrian perked up, like that unruly part of his anatomy
also showing interest. "Tell me, sweet one. Why did you arrange this tryst?"

Ah, there came that flush again. Enjoying the sight, he listened to her
request. "I lost a brooch that day. I didn't realize it was gone until I got
home. It is not a valuable thing, but it has great sentimental value." She
swallowed. "It was my grandmother's. It's round, engraved with her initials,
with a bit of scrollwork around the edge."

"I see." A brooch? Disappointment hit him. That was all she wanted?
But he would behave like a gentleman. That would be the best way to draw
her in, and he fully intended to do that. "How big is it?"

"About an inch. It's of little value." She lifted her face, her eyes swimming
in tears. "I'll pay a great deal to have it back."

Now was his chance. If he behaved true to type, he'd demand a night
in her bed as his reward. And from the expression on her face she'd give
it to him. "Did your grandmother mean a lot to you?"

"Yes. That is—yes."

She was about to say something else. That hesitation spoke volumes.
This demanded research. "Is it a family treasure?"

She shook her head, giving herself the opportunity, he noted, to get rid of those tears. She didn't want him to notice. He'd have to be blind not to. "It's a personal piece. My grandfather had it made for her."

"And it means a lot to you, I can see that." But why? Something niggled at him, something that wasn't quite right about her attachment to this piece of jewelry. For one thing, her grandmother would have had pieces. Surely Livia could claim another token, if she wanted one. What did this brooch mean to her?

The prospect of finding out exactly what lay behind her request intrigued him. He would take on the recovery of the brooch for that alone. Curiosity would be the death of him, his grandfather had always said. But what else was there to stave off the boredom of existence?

"Do you know where you lost it?"

She was so close he could see the gleam of gold beneath her hair powder, and the way her eyes, so heavenly blue, had a darker ring defining the irises.

She shook her head. "Either the cutpurse got it, or I lost it in your house."

"I see."

Unfortunately, that meant he would have to face his erstwhile mistress, a fate he'd prefer to avoid. Her tantrums wearied him. When Ophelia balanced her demands against her performance, he wondered how she'd managed to get half a year of his life out of him.

"I will pay you," Livia said eagerly. "I have no desire to remain in your debt."

"Then I will consider our dance the payment." Good lord, where had that chivalric impulse come from? He should have asked her for something else. A dinner at her house, a sign of acceptance from the powerful Emperors.

"That is beyond kindness." Her soft tones were most unlike the practical, bold ones he'd become accustomed to. "I would give much to have the brooch back."

"I may have to contact you. I assume you wish me to write to you anonymously." Of course she would.

"No. I have corresponded with gentlemen before." That, by itself, was not shocking, although it would be if the letters were sent clandestinely. But he had a reason to write to her. He had a way in.

Now he needed to know if her guardians read her mail. "But not with someone like me. If your mother oversees your mail, she will not allow me to write, surely."

"She does not. She trusts us."

He almost burst out laughing. "Considering the history of your siblings, that is trust indeed."

She shrugged, her smooth white shoulders moving inside the stiff silk of her ball gown in a way that made his mouth water. Could he slip that fabric away, and discover the pleasures beneath? But to do that would be to ruin her. He should not care. He never had in the past. But this time—he did.

"I suppose we are a scandalous family." The melancholy made him want to draw her into his arms, and not for his usual purposes. "I am the last unmarried member, though. And likely to remain so."

"Why would you think that? You are a lovely woman with much to commend you. Not every man wants a girl fresh from the schoolroom. I do not."

She jerked her head up, meeting his gaze, her eyes wide and her light brown brows arched. "You? You're looking for another wife?"

"Perhaps. I remain to be convinced, but one day I must. Either that or lose the estate to a distant relative. Personally I don't object to that, but my other relatives might."

"You have an heir?"

"A distant cousin. He is avidly awaiting my demise. But he has rivals. In that event the estate could be lost in legal fees. I'm doing my best to make that irrelevant by dispersing as much of my fortune as I can, but I doubt I can dissipate it all. So I must at least consider marrying and begetting an heir."

She tilted her head to one side, but whatever she was about to say, whatever stricture she was about to impose on him was lost by the pressure of his mouth on hers. Unable to resist her a moment longer, he drew her hard against him and kissed her.

There it was, that taste that had haunted him since he'd punished her in the street. Still he couldn't identify it, but he wanted more of it. He could sate himself on that alone. The notion of what the rest of her would taste like had kept him awake for several uncomfortable nights. Yearning for a woman, a particular woman, had left him many years ago, and here it was, back again. He'd almost forgotten what it felt like.

Unfulfilled longing had its own rewards, but he had no desire to perpetuate the practice. He'd rather fulfill it another way.

This was much better. This being his lips covering hers, and her soft body cushioning his. Wrapping his fingers around the back of her neck, he held her still for his delectation. Living silk threaded between his fingers from an artfully arranged ringlet, enhancing his enjoyment of this lovely woman.

This time she opened her luscious lips for him when he passed his tongue over her lower lip. Plunging deeply, he moaned into her mouth, and met the vibrations of her responding sound. She tasted sweet, with a faint flavor of wine. He would gladly live off her forever.

No, not that. Alarm sparked, but he gave her no clue, drawing away gradually, and watching as she opened her eyes and returned to reality. "Yes," he said softly, drawing his hand down, taking care not to disturb her elaborate hairstyle.

Her muscles, from being relaxed in his arms, tensed once more. "Was that payment?"

He was glad to hear her huskier, softer voice. Longing filled him, to take her through to the bedroom beyond, lock the door and ignore everything except the challenge of pleasuring her.

If he did, they were both lost. While he didn't care for himself, being lost already, he didn't want to bring that fate to her. "No. That was pleasure given and taken."

Glancing down, Livia smoothed her skirts with hands that shook a little. "Thank you for helping me."

Oh, he'd do much more than that. "I will do everything I can to retrieve your treasure."

Since that was his way to retain contact with her, he'd take it.

* * * *

Ruffled from her encounter with the devilish duke, Livia hurried across the hall to the ladies' room and took five minutes to compose herself. She needed more, but she'd make do. Smoothing her hair back, twisting a curl around her finger to tidy it, and settling her skirts gave her a moment alone to set herself to rights.

Rightly she should object to the ruffian grabbing her and kissing her whenever she came close, but in all honesty she could not. She enjoyed it. Not that she would admit that to anyone, least of all the Duke of Preston.

As she patted her hair into place, standing before the mirror lit by branched candles either side, she could not escape the fact that she was deeply attracted to his grace, whose first name, she had learned, was Adrian. She would have to get over it, that was all.

But a sneaky little voice deep, deep inside asked, *Why not? You're never going to marry, so why not take him as a lover?*

Never could she have imagined doing that again. The first time had ended in total disaster.

Turning, she presented her profile to the mirror. Satisfied with what she saw, she left the room, making her way back downstairs.

The main room blazed with the light from a hundred candles, the scent of beeswax heavy in the air. Camphor, from clothes hastily brought out of storage and lavender sent occasional messages to her nose. Familiar, almost comforting smells. But she couldn't get that new aroma hot, hard male out of her senses. When he drew her close, his musky, clean scent pulled her closer, surrounded her with an odd feeling she didn't quite have a word for. Attraction, desire, perhaps, all those things she'd deliberately put away ten years ago.

Glancing around, Livia couldn't see her family. They had probably moved to the supper room. Although the quartet was still playing, the room was not as full as it had been when she left.

Spotting her cousin, Livia glided over to him. "Spying on me, Ivan?"

Ivan gave her one of his charming smiles. "Why on earth would you think that? Considering this is the only society event of any significance tonight, is it surprising that we end up in the same place?"

Flicking out her fan, she put it to use, setting up a breeze that reached Ivan. Proverbially tall, dark, and handsome, Ivan showed no sign of discomfort, even though she'd aimed the waft at his eyes. "I've not known you avid to attend balls."

Ivan pulled a face. "Not in the season, certainly, but this is more of an entertainment and less of a chase to the death."

"Marriage is death?"

"For the wrong couple, very much so. For the right couple, not so much."

He stepped aside, giving her a full view of the man standing just behind him. "I believe you know Sir Jeffrey Creasey?"

Livia's blood ran cold. Yes, she knew him.

Lowering her head, she dropped into a curtsy, giving herself time to get her breath back. "Yes indeed. I have not seen you this age, sir. How do you do?"

"Better now I've seen you, Lady Livia." Dressed in a blue coat with gold braid, Sir Jeffrey was just as handsome as she remembered.

His responding bow gave her a chance to regain her composure, what was left of it. She forced herself to lift her gaze, masking her expression with a glacial stare. "Indeed. How is your lady wife?"

"Ah." The drop in his voice was echoed by the droop of his mobile lips. Lips that Livia knew well, that she had thought she'd forgotten. "Sadly, my dear Maria died last year. She followed the drum to the last and suffered for it. She caught a fever."

"I'm so sorry. Poor Maria."

"Indeed. Thank you. I lost the taste for the army after that. After my father died I sold out. I'm back for good, newly elected to Parliament and here to attend the House."

Poor Maria. She would have loved a visit to London. She had adored Jeffrey, chased him with a doggedness he had not deserved, nor discouraged. But he had eyes only for Livia at the time.

"You inherited your father's seat in Parliament?" She couldn't think what to say. And because Ivan didn't know, he thought he'd done her a favor by reintroducing them. Small talk seemed the safest way, until she could escape.

"I did. Of course we had to go through the formality of elections, but yes, to all intents and purposes." Supremely confident, he gave her the full force of his dazzling good looks. At least they had no effect on her anymore.

"I'm afraid I have not seen your family for some time," she said. "We did attend your father's funeral." Which was more than he did, claiming the press of events abroad. And yet here he was now.

"A state of affairs we can now rectify." Sir Jeffrey smiled broadly, as if conveying a favor to her. "My father has gone, and I am now the squire. We are once more neighbors. I look forward to seeing more of you." His smile deepened, as if for her alone. "Perhaps we can regain our youthful friendship. I'll be returning to the country soon, and then we will be but a few miles apart."

Livia couldn't welcome that because of what had happened between them. She had prayed in church every Sunday that she never saw him again. She had good reason.

Somewhere in the world, their son existed. Because of their painfully brief and youthful affair, a child lived.

Chapter 3

Adrian instinctively ducked as a Meissen monkey flew past his head. The streak of white porcelain startled a passing horse hauling a hackney cab, halting long enough to make its driver curse and snake his whip over the creature's head. The benighted porcelain beast shattered on the cobbles of King Street.

Adrian dusted his hands. At least he would not have to enter that place again. Finding Ophelia in the arms of her latest lover had not concerned him one bit. The lady needed to make a living, after all. But having her throw curses at him, then, once her lover was out of sight, throw herself at him and beg him to take her back, that had unnerved him.

After hastily explaining that he had lost a piece of family jewelry in the front parlor, she'd actually helped him to search, until he'd let fall that the brooch belonged to a lady. That was a mistake.

If he'd cared more about what she thought, he'd have seduced her and let her new lover see how to control this woman, but the thought of touching her again did not appeal, so he'd let her shriek and hurl ornaments at him.

In any case, the lover couldn't wait to quit the building once he'd seen an example of her tantrums.

Adrian could not find it in himself to be sorry. Except he had not found the brooch. He was certain Livia had not dropped it there.

Which left the orphanage. Not looking forward to the visit, but determined to get it over with, he strode around the corner into a smaller street, and found the place easily enough from the tarnished plaque outside. *Brownlow Street Foundling Hospital*, it read.

Since Thomas Coram had set up his foundling hospital, the fashionable world had seen the rescuing of indigent children as a worthy cause and one that put them in a good light. Several had sprung up, though this example did not appear to be the best example of its kind. The tall building was blackened with soot, the mortar falling out from between the once-red bricks. The windows were bare of covering, and the shutters fastened back against the wall did not appear to have been put to use for some time, slats broken and their fastenings rusting.

Still, good people often worked tirelessly, despite their lack of funds, to do the best they could for the children in their care. Even a cynic like Adrian understood that. He plied the knocker. Then used it more vigorously again.

After a good five minutes the sound of bolts being drawn came from the other side of the door. It creaked open, revealing a small, towheaded child dressed in a pair of filthy breeches and a shirt worn so thin Adrian could see his skin through the grubby linen.

"Sir?"

"Can I speak to whoever is in charge?"

"'Oo's that?" A rough, calloused hand shoved the boy aside and a man stood in the space the child had occupied. His simple, but good clothes were in stark contrast to the boy's worn garments. He folded his arms. "Well?"

When in this part of London, Adrian rarely wore his small sword. The weapon marked him out as an aristocrat, since only they were allowed to wear them in town. But once he clapped eyes on this ruffian, he was glad of the useful knife in his coat pocket. His hand curled around the handle as he gave the man an easy smile. "Adrian Sterling." Best not to brandish his title either. The man would turn nasty in a minute. Either that or obsequious and Adrian was in no mood for either. "I'm a neighbor, of sorts. I wondered if your children had seen a skirmish in King Street the other day. Someone recognized a boy from your house." He skirted the truth. "My lady friend had her purse cut and a brooch stolen."

"Yes?" He raised his chin, his jowls quivering.

"She is offering a reward for its return. At least the brooch. The purse she knows is lost."

"What kind of reward?"

"Five pounds." He amended the amount when the man sniffed. "Guineas."

"What does this brooch look like? And 'oo did yer see? Got a name?"

Adrian shook his head. A noxious odor emanated from the house. He guessed the unfortunates here did not live in particularly salubrious surroundings. The reward would go straight in this person's pocket, which made him disinclined to give it. "No name. My lady friend was attacked by small children."

"My children are good. They'd 'ave been in their lessons or in bed."

Adrian doubted that, but wisely said nothing. "Maybe the lad who took the brooch was known to your children."

The man didn't answer immediately. He stared at Adrian, as if assessing him. "'Appen." He sniffed and drew his sleeve across his nose, leaving a streak of brown slime behind. Snuff would do that, especially the cheap kind. "I'll arsk. Where can I find yer?"

Not at the house in King Street, that was for sure. "I'll find you."

"Is it the brothel at number twenty?" The man eyed him shrewdly.

As was his wont, Adrian was dressed plainly, but in good quality cloth and spotlessly clean linen. Unlike others, he didn't always wear his rank on his back. He could pass muster as a customer at a well-to-do brothel. He nodded. "You can get in touch with me at that address." He knew the place, although brothels hadn't seen him as a client since his early years on the town. Adrian preferred to keep a mistress, someone he could converse with as well as roger, and someone less likely to pass on anything unpleasant.

He could pay the madam a retainer to hold the brooch for him if it appeared. Somehow, he doubted it would. If he offered more than his already generous offer, that would cause suspicion. The man standing before him on the worn step would believe there was something special about the brooch, and then Adrian would never get it back.

"Chances are a gang took it. You'll never see it again." The man smirked, revealing a mouth where teeth were a novelty.

Adrian kept his temper. Barely, although the heat of it simmered inside him. "I'd appreciate it. It's about an inch wide, and it has initials engraved on the front. Not a valuable thing, but it was my friend's inheritance from her grandmother."

Not for the first time he wondered why a small gold brooch could mean so much. Livia's grandmother on one side was a duchess, on the other a marchioness. Both had collections of jewelry. Surely she could claim another piece as a memento if she wanted one? What was so special about this piece?

He showed none of his doubts to this man. Merely thanked him and stepped back.

"Do yer want ter come in and meet the children?" The man gave him a sickly, near-toothless smile.

"Not today, but thank you." If he stepped inside that house, God knew if he would come out again. This was an orphanage in name only, he'd wager his last guinea on that. They'd strip him, beat him, and throw him in the street. If they knew who he was, they'd tie him up and hold him to ransom. If they knew he had a purse of golden coins tucked snugly in the inner pocket of his breeches his life wouldn't be worth a penny.

So he walked away, trying to keep his step rapid, but not brisk. He'd call at the brothel and give the madam a retainer to hold the brooch for him if it turned up. He'd rather give his money to a woman earning a more honest living than this man. One way or another he would get that brooch back, if it was humanly possible.

He had just turned the corner when the scampering of feet behind him made him spin around, ready to confront whoever was chasing him.

There stood the small boy who had opened the door. Wiry, with unkempt, overgrown hair, the lad met Adrian's challenging stare boldly. "You said five guineas?"

"I did. Why?" He took a sideways step, putting his back against the wall. Even small boys had accomplices and they could wield a knife better than most grown men.

Glancing down, the boy shuffled his feet on the cobbles. "I might 'ave seen it."

"Do you have it?"

Grimacing, the boy shook his head. "But I might have information for you." Although he slipped into the vernacular, the lad was obviously making an effort to speak well. That alone gave Adrian pause. He could use this child.

"'Ow much is it worth?" the urchin demanded.

"That depends on the information." He studied the lad closely. The child had obviously made an effort to clean himself, his face shiny but a little streaked with dirt. Adrian liked his initiative in coming forward and his swift appraisal of his appearance.

The youth's guileless blue eyes met Adrian's not-so-guileless ones. "A guinea? I can't get you the brooch, but I can tell you what 'appened."

"If it's worth my while you'll get your guinea. My lady friend is upset about losing her brooch. It's not worth five pounds but it was her grandmother's." If the boy had it, he would see that he'd get more by giving it up than in selling it in any pawnshop.

The boy scratched his head. No doubt his scalp was alive with vermin. "I saw a man. Really well-dressed." He passed a critical gaze over Adrian, hat to shoes and back to his face. "Better than you. Flashier than you, any'ow."

"What else?"

"I didn't see 'im again, but it was our boys went out to get it on ole Smiffy's orders. So if it went, they got it."

"Did you go out with them?"

The boy shook his head. "I was doin' somethink else. Cookin'."

That information brought Adrian closer to the brooch. "Can you find out what the man's name was?"

He shook his head again. "Smiffy doesn't write that sort of thing down. 'E talked well. But 'e won't come back. 'E got what he wanted."

The boy spoke truth. Why would the man return to risk being recognized? Adrian liked the spark of intelligence in the lad's eyes. "What's your name?"

"Mickey. Michael," the boy corrected himself. "Michael O'Shaugnessy."

"Your parents are Irish?"

"Were. My da was a sailor. My ma came to London to be with 'im. Sent me to school. But she died, and 'e died, and I 'ad to shift for myself."

Curiosity drove Adrian to ask, "What is the orphanage like?"

Mickey sniggered. "Orphanage nothing. It's a thieves' kitchen. That brass plate is only out there to put people off. And get a few donations from the nobs. Ole Smiffy sends us out thieving every day. We don't get fed if we don't take back at least a kerchief."

Adrian had suspected as much. He ached to get out of this area, and he doubted he could do any more here. "Come on." He started walking toward Covent Garden. He'd get a cab there and dust this part of London off his feet. "So how old are you, Mickey?"

"Twelve."

The boy was small enough for nine, but Adrian wasn't surprised. Street children were often malnourished, their growth stunted by the lack of good food.

Because he liked the boy and for no other reason, he handed over the guinea. He fully expected the urchin to grab the coin and run off, but the boy continued to skip along, matching Adrian's easy strides with a fast trot.

Adrian had found that the best way to walk in these streets with no pavements and worn cobbles was to march straight ahead, assuming he was the only person there. People dodged around them, cursing occasionally, but neither he nor Mickey cared about that.

"Can you read, boy?"

"Yes, I can," the boy said. "I went to school for a whole year. I learned to add up and to read. But I need a bit of time to make it out."

They turned a corner and entered the piazza. The designers had kept the streets around Covent Garden deliberately winding and narrow, the better to emphasize the space when the traveler finally entered it. They'd meant it for a square of fashionable residences, but society had long moved on, although a few eccentrics still lived here. The streets were a jumble of taverns, coffee houses, private residences, brothels and lodging houses. The square contained ranks of tall, brick-built houses, the piazza in the center a market for the fruit, vegetables and flowers that were driven here every morning from the market gardens ringing the city. At the top lay the church and the Opera House, graciously designed buildings in once-white stone.

As always, crowds thronged the area, but at least they could walk more freely now. Adrian headed for the far side, where a line of chairmen waited to do business. One of those would do, or a hackney if one passed by. At the boy's words, he'd given up the idea of calling in on the brothel. If someone had paid for the brooch to be stolen, it would never show up there.

An idea occurred to him. "Would you know the man again?"

Mickey nodded vigorously. "Oh yes. Spoke proper, tall, good-looking. Yes, I'd know him anywhere."

So who would want to get hold of a nondescript gold brooch? What secrets did it hold? It obviously meant a great deal to Livia. She'd been prepared to meet Adrian again in order to get it back. That must have taken a lot of courage, considering what he'd done to her. Her expression had told him even more than her words had. Did someone want to threaten her with the piece, or make her do something in return for the trinket? If he did, Adrian would expect him to make his move soon.

Mickey was a weapon Adrian could use. He didn't doubt that the boy could recognize who had paid for thieves to steal the brooch. He was sharp, quick and intelligent.

Someone had attacked Livia in the street, putting her in danger of injury or worse. The person who'd paid for this wasn't particular. Perhaps he had approached her body servants with the same aim. Why the brooch, Adrian still didn't understand. But he would.

Raising an arm, he hailed a hackney cab. "How brave are you, Mickey? Do you want to better yourself?"

"I'd like to get out of that place." The boy gave him a suspicious look. "I ain't doing anything, you know, personal."

He wouldn't have expected a child from that place to have such scruples, but it boded well. Most of the poorer children wouldn't think twice about selling their bodies for money. And scrubbed up, Mickey could present well.

"I can give you a job, and I promise it's nothing you won't like."

"Awright. What is it?"

"Then here is the offer. I want you to tell me the minute you see the man who paid you. For now, you'll be my page, so I can take you about. Later we will find something more permanent for you."

His suspicions were coalescing. This person who wanted her brooch; it wasn't for gain. So was it to gain a hold over Livia? Make her do something she objected to?

One of her family? She belonged to a large family group. One of them might want more than he would be comfortable admitting. He'd seen her cousin Ivan Rowley at the ball the other night. Perhaps he knew something.

"You will make a wonderful page," he promised Mickey. And set fashionable London by its ears.

Adrian looked forward to that part.

Chapter 4

Tired of the four walls around her, but not in the mood for riding, Livia took her maid and accompanied her mother to the Green Park.

The park in the autumn reminded Livia of her family home in Derbyshire. The trees were changing color, fading from lime through to yellow, then a muted red and brown. The cows at the end, with the milkmaids who would sell milk fresh from the animal wore cloaks over their rural gowns, and pet dogs chased fallen twigs.

At this time of year the park held enough people to provide an amusing stroll and chat, but not enough to annoy. Livia, wearing her new dark blue gown with silver trim, was enjoying displaying her new finery and for the first time in days, relaxing. That was until Captain Sir Jeffrey Creasey approached.

Livia's heart sank to her stomach when he bowed to her and her mother welcomed him. "It is good to see you so well, Sir Jeffrey. Are you back for good?"

Of course her mother had no idea who had fathered Livia's baby. As far as she was concerned he was a neighbor from the country, a pleasant young man who married and joined the army.

He was wearing red again, darker than the scarlet he'd sported at the ball. Was he afraid people wouldn't notice him? His charming smile curved those lips she remembered far too well. "Indeed, my lady, I am. I felt it my duty to sell out and come home."

"And after you lost your lovely wife."

The smile melted away. "Maria was my aid and comfort. She never felt comfortable following the drum, but she was a game girl. I will miss her to my dying day."

He said the heartfelt words as if reciting something he'd memorized but not completely understood.

"We were so sorry to hear of her death," Lady Strenshall said, always on point with the correct sentiment, though in fact she'd confided to her husband only that morning that she barely remembered the poor young lady.

Livia found another meaning to her mother's words. One day people would say that about her. She was the twin everyone overlooked in favor of her vivacious sister. Happy that way, she had thought, until she was left behind. But she had shrunk back for so long she had no idea how to make herself stand out. Even if she wanted such a thing, which of course she did not.

Trying to step back, she stumbled on a piece of uneven ground. Sir Jeffrey leaned forward, catching her elbow. He let his hand linger, and when he withdrew it, stroked down her forearm, touching the only part of her arm open to the elements, a patch below her wrist. She should have worn her long gloves instead of the short kidskin pair. She experienced no thrill, no excitement, nothing. So sad. That was how love died.

If he'd stayed away, she could have held her memories close, retained that brief few weeks as a golden time in her mind. But seeing him again, the bubble burst. There was no going back.

She put what she'd learned since that time to good use, keeping her expression clear while she faced him. Once she'd have excused herself, let her face crumple or simply walked away. No more. Memories mingled with deep hurt, but nothing showed as she smoothly thanked him for preventing her fall. When he offered his arm, she had to take it.

"I will be traveling to my estate in a few weeks," he said. "I assume I will see you over Christmas?"

Damn, he would. He lived less than ten miles away. In their youth, their parents had allowed Jeffrey to run free with Livia and her siblings, playing on the estate. He'd gravitated toward Livia, and they'd become the best of friends.

Of everything she regretted, the loss of that friendship featured high on the list. Not top, though. That was reserved for a being she'd only had a glimpse of before they'd taken him away. She couldn't even blame Jeffrey, because he'd never known. By then he'd married sweet little Maria. Even though Livia had wanted to tell him, there was not much point anymore.

Her shorter skirts skimmed the still-damp paths, so when he suggested walking across the grass, she demurred. "Should we head for that pavilion over there?"

The small wooden structure appeared a long way in the distance, but it was that or allow her skirts to blot up the damp from yesterday's rain and the dew from this morning. Her mother could walk for miles and call it a stroll.

Worse, her mother met one of her old flirts, and happily accepted his support while she laughed with him. They hung back, allowing Livia and Jeffrey to walk forward. She could not check her pace without making her dislike of being with him obvious. With her mother's voice growing fainter, they had relative privacy. She cast her gaze up to him, meeting those blue eyes she had, for a short time, thought she wanted to see above all others. She'd been wrong. How could she ever trust herself again?

"No doubt you're working on the new bill."

"Oh yes, we're working night and day. Tedious stuff."

Were they talking about the same bill? "The one to fund more hospitals?" Her father was passionate about the bill, discussing it at the breakfast table and at dinner.

"Yes, that's the one. Why we cannot leave it to the charities I do not know. I still believe that is the best path to take." So the poor could continue moving, becoming nobody's responsibility until they died in a ditch.

Livia did not say that. Obviously Jeffrey was taking the diehard county view, and she couldn't argue against centuries of tradition and avoiding responsibility.

"The deserving poor should be attended to first," he declared, as if his point was obvious.

Livia bit her lip.

"I'm sure your father would agree."

As if she had no opinion of her own? Strange that she'd never noticed what a pompous ass Jeffrey was. "I doubt he would. He is a big advocate of the bill, even though he says it is unlikely to pass. This time, at least. I believe his stance is more Christian."

"So are the charities." He sounded as if argument would be a waste of time. He patted her hand. "My dear, surely we can find more interesting matters to discuss? What do you know of politics?"

"The women of my family have always been involved in the topic." Of course they had. Her great-aunt had been a great political hostess in her time, universally praised for the intellectual rigor of her arguments.

"Women have far more important things to do." He left his hand on hers, gazing at her in a meaningful way, waiting for her to ask.

So she asked him. "Like what?"

"Marriage and children."

This man had made that future impossible for her. How could she think of bearing another child when her first was God knew where?

"You know I cannot." Try as she might, Livia could not take the bitterness from her voice.

When she faltered, he pulled her along until she regained her footing. "Yes, you can. You can with me. I know your secret, Livia."

Not the baby. He didn't know about their son.

She sucked in a breath. Gazing deep into his eyes, she tried to find the truth, but she could not. His face was as handsome as ever, his complexion smooth and pale, the epitome of the fashionable man. Over the years he'd added bulk, but no fat. All she felt under the soft wool of his coat was hard muscle.

"I know, but the one I'm talking about is your maidenhead."

Which he'd taken. Shock arced through her, freezing her. Only her determination to hide how much he had affected her with that remark kept her moving.

She said nothing. What was there to say?

"You should not have given yourself so easily."

"But it was—" *You.*

He cut her off. "Say no more. Even here voices carry." He hadn't appeared so concerned when they were discussing her part in the affair. "I want to compensate for what our parents did to us."

"*They* did?"

Her parents had dealt with her dilemma practically, until everything had gone wrong. His parents had married him off to Maria, the girl who had always hankered after him.

Determined not to foster bad blood between the families, Livia had flirted with every man who would look at her at the house party going on at that time to deflect interest in Jeffrey.

"My parents betrothed me to Maria faster than I could register. They did not approve of your family." Livia knew that. "Then they bought my commission and rushed the marriage."

Everyone at the house party had attended the wedding, declaring it charming to see the young lovers united. Livia had shrunk at the back of the church, filled with horror and shame.

He'd smiled at Maria the way Livia thought he'd kept just for her. That was her first disillusionment. The rest had come later.

He shook his head. "I was told you wanted nothing more to do with me." His assertion shocked her. "Really?"

He nodded, the melancholy expression in his eyes soul-deep. "What else could I do? At least I could make one person happy, even if I lost the love of my life."

"I'm sorry."

Had their affair really been broken apart by his parents? At the time she'd assumed so, but later she'd wondered. Too late now.

He gazed straight ahead. "I would like to make amends. I intend to come a-courting once more. I have never forgotten you, Livia. And now I need an heir." He spoke as if passing the time of day, an easy conversational tone.

He turned his gaze onto her, his eyes clear and true. "Will you receive me this time, Livia? Will we find the future we were once denied?"

Everything in her stilled. The one man who would not care about her lack of virginity was free again. She could have him. Nobody would stand in their way this time.

She should want this. Once she had desired nothing more. When she was sixteen, before she'd tasted the bitterness life could hold.

She didn't want him anymore. Didn't want to become the quiet, respectable wife of a man who did not consider his wife's opinion important.

But what alternative did she have? That was why she had refused or deterred any potential suitor. She would have to confess to him, because she refused to lie to a man who wanted to make her his wife. And then, if she chose the wrong man to confide in, her secret would spread and she'd be ruined. "It's too late for us, Jeffrey. So much has happened since then."

He deserved to know about the baby. But how could she tell him?

He stopped walking, faced her and took both her hands in his, his gesture obvious to anyone watching. Fear and fury rose in equal measure in Livia, but she stood, waiting for him to try to push her into something she was no longer sure she wanted. Would he propose to her now? Sink onto the wet grass and risk ruining the knees of his smart new breeches?

But all he said was, "It is not too late. It will never be too late for us."

She opened her mouth and took a breath, ready to reply, but a voice from behind her gave her pause. "Well met, Lady Livia. I trust I find you well?"

Tingles coursed over her skin when she sensed the Duke of Preston's presence. Moving aside as Jeffrey released her, Livia savored the relief washing through her.

Making her curtsy gave Livia a chance to compose herself. Why the duke always unnerved her she had no idea, but she had best accept that he did and learn how to cope with her unfortunate reaction.

"Your grace, may I introduce a neighbor of ours from the country, Captain Sir Jeffrey Creasey?"

The pause gave her mother a chance to catch up with them.

"Sir Jeffrey has come to town to attend the Commons." Her ladyship smiled, seemingly oblivious to the currents passing between the two men.

The air prickled. They had taken an instant dislike to each other. The duke was better at hiding his animosity, but Livia felt it just the same.

"Lady Livia is an old playmate." Sir Jeffrey smiled fondly at Livia. "I have known her almost as long as I've known myself."

"And the rest of the family, presumably." Preston glanced around, as if bored and looking for amusement elsewhere.

"But her ladyship most of all." Jeffrey moved a little closer to her, as if claiming her already.

This was ridiculous. The two men were butting heads over her? No, they were disputing their territory, that was all. She might as well be a log of wood or a favored dog. They didn't care.

She stepped back to stand with her mother. Preston sent her an amused smile, as if he knew what she was thinking. Instead of responding, she met his gaze without expression before looking away.

He turned back to Jeffrey. "By your title I gather you have been with the army?"

"I have, sir. The fifth dragoons. But I needed to return home after my father died. Settle down, as my mother puts it."

Now it was his turn to send Livia a meaningful glance. She gave him the same response. However she felt about the men, and she was no longer sure of her response, she would give neither dog a bone.

"Sadly," Jeffrey went on, "I lost my dear wife abroad. I understand you are also a widower?"

So he knew about the duke. Interesting, since he'd never had any business with Preston before.

"I lost my wife five years ago," he said. "Unfortunately, with no issue. My mother does not concern herself with my affairs." He gave Jeffrey a short bow. "You must forgive us, if you please. Lady Livia asked a favor of me, and I wished to inform her of my progress. Would you walk a while with me, ma'am?"

Neatly done. He'd cut her out of the crowd and claimed some privacy at the same time as claiming a special relationship with her. He'd also put Jeffrey's nose out of joint, which Livia was not at all averse to.

"Do not go out of my sight," her mother warned. "Sir Jeffrey, your arm please."

Livia and the duke strolled toward the blasted pavilion. She didn't care if she never saw it again. "Do you have any news?" she asked when they were out of earshot.

Glancing at her, he raised a brow. "In a hurry, are we? I haven't recovered your brooch yet, though I have a better idea of where it was. You did not drop it in the house in King Street, I am certain of that. So we are left with the orphanage, which in truth is no orphanage at all, but a school for cutpurses and pickpockets."

"Goodness!" He gave her the information so calmly she thought she had mistaken him at first. "Such places exist? I thought they were the result of the journal writers' vivid imaginations."

"Not at all. A child makes the best thief. They are fast, and they may appeal to the soft heart of the magistrate, if they are caught. As far as their supervisor is concerned they are also eminently replaceable."

"Can't we do something to stop it?" Her heart went out to those poor children, who through no fault of their own were condemned to a life of drudgery and worse.

"The best approach is from the top. That is what Parliament is for." Unlike Jeffrey, he had not dismissed her concerns.

"And why the new bill should pass."

He shook his head. "Sadly, this time it has little chance. But we will persist."

This did not seem like the duke she knew, the careless wastrel who cared nothing for anyone.

"Children deserve a better start in life than they have. However, we are straying from the subject of your brooch."

When she caught her breath, he gazed down at her, genuine concern in his eyes. "Are you quite well?"

"Yes, I assure you." Except—had her own child become a thief? Had he appeared in court, been transported? She refused to consider the other possibility, that he was dead. That small, helpless innocent, wrenched from her and taken to who knew where? She had tried to find out, but the effort had proved impossible.

Smallpox, the scourge of their age, had struck again, killed the messenger before she could tell anyone what had become of the child. Her baby was gone.

The duke did not appear to notice Livia's momentary lapse of attention. What must he think of her, making such a fuss about a trinket? "The brooch is still beyond my reach, but I have taken steps to retrieve it. I know where it was, and I have a better idea of what happened to it. However, we must face the possibility that it has gone to a pawnshop, and in that case, I fear we may never get it back."

"Yes, of course. Please don't concern yourself with it any longer. It's a small matter. I allowed myself to become more upset than I should have done. Probably the result of the attack."

She didn't want to arouse any more suspicions from this alarmingly perspicacious man. She had turned to him in her grief at losing her one link with her baby when she should never have done that. But it was time to let go. Somehow, she would do that.

"Ah but then, sweet Livia, I would have no excuse to see you again. I take leave to tell you that you are enlivening my sojourn in London this season. I have rarely been so diverted as since I met you."

"We will meet, sir." Her feathers ruffled at his casual use of her first name, she tried the tactic of standing on her dignity. "In ballrooms and the like."

"So we will."

Relieved at his agreement, she strolled on. But deep inside her, disappointment lowered her mood. He was giving up so easily. Of course, all he knew was that she had lost a sentimental memento. Why should he care? And he obviously did not want to pursue a connection with her, something else that should fill her with joy, but did not. She could never marry, so she should not lead him on.

Glancing around, she saw Jeffrey bow to her mother and briskly head for the gates. At least he had gone. Preston followed her gaze and grinned. "He's left the field to me."

"That makes me the field?"

His grin broadened. When he did that, she warmed to him. He looked like a much younger version of himself, transformed into a carefree young man, instead of a cynical, worldly aristocrat. She wanted more smiles. "I would say you were a whole estate full of fields, Lady Livia."

"Oy, sir, marster—" The childish voice behind them broke off and recommenced with some very unchild-like cursing. "Sorry, your gracious, but Mr. 'Erring says the 'orses are getting restless and do you want them walked a bit more?"

Brimful of laughter, Livia swung around to confront a child wearing an ill-fitting suit of clothes. The boy snatched his cocked hat off his head and bowed, his face and neck crimson. "Oh, ah, yes. Sorry, ma'am."

"Your ladyship," Preston said from behind her, but laughter rang in his voice too. "I beg your pardon, Lady Livia. This is Mickey, my new page."

She turned her head to meet his eyes. "Truly? Where did you find him?"

"At that benighted orphanage you were visiting. The boy did his best to help, although he could not say much."

He shot a glare at Mickey, now silently waiting, turning his hat around in his hands. His dark hair had obviously been shorn recently, a white line on his neck showing where the skin was usually hidden from the elements. "I beg your pardon for presenting him bare-headed, but his wig has not arrived yet."

The boy made a sound Livia could have sworn was a snort. "Never wore one of those fings before," he muttered.

"I daresay." She did her best to sound stern. "But you must learn to do so now. Put your hat back on."

The boy settled the hat on his head and lifted his chin to stare at her. She met his blue eyes steadily.

"You should not meet a lady's eyes directly," Preston told him. The boy grimaced but obeyed the duke and looked down. "You see how quick he is? I have expectations that he will make an excellent servant."

"You have set yourself a hard task, sir. You might prefer him to work in a position less public. Your stables, perhaps."

"Oh no. I am quite convinced he will make an excellent body servant if he works hard. Besides, I'm not sure I fully trust him, so keeping him close is the best way for now. He is my new page and he will remain so for the time being."

"And you are training him yourself? That's very Christian of you."

"Isn't it?"

Whipping her head around, she caught an expression of unholy glee before he masked it with bland politeness. "You're inflicting this child on society."

"I cannot deny that the training may not go completely unobserved. But I am doing my duty, don't you agree?"

She could hardly say no. Anyone taken out of that appalling place would have a better life. When the duke had told her the orphanage was little better than a thieves' kitchen, she could not be surprised, and not only because of her reaction to the children there. "I had thought to send money to help them. But that would not have helped, would it?"

"No. The supervisor, who my new servant informs me goes by the name of Ole Smiffy, would have pocketed it. I will inform the authorities of the use the orphanage is put to. Since the place is in the City, the magistrates at Bow Street might be interested."

"Thank you." She swallowed, aware her response still did not explain why she had abandoned the building so fast. Nor could she explain it, not without giving her real reason for doing so, and that, of course, was out of the question.

"I may need some help schooling this reprobate." His smile took some of the sting out of his words. But not all. "May I call on you, Lady Livia, to help me in this endeavor? After all, with the good example you set, I could hardly do less."

Her mother had joined them. "I'm glad my daughter has had some ameliorating effect on you, duke. However, I fear we must be on our way. Good day, sir."

Summarily dismissed, the duke bowed and moved away, beckoning to the boy, who scuttled behind him.

"Does he know he is making a laughing stock of himself?" Lady Strenshall asked her daughter.

"I think he is relishing it," she said, staring after his retreating form.

Chapter 5

"Try to keep up, boy," Adrian told Mickey. The boy scurried to catch him, but Adrian gave no quarter, striding ahead along the broad, smooth pavement. He'd seen Mickey move, and he knew the boy was trying to elicit sympathy. He refused to give it. If Adrian, in his privileged world, could learn to live without sympathy, so could this boy.

"You're a shameless child," Adrian added, as he paused outside the imposing entrance of White's Club. "Be at your most endearing, otherwise they won't let you in. You know where you are?"

The boy nodded. "Never bin inside, though."

"You surprise me," he drawled, before switching to more incisive and lower tones. "I want you to listen and tell me what you hear. Clear?"

The boy nodded. "I do that sometimes. Surprise people. What do you want to know?"

He raised a brow. "Your accent is markedly better."

"I listen and learn."

Adrian was sure of the boy's native intelligence. Equally sure that he would surprise a few more people before he was done. One thing he knew for sure—Mickey wasn't going back to the place he'd come from. He was far too good for that.

"Come on, then. Behave yourself in here."

"Your grace."

No errors with his title now. Adrian led the way up the steps, threw his hat and gloves on the counter to the usher on duty, handed over his sword and led the way up the broad staircase to the club rooms. Nobody questioned him about Mickey, which would have been a bore.

While Adrian chose not to attend most social events where he could expect to meet hopeful brides-to-be, they knew him well in this exclusively male preserve. As an unmarried duke he bore a target on his back for young, unmarried women, and until now he hadn't been ready to accept that challenge. But now, here he was, working hard on behalf of a young woman.

Had he been caught? If he had, he doubted Livia realized or wanted it. That would be the ultimate irony, to be caught on a hook that wasn't dangling for him. But he liked her independent spirit, her ability to fight back. She would not cling to him, or demand things he had no ability to give. For the first time since his wife died, he was considering the prospect of remarrying. He could hardly believe it himself.

Only considering it, though.

With a careless shrug, he strolled into the main club room.

Essentially masculine, the room was filled with comfortable seats, arranged in informal groups, and small tables, with a few shelves and sideboards holding decanters and journals. Men sat around, chatting, the hum of conversation a buzz in the air. A significant pause occurred when he entered, and a few heads turned his way. Most glanced away again, but a few watched him curiously as he sauntered around the tables until someone hailed him. "Preston, would you care to join us?"

He deigned to notice the Marquess of Strenshall and his eldest son, Lord Malton, sitting with the youngest of the male set of twins, Lord Darius Shaw, who watched him from under heavy lids, his gray eyes shrewd. Adrian had clashed with him before, an enjoyable discussion on a point of law. He regarded the whole family as intelligent, but Darius had a particularly fine mind.

Pulling back a chair, he seated himself and accepted a glass of wine, shaking his lace cuffs back before he took a sip of the ruby liquid. Although he didn't look around, he felt the presence of Mickey just behind him, on the left side. Exactly where a servant should stand. "You have a new follower," the marquess remarked.

"A page."

"Appropriate," Darius remarked.

The air froze. The last time anyone in his family had a page, disaster had resulted. But that page had been black. Adrian gripped his glass, forcing himself to pause, not to throw the contents into the man's face. "And your meaning, sir?"

"Merely that a duke should have an attendant." Darius raised his own glass. "Your health, sir."

He didn't mean that in the least, but Adrian had no way of challenging him. He always faced direct accusations head-on. The heir to a powerful dukedom not descended from the male line, people said. An impostor, they claimed. He could do nothing to counter that argument, short of throwing himself in the river.

Or perhaps…yes. Adrian nodded and raised his own glass. "Yours. The irony is not lost on me. I daresay many people will also note it. I found the lad in an orphanage close to the home of my last mistress."

He lifted a brow and allowed his lips to quirk. "Perhaps, sir, since I've done with her and she has a cozy house as a consequence, you would like to take her over. I believe she is still without a permanent protector. Just let me know and I'll give you her direction."

Malton shouted with laughter. His jest had hit home. Darius glared at Adrian frigidly, before he gave a reluctant nod. "Touché, sir. I thank you for your consideration, but I believe I will reject your kind offer."

A hit on both sides and honor satisfied.

Most of society knew Darius's preferences did not lie in the direction of the female sex but chose to turn its collective blind eye to the fact. Darius belonged to the extended family known as the Emperors of London. Few people dared to cross them.

Adrian would. Frankly he didn't care. They could only hurt him if he cared about what they did to him and he'd lost that ability years ago. Caring would open him up to hurt. He'd had enough of that.

Not a flinch marked Lord Darius's easy demeanor and the surface of the wine in the glass he held wasn't marked by even a quiver. "But thank you for the offer. Does the lady not have a say in her future admirers?"

"This one does." Adrian took a sip of his wine, quietly toasting Darius. "It's Ophelia d'Arblay. Currently the toast of the Theatre Royal."

"But not for long," Malton commented. "Her spectacular beauty is only surpassed by the woodenness of her acting."

"Indeed," Adrian said. "It matches her prowess in other pursuits." Not even a good actress in bed, she would have to learn better if she wanted to progress in the world of the demi-monde. "I found someone else in the district too," he continued smoothly, "as well as my new page. Much prettier and far more ill-suited to the neighborhood."

Lord Malton's fine lips firmed. "My sister."

Nobody could overhear them in this corner if they kept their voices down. "Indeed. She escaped the orphanage before the carriage arrived to take her home. I found her in King Street."

"We have to thank you for your help in that situation," the marquess said smoothly. "Also for your discretion."

And taking her into the house of his mistress, but Adrian guessed Livia's father didn't know that part. Or preferred to skim over it. The kiss—he would know about that, but no significant scandal had ensued, so perhaps he was forgiven. "You're welcome. If I had a sister, I'm sure you'd do the same favor for her."

"Lady Livia is my only unmarried daughter," the marquess said steadily. He didn't have to make the point quite so forcibly.

"I am aware of that, sir," Adrian answered gravely.

"If you are seen in her company much more, society will expect tidings. Any failure in that direction will reflect on her rather than on you."

Adrian tilted his glass and examined the weak late autumn sunlight striking off the deeply cut facets. "I am aware."

He wasn't here to make assurances. Much better was having people on edge around him. That gave him an advantage, especially if he knew what they were nervous about. "I will do as I see fit. You will have to trust me, gentlemen, will you not?"

"Not at all," Malton answered, cool as you please. "Merely that if you compromise my sister in any way, you will suffer for it. Or you will marry her."

"Surely that would be my decision. I take it, then, that you would welcome me into the family?"

Strenshall looked uneasy. Adrian knew that expression—he'd seen it often enough. "We would prefer that matters did not progress so far."

"Why? What could conceivably deter your daughter from receiving my suit?" Gently, he placed the glass on the round table at his side. "Gentlemen, I give you good day. I do not expect you to answer that last question. I know the answer well enough. God knows I've heard it enough times."

Sick of this place, sick of being warned off, because this wasn't the first father to issue a warning, sick of constantly fighting against something that was not his fault, Adrian got to his feet. Followed by a silent Mickey, he left the club, taking his time collecting his hat and gloves at the desk in the lobby. He had to give his temper time to dissipate before he punched the nearest wall and made a total fool of himself.

Maybe smashing a room full of china knickknacks worked. It had certainly seemed to work for Ophelia.

What had angered him the most was the notion of being compelled to marry Livia. No warning sounds, no prickling sensation up his spine accompanied that warning. Nothing. If he married her, he would do it on his own terms, not dictated to by anyone else.

Adrian strode away, uncaring whether Mickey followed him or not. How could that happen? How could he not feel the warnings when marriage came anywhere near him? He couldn't marry anyone. He was tainted, a byword for disreputable behavior. He couldn't bring that to her. Neither could he give her his defiled blood. And by that he didn't mean his father. Either of them.

"Hey, sir, mister, your grace." Muttered curses followed in his wake. "Hold up!"

"What?" Exasperated, he swung around, the weighted skirts of his coat catching the boy around the shoulders and knocking him over. Undeterred, Mickey scrambled to his feet and stood, arms akimbo, glaring at Adrian.

Adrian liked that. He wanted people who were prepared to face him. "What is it, boy?"

"That man. That cove 'oo paid us for the brooch. 'E passed us on the way out."

After a string of inventive curses, Adrian felt better. Marginally. "Did you recognize him?"

The boy grunted. "Yes. It was him, I'm sure it was. But I don't know who it was." His h's were the first thing to leave him and the first to return, Adrian noted with interest. Followed swiftly by the g's.

"Did he recognize you?" That might put Mickey in danger or warn said cove that someone was after him.

"Naw. Didn't bother to look. He was glaring at you. I'm surprised you don't have a hole in your back."

That was nothing new to Adrian. "That could be any number of gentlemen."

"All the ones wiv wives you've tupped?"

Adrian knew better than to reprimand the boy for knowing. For one thing, he was older than he appeared, and for another, a person could hardly live on the streets of London without knowing. "Among other things. Keep your eyes peeled."

He debated whether to leave Mickey behind to watch for the man. But he might not be as lucky twice. His quarry could recognize the boy and then the game would be up. And Mickey might be in danger. Adrian still didn't know why this brooch was so important, but every time he made a move, something happened that convinced him there was more to it than a sentimental memento.

"You, my boy, are with me until further notice."

Mickey eyed him suspiciously. "So what when the job's done? You'll pay me off and send me back?"

"Is that what you want?"

Someone passed by and sniffed in disdain. Adrian ignored him.

"Maybe." Mickey stared at the pavement at his feet.

"I see. I can find you a position in my household, if you'd prefer that."

"Kitchen boy?"

Somehow Adrian thought not. This child was too intelligent to waste. "Don't worry. We'll work out what is best for you. Be assured I won't give you a few guineas and throw you back on the street. Not, at least, if you behave. Remember what I told you?"

The boy scraped his new shoe along the ground. "No thieving and no gossip."

"I'll amend that. No thieving unless I tell you. No gossip unless I tell you to repeat it." How better to spread a rumor than to ask a servant to do it?

He didn't need Mickey's cynical grin to tell him that double standards were involved here. All for a good cause.

To his surprise he discovered his temper had melted away. He might keep the boy as his page and annoy the fashionable world full-time. That would certainly enliven his life.

That would also happen if he married Livia. The Emperors tended to absorb the spouses that came into their fold, wrapping them into the powerful family that controlled so much. Adrian didn't know how to live in a group. He was an only child, brought up by his dynastically minded grandfather rather than his largely absent parents, his nearest relative a cousin who was currently his heir.

They did not share much of a social life. His cousin lived in another part of the country, only visiting occasionally to familiarize himself with the house and its methods, in case Adrian died in some duel, or in his mistress's bed.

So far neither had happened. He had increased his skill on the dueling field, and these days fought few to none. He had taken to having one mistress at a time. Doxies had lost their appeal a long time ago. What a sad rake he was turning out to be! If he didn't do something soon people would think he had turned over a new leaf. That would never do.

"Come on," he said, infused with new purpose. "We'll find a gambling hell. Let's see what we can wreak there."

* * * *

Lady Bradford had engaged a good crowd for her musicale, probably because she had promised the presence of the latest soprano to astonish the crowd at the Italian opera.

Livia enjoyed a good opera, but tonight left her wanting. She could not understand why. Especially when the soprano appeared and made everyone understand why she was so very good. She even managed an English ballad with a creditable accent.

After they passed through to the elegant salon where supper was laid out for them, they could talk. The room was crowded, people crushing close, but Livia wondered how much was from necessity and how much concerned their wish to overhear. She was only too aware that the current gossip centered around her and the Duke of Preston.

"A refreshing change," her mother said, "to have such a modest young lady with a truly excellent voice."

"The last song didn't interest me at all," her brother said, "but she sang it well."

And that was another thing. Marcus had come to town, bearing his wife, Viola, with a complete entourage to care for their precious baby. Livia was overjoyed, then dismayed. Viola had been the daughter of their land steward, and she'd belonged to their group of playmates. She knew Livia better than was comfortable right now, and Livia hated hiding her secret from her old friend. But not even Viola knew.

Viola was standing at Livia's elbow, watching her. Livia felt her perceptive gaze, warmth creeping along her left side as she forced her calm and interested demeanor. Her secret, dormant for so many years, threatened to rise up and drown her. She had thought it gone forever but recently everything she had done, every sight, had reminded her of her lost child. He'd be ten years old now. She refused to accept the alternative. Surely she'd have known if the baby had died?

Viola touched her shoulder. "Are you quite well, dear?" She must have felt Livia's shiver.

"Perfectly, thank you." Forcing a smile, Livia turned her head to meet Viola's gaze.

Out of the corner of her eye, she caught sight of the new entrant. Adrian—the Duke of Preston, that was—stood at the back of the crowded room, his rich blue coat a flag in the middle of a sea of pastel colors. Did he select where he would stand based on what he was wearing? Of course not. A man in somber black stood close to him, now she spread her field of vision to take in his surroundings. But Adrian sucked all the attention. Unless that effect purely affected her, that was.

Her foolish heart leaped, and her pulse throbbed in her throat, making breathing evenly difficult. Unfortunately, in her low-cut gown, that could easily be perceived if she did not control her reaction.

"Has someone attracted your interest?" Viola murmured.

Livia hated lying to her friends and family. She rarely did so. "No." But sometimes it had to be done.

"A shame. It's your turn, Livia." Viola glanced up, meeting her husband's gaze. They did that a lot—acted in concert, as if they were linked in some odd way. They adored each other, and Livia suspected they always had. But they hadn't realized until recently.

The duke made his way through the room to join her. Livia didn't have to see him, she sensed every step. As he came closer, his voice murmured through to her, exchanging platitudes. He was much better at meaningless chit-chat than she'd imagined, especially for someone who claimed they had no patience for society and its ways. On the other hand, the nearer he came, the more she lost her ability to think rationally.

She had to stop this nonsense. Not that she knew how.

"Ladies, well met," he murmured as he gave a perfect bow, but without the flourish at the end that many men preferred. Rising, he met Livia's gaze directly. To hide her reaction, she bobbed a curtsy, but he knew. She saw the knowledge in his eyes when she rose and lifted her chin. "It is good to see you all in such good heart. My lady, I merely wish to report that there has been some progress in retrieving your trinket."

Her stomach plummeted to her toes. "Thank you, but you need not concern yourself any longer."

"You have found it?" His raised brow told her he didn't believe her.

Where was that blasted soprano? Surely she'd rested enough by now? "No, sir, I have not, but it is a mere nothing. Of no importance."

"A memento of your grandmother, you said."

A gasp told Livia that her mother had got the gist of the discussion. "That little brooch? Goodness, Livia, you need not make such a fuss about it."

"I happened to mention it to his grace, but I didn't mean to put him to such trouble."

Lady Strenshall furled her fan, examining the glittering pattern on the sticks before addressing Preston once more. "Indeed, it is wrong of my daughter to request your help to retrieve it. It is true, the object is of sentimental value, but I'm sure if we speak to Kirkburton he will find something of our mother's to replace it."

"Oh, but…" Livia bit her tongue. Her mother knew the true value of the brooch, and how important it was that nobody understood its significance. "Yes, of course."

Preston would not have missed her small protest. He was entirely too quick for her liking. "I insist. Lady Livia did not ask for my help, but she mentioned it in my presence. What can a man do?" He spread his hands in a gesture of despair. "London is devoid of amusements. Pray allow me to fill my time with something a little more diverting than the usual distractions."

"You do not mean this charming evening, I am persuaded," Livia said, wickedness and a strong desire to get her revenge invading her.

"Naturally."

"The soprano is delightful. The toast of the Italian opera. Did you come to see her?"

Maybe he was looking for a replacement for Ophelia. The singer's dark hair and flashing eyes would provide him with the best diversion. Her protestations that she was a respectable woman would not last long in the face of this man's determination.

He gave her a bland smile. "No, I came to see you."

A few people sucked in a breath, not only the family but the others crowding close. He had equated her with the soprano? Well, it was her fault, after all. He'd turned her sally right back at her. She could do nothing other than smile and deploy her fan. "Thank you, sir. You know how to flatter a woman," she said, keeping her voice flat.

His smile, far too intimate, attacked that warmth inside her. If she wasn't so well-bred, she'd have squirmed under his perceptive gaze. "I do my poor best."

A movement from the door revealed their hostess, indicating they should return. The crowd moved slowly toward the exit, but Livia found an arm hooked firmly around hers, holding her back.

Patiently, she waited until everyone had filed out. Her mother turned, glanced at them and her eyes narrowed. "Five minutes," she said.

"You know," Livia said when everyone had left, leaving only Livia, Preston, and a few servants clearing up the mess the guests had left behind, "if you insist on hovering so close to me, people will get the wrong idea. And we will be forced to a position neither of us wants."

"I don't know," he said, gently turning her to face him. "I've been thinking that might not be a bad idea. Are you so averse to it?"

She blinked. "We are talking about the same thing, are we not?"

Not at all put out, he inclined his head, bringing his mouth closer. "A betrothal. Shall we set London by its collective ear?"

"Such address that you have!"

He laid his hand over hers. She hated that she couldn't control the trembling. "Why not? I will take the greatest care of you."

"You don't mean it. You're joking me." He could not do this. She could not do this. "I decided many years ago that I should remain single."

"Why? Why must you? You cannot shock me, Livia."

"Your grace—"

"Adrian. My name is Adrian."

Swallowing, she dared to lift her head and meet his calm gaze. "You merely look for another scandal, Adrian. Please, leave me alone. The brooch is of no consequence."

"Livia, you are lonely and troubled. I don't wish to leave you to this."

She said the only thing she could. "Sir Jeffrey Creasey is back from the army. We are old friends."

"Is he more than a friend?"

She nodded. "We grew up together."

"And you prefer him?" He sounded much steadier than she felt.

Around them the subdued clink of servants stacking plates and flatware kept her grounded. "We are childhood sweethearts."

"But you are not sweethearts now. I did not hear you say that. And until you do, I will not leave you to his mercies."

He straightened and stepped back. Already she felt his absence. She could not go on like this, pining for the wickedest man in London. In the country, most likely. She had to send him away before he tempted her beyond reason.

Already she was having thoughts and notions she must not. He was leading her into a place where she had firmly closed the door years before, showing her glimpses into a world she could never have.

"I don't like your Sir Jeffrey. He assumes you are his for the taking. Are you?"

Numbly, she shook her head, realizing a fraction too late that she should have nodded. Sent him away. "You only want me because I resist. Because you can't have me."

"I did at first, I admit. I sought to amuse myself, without compromising either of us. I never thought to marry again, but I never met anyone I could stomach for more than a few hours at a time."

A smile curved his lips, altogether different from the cynical face he showed to the world. This one revealed warmth, true humor and kindness. This was the man she could not resist. Seeing him like this made her understand how dangerous he truly was. "So no, my lady, my Livia, I will not go away. Not until I discover what you are hiding and what that brooch truly means to you."

Lifting her hand, he kissed it, never letting his gaze leave hers. His caress was as intimate, as meaningful as any she had ever received. Like the sealing of a vow, that kiss marked a turn in their relationship.

From what and to what she did not know. But something had changed between them.

Chapter 6

What was he thinking? He had shown her more than he intended. Her sweet face, her eyes fierce with tension she would not admit had called to her, demanding his help. Her words had said otherwise.

As Adrian left the house, not bothering with the second half of the evening's entertainment, he strode up the street, heading for the less salubrious and far more enjoyable parts of the city.

Entering into society again had proved interesting but snared him more than he wished. However, he had discovered the one woman who would not bore him. For the foreseeable future, at least.

He could promise nothing, but perhaps he'd found the woman who could keep him for long enough. He could make a child with her. An heir. After Anna had died, he had turned his face against marriage. They had torn through London, turned the city into their playground. He led the way, and she'd followed, but that way he could keep her at the correct distance. He'd imagined when she tired of their play they would breed, but she wasn't ready. Now she would never be.

Reaching Covent Garden, he gazed at the scene with mixed emotions. This place had provided distraction enough over the years. He'd brawled here, whored here, gambled in a cozy den not far from here, at the back of Maiden Lane. That was where he'd decided to go tonight.

The square was alive with people, whores calling out for business, bullies roaring outside gambling dens, lights everywhere, as if beeswax was free. Usually he loved the sight, a welcome change from the careful manners of the fashionable salons, but tonight he felt none of the excitement. That had all gone.

Having won the other night, despite the house being against him, he needed to lose a few thousand pounds. Throw it away heedlessly, donate it to the wickedness of the city. Get that temptation out of his system. He might even find a comely whore or two, although after Ophelia's spectacular tantrums, he was in no mood for careless swiving.

Only drawn by the allure of a perfectly respectable woman of fashion. That above all. His desire for her was running out of control, and if he did anything in this life, it was to make his lesser appetites serve him, not the other way about.

A few men nodded to him, and women swayed toward him, but he did not stop until he reached the door of the gaming hell. The paint was faded and peeling, the door rotting where it stood, but sturdy timbers were nailed across it. He knocked, recalling the specific tattoo he would need to use in order for the place to be opened.

A bully slid the door open a crack, grunted, and opened it wide enough for Adrian to enter. The glow of candlelight and the scent of beeswax greeted him. In this area a person would think that cheaper tallow would be the order of the day, but this den catered for the wealthy, and provided the amenities they expected.

As he descended the stairs, the hum of voices made themselves apparent. This was one of Adrian's favorite haunts, but he had none of his usual sense of homecoming as he entered the large room created by knocking together several cellars belonging to the houses above. He knew all the exits, and the signals, but the authorities tended to leave them alone. Rarely did they create any trouble.

A waiter hailed him. "What is your pleasure tonight, sir?" Titled gentlemen rarely went by their real names in this place. Unless they volunteered the information, they were never asked.

He waved a hand. "Whatever you consider interesting."

"The loo table is lively tonight, sir."

He nodded. "That will do." A pure game of chance would give him time to think about other things and try to calm his tempestuous thoughts.

As he took his seat, he swept a disinterested glance around the table, not allowing his attention to linger on anyone.

Not even Sir Jeffrey Creasey, who sat regarding him, turning a golden guinea around in his fingers.

Adrian favored him with a cool nod. He inclined his head. "Welcome, your grace. I take it I am dealing you in?"

Using his title was in direct contravention to the rules of the house. Sir Jeffrey could have used "Preston," or "sir," but he had chosen to go with Adrian's honorific. Adrian said nothing but let his eyelids droop in an expression of disdain. He did not care who knew his name, but others might. The implied disrespect niggled at him.

Seven men sat at the table, all of whom Adrian knew, at least by sight. He let the slur pass. Digging in his pocket, he found a handful of guineas, which he stacked next to him. In a better-furnished establishment they would have a table with recessed dishes for the money.

A waiter took his money and exchanged it for counters. Adrian understood the reasoning well. Players would throw these bone discs into the pool where they might hesitate if they had golden guineas before them. But they had to cash in their winnings before they left, because the tokens became worthless if they were taken out of the house and brought back in again.

That was also understandable but another win for the house. He found more guineas and had them exchanged. Soon he would move to notes of hand, all of which he would honor. Perhaps recklessly throwing his money away would help to cure the nagging feeling deep inside that he was waking up, turning into somebody he didn't know. Threatening to get out of control.

They cut for dealer, and the gentleman three away from Adrian won. He accepted his hand of three cards, glancing at them before laying them back down before him. He would pass, even though this hand was good. He wanted to see how Sir Jeffrey played.

He played well.

Over the next few hands Adrian watched him, aware that he was being scrutinized in turn.

Lord Blackburn tossed a counter into the growing pile in the center of the table. The last hand had gone unclaimed, so they were playing on. "Of course you have that gorgeous creature, Ophelia d'Arblay, in tow."

Adrian handed the girl a guinea—a real one. The woman made a show of biting it and tucked it into her pocket. She could hardly put it into her bodice, since that item of clothing was virtually nonexistent. Sir Jeffrey beckoned to her. "Come here."

The woman sidled around the table and Sir Jeffrey tugged her into his lap. After pushing down her shift, he played with her nipples, pulling and tugging them as he glanced at his cards.

Adrian winced for her. She must have nipples of steel to put up with that treatment. "You learned some interesting habits in the army, sir."

Sir Jeffrey didn't appear perturbed, but tossed a few more counters into the pile. "When a man doesn't know if tomorrow will be his last day on earth, he takes his pleasures when they appear." He pinched the girl, and when she yelped, he laughed.

All three of Adrian's cards were trumps. He couldn't refuse this challenge. His suspicions were roused when Sir Jeffrey beat him, but only just each time, one card above his. That was clumsy. A man learned to expect to lose in these dens, but not to another gentleman.

Sir Jeffrey had bribed the house. That doxy was probably feeding him the cards. Her skill must be prodigious, since she didn't have many places to hide them.

In this game a little luck went a long way. So did skill. While the man was a good player, he didn't have Adrian's experience of Covent Garden gaming hells. His next hand was equally tempting. Since the pot was small, Sir Jeffrey having won the previous one, Adrian played, knowing he'd lose.

Calling for another bottle of wine, he glanced at the cards dealt by Walton, who sat to his left. Walton met Adrian's eyes, his brows slightly raised. He'd guessed as well. Damn, if two of them had worked out the play so quickly Sir Jeffrey could be in trouble. If exposed, he'd never get over the scandal. He didn't have a title like Adrian's, one he could fall back on. Didn't he realize that?

Obviously not. Adrian sensed a bully-boy. Or maybe he was biased, because of Sir Jeffrey's friendship with Livia. His mouth firmed. Of course, everything went back to her these days.

A moderate hand worked for him. Although he didn't win the game, he won a trick, which stopped Sir Jeffrey taking the pot. Since he elected to leave his stake in, the pot grew.

Adrian played judiciously, waiting until the pile at the center of the table swelled to over a thousand guineas. Regretfully, he would have to bring this game to a close. If his guess was correct, the man was playing far too deep. On army pay and with a small estate, a thousand guineas would wipe him out. Or put him right. Perhaps Adrian should let him win.

The less he had to do with this man the better, but for Livia's sake, he'd find out what he could. For his own sake too. He liked to know his enemies, and he would take on the challenge with absolute pleasure.

Lounging back in his chair, feeling the worn leather give way as he moved, he gave every impression of bored acceptance, playing the game as a gentleman should, without too much attention. Another kind of play, subtler and infinitely more interesting than the one going on before them.

His deal, so he shuffled. There they were, the notches on the sides of the cards that showed Sir Jeffrey which cards others had. Adrian dealt the cards fairly, receiving an excellent hand that he could use, but this time when he picked them up, he took care to cover the notches. Sir Jeffrey would spot what he was doing, but what of that?

He played and won. He pulled the counters toward him as if they were worth as little as the bone they were fashioned from. Picking up the five hundred guinea chip, he played with the disc, winding it around his fingers deftly, a childish trick but one that gave him a great deal of satisfaction when he saw the expression Sir Jeffrey was unable to hide.

His opponent pulled back his coat and drew out his hunter watch, dislodging the woman on his knee. She got up with an affronted squeak, pulling her shift back into place. Ignoring her, he flicked open the lid of his watch. The glint of gold attracted Adrian's attention. He had something pinned to his waistcoat pocket, securing the watch chain in place. Then he dragged the woman back down.

Not before Adrian had seen the small, circular gold brooch. The fluting and twists around the edge gave the piece a feminine appearance. Although difficult to see in this flickering, dim light, Adrian was sure the brooch was engraved with initials.

The man was flaunting his possession of the brooch Livia was searching for. Either that, or he knew nothing and the appearance of the piece was pure coincidence.

Adrian didn't believe that for a minute. He couldn't challenge the man, who was now staring at him, his chin stuck out, as if waiting for the accusation. A clever move would be to obtain something similar and taunt Adrian with it, force him to come out into the open. Then make a fool of him. Ridicule worked much better than duels or outright opposition, especially when Adrian outranked this man. Hell, he outranked everybody at the table this evening. He didn't hold much store by that, but society did. And Adrian had never thrown a weapon away.

"That pin—have I seen it before?"

"This?" The rascal knew exactly what he meant, his fingers going immediately to the brooch, fingering it, stroking over the engraved surface. "It's a common enough design."

"So it is. Have you had it long? It occurs to me that my mother might like something similar."

A grunt came from his left as Blackburn registered his surprise. Adrian never mentioned his mother, who lived in discreet seclusion in the country. Sir Jeffrey did not appear to see this as strange. He had obviously not studied Adrian too closely. Perhaps he did not consider him a strong enough rival. Adrian would see about that.

"I believe most jewelers or goldsmiths will have something that will do. I've had this one for years. It belonged to an aunt, now sadly deceased. I use it as a good luck token." Sir Jeffrey's fingers closed over the brooch, as if protecting it.

"I see. Then of course it cannot be the same one." Except Adrian wanted a closer look at it. He didn't trust Sir Jeffrey, and from his behavior here tonight, Adrian was right in his instinctive judgment. The man was pure slime.

He won that trick, as he'd expected, and the pot. Sir Jeffrey sucked in a breath, his nostrils contracting and his mouth going into a hard line before he forced himself to relax. Although not all thousand guineas were his, Adrian had struck a blow.

The cards came to him and he dealt another hand. This time he had the kind of hand card players dreamed of. The game was his, or not, as he chose. That depended on Sir Jeffrey.

The man in question fingered the woman sprawled in his lap as he took his cards. "I need to make the most of this. I'll have to be more discreet if I'm to wed soon."

Adrian's senses perked up. "You are? Who is the lucky woman?"

"You know her." Sir Jeffrey met Adrian's gaze, his gray eyes bloodshot but alert. "The owner of this." He touched the brooch. "She's been waiting for me all this time." He smirked. "I click my fingers and she comes." He demonstrated, the sharp snap loud in the sudden silence.

"You are referring to a mutual acquaintance?" Adrian's voice could freeze water if he chose.

Sir Jeffrey either didn't notice the warning tone, or alcohol had given him the bravado he needed. "Indeed. The beautiful strawberry-headed wench who waited for me all these years. You see..." He leaned forward as if to vouchsafe a confidence, but he didn't moderate the volume of his statements. "I've been there already. And no man can compare to me, or so she told me at the time." Leaning back, he tweaked the whore's breast. "As you will shortly discover, my dear, if you behave yourself."

Adrian's blood ran cold, then hot as if someone had whipped back a screen before an inferno. The man dared to speak about Livia in a place like this? Nevertheless, for her sake, he moderated his tone. "I suggest you retract that statement."

Blackburn stared at him in alarm, as did everyone except the knave sitting across from him. They knew what that tone meant. Sir Jeffrey had pushed Adrian as far as he was willing to go.

"What, about Lady Livia?"

Adrian stood, shoving the table aside. Counters, cards, and wine tumbled to the floor in a huge crash, but Adrian didn't take his eyes off the man before him. He needed impediments out the way because he was going to kill him.

The whore leaped up and hurried out of the way, breasts bouncing. The others at the table sprang back. Blackburn stood more slowly. "Preston?"

Adrian drew the only weapon available to him—his dress sword. A thin blade, the hilt elaborate, and glittering with jewels, it wouldn't stand much punishment. So he'd use it wisely. One thrust in the right place should do the job.

His habitual coolness made its presence known but could not overcome the blaze of fury sweeping over him.

Sir Jeffrey knocked the blade aside, taking a scratch on the back of his hand. Slowly, he got to his feet. "That thing?" He gave the blade a sneering look. "What are you going to do with that? Prick me?"

A chill swept through him, the cool of white-hot anger. He'd gone beyond fury. "Kill you unless you take that remark about our mutual friend back." Naming her was unspeakable. Unbearable. He refused to allow it.

From the way Blackburn stood with him, Adrian was not the only man who felt that way. "I'm your second, if you need one."

"Much appreciated, sir." He kept his attention on Sir Jeffrey. "Take it back."

"Is that a challenge?"

"Now or tomorrow morning."

"Oho." Sir Jeffrey glanced around, assessing his audience. Nobody was playing cards now. They were baying for blood, shouting encouragement. "Then let's deal with it here, shall we?"

Lazily, Sir Jeffrey stood and faced Adrian. "Fists or swords? Or maybe pistols?" He glanced around the cramped space. "Although where would be the sport in that? We could hardly miss at this range."

"Blow each other's heads off," Blackburn murmured. "It might be interesting, at that."

Adrian lifted a shoulder in a half-shrug. "I don't need a pistol to take his head off."

Someone thrust two swords between them. Army-style sabers by the look of them, thrust into cheap, cracked leather sheaths. Adrian took them both, ignoring Sir Jeffrey's "Hardly fair."

Nobody commented as Adrian examined the weapons, running his thumb lightly against the blades. They were true, straight, keen with sharpening and freshly oiled. Despite the lack of space, he could use these. He glanced at Blackburn and handed him the swords. Blackburn went through the same process before he nodded at both men. "Are you sure about this, gentlemen? Can you not discuss the matter peaceably?"

Adrian's answer was a snort.

"You think you can beat me, a trained soldier?" That was why Sir Jeffrey was smug. He assumed he had the upper hand. Especially with army weapons.

Oh dear. Did the man think there was nothing but padding under Adrian's coat?

Adrian disabused him. Peeling off his coat, he handed the heavy silk garment to a man standing close. Startled, he recognized Lord Darius Shaw, one of Livia's brothers. "I didn't know you were here."

"I wasn't. I was in the theater, but you know how fast word travels." Darius glanced at Sir Jeffrey and bestowed a small bow on him. "Sir."

"Shaw." The air between Darius and Sir Jeffrey turned decidedly icy. Did the two have bad blood? Another black mark against Sir Jeffrey, as far as Adrian was concerned.

"I would take your place, sir," Darius said. "I believe the traduced lady is closer to me."

"Stand in line." Adrian snarled.

Blackburn held out the swords, balanced on the palms of his hands. Without paying attention, Adrian accepted the first.

Sir Jeffrey took the other, and made play with it, swinging it and testing the blade. The others made themselves busy shoving the tables against the stone walls and piling the chairs on top.

A gentleman would have waited for them to finish. Before tonight Adrian would have said he was no gentleman, but Sir Jeffrey proved him wrong by coming at him swinging. The blade sliced through the air.

Alarmed shouts of "Get out of the way!" and "Watch out, man!" came from all sides. The whores had long gone, as far as Adrian could tell, but he concentrated on nothing but this man. They had not even agreed to the terms.

Forget that. If he could kill the bastard, he would do it.

He timed his block perfectly, cutting his sword up to block Sir Jeffrey's slash, the blade at an angle so the sharp edge wasn't damaged. Lifting farther, he swept Sir Jeffrey's attack aside, and sprang back.

Rough floors, lots of grip, no slide. He marked it, and waited, poised, for Sir Jeffrey's next attack. He would learn his opponent's style, the way he preferred to work. Army trained men usually had a straightforward approach, with none of the tricks that marked the expert swordsman. And Adrian was, despite the wealth and privilege Sir Jeffrey obviously despised, an expert swordsman.

Sir Jeffrey smiled, baring his teeth. He jerked his head. "Come on then. Or are you ready to give in?"

Adrian let his lids droop over his eyes. "Hardly. I am like to die of boredom, waiting so long."

He would not allow Sir Jeffrey to taunt him into making a premature move but try to get him to make one.

The murmur behind him swelled as the men increased their bets. "I'll take those odds," he called out. They were already close to evens. Nobody knew Sir Jeffrey's prowess, but he had been a military man. Most men here knew Adrian's reputation with the sword.

Adrian pretended to fumble for his watch. "For God's sake, man, I don't have all night."

His lack of attention on his opponent did the trick. Sir Jeffrey came at him, a hard drive, which, had it found its mark, would have skewered Adrian through his belly. A good place to aim for, since a man sliced through the stomach didn't fight well and bled a lot. Not good because a man hit there tended to die.

Adrian curved back, moving aside at the last moment and catching Sir Jeffrey's sword with his own, forcing the man off-balance.

Sir Jeffrey surged forward, men diving out of the way, but caught a nearby table with his free hand, steadying himself.

Before he could recover, Adrian was on him. The fierce temper had left him now. With cold calculation, he went for Sir Jeffrey's sword arm to put him out of the game.

The man spun around and met the blow, knocking Adrian's weapon aside in a clash that could have been heard in the street.

Adrian didn't hesitate, stepping aside fluidly and turning his sword in his hand, a drop and catch that few could have emulated. It ended in a lunge, still to Sir Jeffrey's right side, high, carefully avoiding the vital organs.

Sir Jeffrey had no such finesse. He went for the heart. This time Adrian ducked under the blade at the last moment he dared and came up, one knee collecting splinters on the floor, the other firm and true, aiming for Sir Jeffrey's arm.

He must be aware of what Adrian intended now. He spun around, the movement hampered by the uneven boards under his feet, sweeping his weapon around ready to collect any attack from the flank or his front.

Adrian did not attempt to attack until Sir Jeffrey over-spun and had to stop himself abruptly. With a tight grin, Adrian took his chance and went up. Sir Jeffrey parried the attack, and suddenly they were close, sword sliding against sword, hilts connecting.

Their gazes met in a single piercing, accusatory exchange, as pointed as the finest steel blade. "You shall not have her," Sir Jeffrey said, spittle marking his lips. "She is already mine."

Adrian didn't bother to reply. Releasing his hold on the sword, he brought his left hand up, catching his opponent squarely on the chin.

Sir Jeffrey's head snapped back and he fell, solid as a tree trunk hitting the forest floor. Dead unconscious, but not expired. Sir Jeffrey had gone for killing blows, which had made him predictable. Adrian merely wanted to disable him. Not that he didn't wish the man harm, but he didn't want to be accused of murdering the ruffian.

The only sound in the room was Adrian's breathing, until Blackburn sprang forward. "Well done, sir!"

Adrian didn't show it, but he was shaken. He'd come close to losing his rationality, his capacity for isolation that had kept him alive.

He'd begun the fight with murderous intent. Somehow he had found his sangfroid once more, his common sense and drew back.

Without a word, he turned and left, dropping the sword as if it burned him.

At the end of the street he paused, hearing the patter of feet behind him. Mickey caught up with him, his hand over his heart, his chest heaving. "'Ere." He thrust a handful of coins and papers—IOUs—at Adrian. "Your winnin's."

Despite his ill-temper, the boy's gesture astonished Adrian out of his mood. "You could have taken it and run."

"Nah." The boy shook his head. "I'm in this for the long run, me. What's the point of takin' this, when I can't collect on the paper and all I get is back on the streets?"

Adrian was impressed. "You're a perspicacious boy."

Mickey didn't seem concerned, giving a cheerful shrug. "If you say so."

His face cracked in a reluctant and unexpected grin. "I shouldn't keep you up so late. I'm convinced Lady Livia disapproves of me employing you in this way."

"If she knew where you took me tonight, she'd 'ave a fit." Mickey grimaced. "And she's going to get to 'ear about it."

Adrian had already worked that out. "Her brother was there, but he won't tell her. Nevertheless, the story will be all around London tomorrow. Damnation, I meant to protect her."

"'T wasn't you wot did it. The other cove threw the name around."

And he'd said something that had riled Adrian's temper. "I had her first," he'd said. Adrian was inclined to believe that was an empty boast. The man would have said anything to drive him away. Or to prove a point, maybe. Dismissing the statement, he decided Sir Jeffrey had only said it to touch a sore point and make Adrian do something rash. Lose at cards, maybe. Because Sir Jeffrey had appeared somewhat desperate. Was he running short of money? Living in society, particularly in London, was far from cheap. And Sir Jeffrey had political ambitions. There were great rewards in politics, most of them of the gold, clinking kind. Pitt claimed he was incorruptible, but then, as one of the wealthiest men in the country, he could afford to be. But his companions played deep and hard. To run with that crowd, a man needed deep pockets.

"I meant what I said when I promised you would never go back to the rookeries."

"Thanks. I think." Mickey peered up at him, his head tilted to one side as if assessing his chances. "You've got a rare temper on you."

"So I have. But I can control it, mostly. Notice I didn't kill him."

"Pity. I don't like that cove." Mickey had recovered his sangfroid, and his accent. "He's sly. You know? Oh, and I got something else for you. You seemed interested in it." Digging his hand in the deep pocket of his coat, Mickey came up with a small, gold object, no bigger than a guinea. It gleamed in the moonlight.

Adrian took it and replaced the brooch with a real guinea. Mickey didn't bite it. He shoved it in his pocket. "Much appreciated. See? If I'd taken your coins I'd be fifty guineas in pocket and some bits of paper I couldn't redeem. This way, I get it back a coin at a time."

"So you do. And my sponsorship." The boy was quick, honest by his own standards and knew how to hold his tongue. He made a useful companion. He could also pass unnoticed in many places, due to his speedy assimilation of accents and styles. He could ape anyone, from a beggar to a duke.

"Thank you for the brooch," Adrian said, because he believed in credit where it was due.

Chapter 7

Another day, another ball. Unlike the ones Livia had attended previously, this was the full-blown extravagant affair. Other balls had been smaller, limited, but Lady Calman had thrown open her doors and invited everyone in. Her daughter had snagged a duke, and her second daughter needed another.

Livia had to go if only to face down the critics. The story of the duel had spread around town at the speed of lightning. At least her name was somewhat obscured, but Livia had no doubt they'd fought over her. That wouldn't add to her reputation, but at least it put her squarely in the "scandalous Shaws" camp. Finally, she belonged. They might have known, people said, blood will out. She'd actually heard one woman say that today, at the Royal Exchange, until she'd seen Livia and her mother approaching.

For that reason, Livia doubted she'd meet Preston—Adrian—there, but the first thing she saw when she glided through the doors in the wake of her mother was his grace. Resplendent in royal-blue velvet, his buttons gleaming richly. She'd wager they were real gold, marching up one side of his coat and even more, slightly smaller, on his red and gold embroidered waistcoat. His linen was on point, and lace foamed at his throat and wrists. Anyone would think he was a civilized member of society.

He was talking to the aforementioned young lady in search of a duke. Everyone in society knew Lady Calman wanted a duke for each of her three daughters. Earls wouldn't do. That was the ultimate in idiocy, since Livia could think of at least three earls who had more wealth and influence than most dukes, but if Lady Calman wanted to fill her lottery card, then she was welcome to do so.

Just not with Adrian. *Her* duke.

Oh Lord, she was in trouble. When had she begun to think of him in those terms? She was a fool, she castigated herself harshly. The news of the duel was all over London, but she could not blame Adrian for that. She'd heard from people she trusted to tell her the truth, and they said that Jeffrey had started it, he'd been the person to use her name.

Still, both men had visited a notorious gaming hell.

While she appreciated the defense of her name, the fact Livia doubted he wanted her any more than he wanted Miss Horwich, currently smiling and simpering at something Adrian had just said. Yes, simpering. What was more, Livia had rarely seen anyone do it so well. Miss Horwich, second daughter of Viscount Calman and all of eighteen years old, could give lessons in the subject. Not that Livia wanted to take any. She had never felt the desire to simper. Especially when Adrian smiled and lifted Miss Horwich's hand to his lips, as if she'd done something really clever.

Irritated by the display, Livia turned away, and shocked Lord Wigmore with the dazzling brightness of her smile.

Five minutes later she found herself dancing with him. A minuet, moreover, where she would have to keep the same partner throughout the dance. Lord Wigmore, a jolly man of generous proportions, attacked the dance with vigor, prancing where he should have glided, bowing so low he nearly knocked heads with her as she curtseyed.

Even her immaculate training in society manners, even a lifetime of living with these people did not help Livia now. At Lord Wigmore's first gallop, she forced her snort down, swallowed it, but when he followed with a leap not unlike a cat pouncing on a mouse, a giggle escaped her.

Turning her head, she caught the too-perceptive gaze of Adrian, dancing with pretty Miss Horwich. The last person she wanted to share a joke with. Turning to her partner, she dodged aside as he planted his foot on the polished and chalked dance floor. The boards sagged under his weight. She would not call his lordship stout exactly, but he had the bulk that suggested he rarely missed a meal.

Made worse by his choice of pink satin for coat and breeches. Perhaps he'd have appeared to advantage in dark green, something more subdued. At least then he wouldn't clash so badly with her shade of peach. Everybody not dancing was watching—their gazes bored into her back, creating hot spots that made her want to shrug to get rid of them.

She was too well bred for that. But when he stood on her skirt, and the sound of ripping fabric rent the air, an audible gasp escaped her lips. Forcing a shaky smile, she began to back out of the situation when he began to apologize profusely. "Believe me, it is nothing, my lord. A mere accident. If you'll excuse me, I'll go and repair—"

She didn't get a chance. Reaching out, Lord Wigmore wrapped his hands around her upper arms, dragging her close. Far too close. His wine-scented breath filled the narrow space between them. "I am so sorry, Lady Livia. I am far more accustomed to the hunting field. I will, of course, replace the gown, but allow me to help you." The gleam in his eyes didn't bode well for whatever he had planned. In fact, she was almost certain he had trodden on her skirt deliberately.

"My mother is in the other room. I will find her."

As she turned, another pull on her skirt sent her tumbling forward. Hands out to brace her fall, Livia gasped when a pair of strong arms grasped her waist and lifted her.

Adrian gently set her on her feet and immediately released her. After a short bow, he scanned her face, his eyes wide. "Are you well?" He turned to his dancing partner, but she had wisely retreated to the edge of the floor, back to her mother, putting distance between herself and the disturbance.

"Yes, yes, I'm sure. I'm fine." She wasn't. Her heart thrummed hard, and she wanted nothing more than a glass of wine and a quiet seat somewhere.

The viscount was blustering. "I could carry you to your mother."

"Sir!" Her face flaming, Livia spread her fan and covered her burning cheeks. "As if you could do that."

"Would you allow me to escort you there?" Adrian smiled, meek as a lamb.

Rather than allow the viscount anywhere near her, Livia nodded and took his arm. "If you please."

Everybody was staring. Livia hated being the center of attention. This meeting was playing into their hands, and their tongues. Adrian had fought a duel over her and now he came to her rescue at a ball. She tried to move gracefully as she walked across the dance floor, but she stumbled before she recovered and bit her lip against the pain.

"I regret the disturbance," Adrian said to the young lady he'd been dancing with. "May I seek the pleasure of your company another time? I would escort Lady Livia to her mother."

Miss Horwich's mother had swiftly caught up to them.

"She went into the supper room," Lady Calman said, tight-lipped. "Of course you must do so, sir. Lady Livia, I can put a room at your disposal if you wish to use it. Up the stairs and turn right. Take the first door along the corridor. It is a guest room and you are welcome to stay there as long as you wish."

So Livia's stumble had not escaped her. Of course it had not. "Thank you." In truth she would welcome the use of a quiet room.

The supper room was next door. Taking his time, Adrian led her there. Leaning close, he murmured, "You're hurt."

"Just a wrench. I'm sure it isn't serious." Although she tried to keep her air of calm, Livia couldn't stop the tremor in her voice.

He paused, then stepped forward once more. Quickening his pace, he took her through the supper room and out of the suite of rooms put aside for the ball.

A small staircase led up. Without hesitation, Adrian bent, tucked his arm under her knees and lifted her.

She could hardly scream. That would create even more attention. Anxiously casting her gaze around, she discovered nobody in sight, but he was halfway up the stairs by then. "What are you doing?" Keeping her voice low took effort.

He glanced at her. "You heard her ladyship. You're going to rest and I'm taking a look at your injury."

"Sir!"

"Hmm?" He refused to speak again until he'd shouldered open the door and entered a room dominated by a canopied bed draped in apple green. He dumped her on the bed. Squeaking, her voice gone, Livia hoisted up her hoops so she would not reveal everything to his marauding eyes, and winced.

"You are hurt." He went down on one knee, lifting her skirts to reveal her satin-clad feet. He made swift work of the buckle on her left shoe, easing it off gently. "This needs some cold water." Getting up, he glanced back at her. "Don't move," he commanded.

Still taken completely aback by his high-handed actions, she had enough sense to realize he was not about to leave her alone or call for her mother. Who was not in the supper room. She must have gone the other way, to the card room.

The sound of water being wrung out of a cloth brought her to her senses. He would put that thing on her delicate silk stockings and ruin them. Either that, or he'd reach for her garter, and Livia was not at all sure she wanted his hands that high up her legs.

With a little fumbling, she managed to get the garter undone, only to meet his amused gaze, a smile lighting his face in an irresistible way. "Don't worry," he said. "I try to retain my gentlemanly behavior."

"But if you did, you would not have brought me here. And you would not have fought Sir Jeffrey in a duel in a—whorehouse!"

"A gaming hell," he corrected her calmly. "The whorehouse is a side business. I was playing cards. I did very well too." His lips opened, as if he would say something else, but he refrained. He began again. "But he should not have cast insinuations on you and he should not have mentioned your name. I merely punched him."

"I heard there was swordplay."

"There were, but we did not hurt one another with them." His glance betrayed his amusement, a smile and a gleam of his eyes. "I stopped his impertinence. I'd call it an undignified brawl. Do not worry."

"Worry? About men fighting over my honor?" She gave an indelicate snort. "In a gaming hell? Dear God, if I wasn't ruined before I am now." Honor she didn't have anymore, come to that. She worried her bottom lip between her teeth. What exactly had Jeffrey said? "You should have let my mother help me. Tongues will wag."

As he knelt down once more, he shook his head. "They're already wagging. We'll talk about that by and by. You were upset, as well as hurt. I couldn't leave you to the cats downstairs. Don't ask it of me."

"What if they'd seen you pick me up?"

He didn't reply. Gently, he rolled her stocking down. "Did that hurt you?"

Her wince wasn't from pain. His touch, stroking down her bare skin, shocked her. Mutely, she shook her head.

He eased the stocking off her foot and wrapped the cold cloth around her ankle. "I think you're right. A wrench. Still, they can be painful."

"C-could you leave me and find a maid to attend me?"

"Not yet." He smoothed her skirts down, and she didn't imagine it; he let his hands linger. She felt the touch as if he'd touched her skin. Her ankle throbbed, but already the pain was subsiding. Getting up, he sat on the bed next to her. She folded her hands together, pleating the fabric under her fingers.

"You saved me from the blatant advances of Lady Calman on behalf of her daughter."

Despite her good intentions to freeze him out and get him to leave, she smiled. She really should not feel so relaxed in his presence, as if addressing a member of her family, or someone she knew well. But his person and his behavior toward her belied his reputation and she felt strangely safe with him. "Didn't you know she wanted a duke for each of her daughters?"

He humphed. "She does? Nobody told me. I could no more marry that child than I could marry the Princess Amelia." One of the King's unmarried, older daughters, Princess Amelia would marry no one.

"You'd have more amusement with the princess." Livia bit her lip. "I should not have said that. Miss Horwich is a pretty girl with a sizable dowry. You should consider her. You could mold her exactly the way you wanted her. She's pretty and eager to please."

"That would drive me mad in a month. If I marry I want a woman who knows her own mind."

"Like me?" Something else she should not have said.

"Like you," he readily agreed.

"But you're not ready to remarry. You said so."

He moved closer. "Did I? Perhaps I was too hasty."

"Oh!" Her heart leaped. Did he mean to propose marriage? Why would he do that? "Why did you come tonight?" A pulse beat in her throat, so hard she could barely breathe.

"To see you." Reaching for her hand, he took it in his. Something metallic and hard pressed into her palm.

She looked down. "My brooch!" Tears sprang to her eyes as she turned the piece of jewelry over to check everything was there. There it was, the light brown baby hair. Instinctively, she stroked it, then folded her hand around the brooch and, heedless of everything except her gratitude, flung her arm around his neck and kissed him.

Adrian took command of the kiss. He opened her mouth with a flick of his tongue, pausing to trace her lips with the tip before licking gently within. Livia had meant a kiss of thanks, nothing more, but she fell into his caress. He urged her into his arms, to lean her head on his shoulder while he explored her and she explored him back. Relief flooded her.

Yes, relief. After that first kiss on King Street, she'd longed for more. She'd tried everything she knew to forget it, from pretending it never happened, to explaining it away as temporary madness, but nothing had worked. She still woke in the dead of night, longing to feel his arms around her and his mouth on hers.

And now here she was. Exactly where she wanted to be. Exactly where she should not be.

He lifted his lips, gazing down at her from eyes slumberous with desire. "Livia, we should go."

Anger and pain arced through her when she thought of going downstairs, hiding their interest, pretending nothing happened. "Just a few more minutes."

Hooking her arm around his neck, she drew him back down. With a groan, he acceded to her unspoken request and kissed her again.

He stroked over her torso. Even inside her trussed-up, boned, and corseted body, she felt that touch as if he caressed her bare skin. Then he did, following the line where her breasts swelled up from her gown, the single frill of lace the only barrier, easily pushed aside.

With a groan, she pushed her body into his hands, eager for more. He drew his lips fractionally away from hers and glanced down. "Yes, oh, you are so lovely. Move with me, sweetheart, let me feel you. Touch me." He sounded breathless, as enthralled as she.

Livia fumbled for his waistcoat buttons. Why did there have to be so many? His skin, so hot, was a layer of cloth away from her, the crisp linen tantalizingly thin. She could see the dark strands of chest hair, the small brown discs of his nipples, but she wanted more. Everything seemed so easy now.

He eased his fingers into the tight top of her stomacher and stays, made her shudder as he caressed her skin. Her head fell back, and his other hand was there, spread over the top of her back, supporting her as he ruthlessly took her mouth again. She attacked right back, exploring his mouth, skimming her tongue over his sharp, white teeth.

She barely heard the click, but her mother's "Oh, my God!" brought her back to reality with a sickening thud.

Her squeak as she regained her senses was overshadowed by Adrian's low groan. He touched his forehead to hers, and murmured, "Trust me," before he pulled away, flicking out his coat as if to straighten it, but also giving her a chance to put her bodice to rights. Shame flooded her, as she became aware of the room filling up.

Adrian glanced back, and finally moved away, but not too far. Picking up her hand, he placed it on his arm. Unfortunately, Lady Calman and her daughter had accompanied them, standing, mouths agape, in the open doorway.

Livia's mother was at her haughtiest—she lifted her chin and flicked out her fan with a snap, flashing Livia a glare and a warning Livia had seen directed at her sisters before. It was her "Let me deal with this" look.

However, she had not bargained for Adrian. He wouldn't let Livia move away, although she tugged at his arm. He merely clamped it to his side, trapping her hand. He waited until Lady Calman's initial outburst had subsided, ending with "I will not have such behavior in my house! Please leave immediately." She glared at Lady Strenshall. "I regret the necessity, but surely your daughter knows better. Did you not teach her the correct way of behaving?"

The marchioness turned a freezing stare onto her that would have frozen a lake of water under the midsummer sun. "My children are not your concern, my lady. They have behaved well enough to engage themselves in useful occupations that are valuable to this country." A not-so-subtle warning lay in her words.

"I regret that I did not moderate my behavior," Adrian said gravely. His cravat was torn aside, and the top half-dozen buttons of his waistcoat were undone. She'd managed to tousle his hair too, pulled some out of the neat black velvet bow at the back of his head. Despite that he spoke with all the hauteur of a duke. Livia had never seen him do that before. She had not even considered him capable of it. "When Lady Livia consented to accept my hand in marriage, I fear we were both transported by joy."

Then he released her, only to sink to his knees before her.

Her heart sank before he lifted her gown slightly to reveal her cloth-wrapped ankle. Tenderly, he unwound the fabric. "Slightly reddened but the swelling is much reduced. I'll find a maid to help you restore yourself, my love." Getting smoothly to his feet, he lifted her trembling hand and kissed it before laying it gently on her lap. He turned, his stance still protective of her, to address her mother. "And I beg your pardon, Lady Strenshall. I had merely intended to ask Lady Livia if she would accept me, should I approach her. I had meant to pay the marquess a visit in the morning. But I was so overjoyed by her acceptance we perhaps became a trifle over-enthusiastic. The blame is all mine. Of course we remain at your husband's disposal."

But her father would hardly deny him now.

"Do I not have a say in this?" Her protest might be futile, but she would be damned if she'd allow them to believe her a milksop miss, overwhelmed by a duke's passion. What a fool she'd been. But however tight this corner, they would emerge unscathed. The Shaw family always did and she would not let the family down.

"Of course, dearest." His tender smile warmed her inside, despite her anger. They could have got past this without any word of marriage. After all, Lady Calman wanted Adrian for her daughter. They could have agreed not to say anything. Livia would wager that would have worked. "You have every right."

Oh, now he said it. Far too late. "I did not exactly accept you."

"As you should not," her mother said briskly. "You know you will not do that until his grace has spoken to your father. But we may take it that he will accept his visit to you." She shot Livia a scathing glance. "Your appearance says as much."

Livia sighed. She would speak to her father first. Perhaps he would reject Adrian's request. "I beg your pardon, Mama." She would not do so in private, but the Shaws never engaged in public squabbling. How could she even consider marrying the man? How could her mother consider it? She suspected she did not, but was making the best of a scandalous situation. Someone would talk, if only to remark on the length of time the duke and Livia had spent together in an unoccupied bedroom.

The print shops would be full of the story in the morning and that, in many ways, was worse than the scandal-sheets. Livia did not doubt that Lady Calman would spread the story, if only out of spite. She had invited every eligible duke in London to her ball tonight in order to snare one for her daughter, and Livia had snatched one from under her nose.

Her mother examined Livia's ankle and sighed. "I do not want you walking again tonight. I would appreciate the services of a footman to carry her home immediately."

"Indeed," said her ladyship. No doubt eager to spread the scandal, she scurried from the room, her daughter at her heels.

Lady Strenshall quietly closed the door. "We must steal a march on her. Can you walk, Livia?"

"I daresay I can manage. It's only a wrench."

Her mother nodded. "Very well."

"I can take her," Adrian said.

The marchioness fixed him with a steely glare. "You, sir, have done enough for one night. If you wish to ameliorate this situation, then pray go to the clubs and carry your news. You are excited and pleased with your choice of bride."

"Mama—"

Livia's mother cut her off by raising one hand. "Please, we don't have much time. You will go home and let the maid put you to bed, Livia. Please don't argue. The footman will not accompany you. The coachman will be enough. Our man will go to the offices of the London Gazetteer. He will allow them to bribe him and he will tell them what I tell him to."

"And that will be?" Adrian drawled.

Anyone else would have heard the menace in his voice, but either Lady Strenshall chose not to or she truly did not notice. Or did not care. "That the Duke of Preston anticipated his prearranged visit to the Marquess of Strenshall and proposed to Lady Livia. The duke was searching for a place to conceal himself after the shameful chase by Lady Calman to attract his interest for her daughter, and he found Livia recovering from a badly damaged ankle, after Lord Calman had danced with her and trodden on

it heavily. Distressed by her condition, the duke blurted out his proposal."
She frowned. "Yes, that will do. Can you do that?" She lifted her chin,
challenging the man who was fully a foot taller than she.

Livia enjoyed seeing such a large man confronted by her mother in full
flow. Few people could resist her.

"I may," Preston said. "But are you sure you want your daughter
associated with the Blackamoor Duke?"

"Pshaw!" Livia had always admired her mother's capacity to find the
right words in any situation. "What has that to do with anything? We
will discuss your association at another time. However, if you ever want
to maul my daughter again, you will comply with my plan. Considering
I had so little time to develop it, I think it will serve. We must go on the
attack as fast as Lady Calman. I saw the light of battle in her eyes, even
if you did not."

Abruptly Adrian turned and went to the mirror hanging on the wall. As
he swiftly buttoned his waistcoat and retied his cravat, Livia caught sight
of a slight indentation in one cheek. He was suppressing a smile. "I did,
ma'am. I will do as you wish, if only to protect Lady Livia." He tugged
at the ribbon at the nape of his neck, letting his hair swing free, and set
to smoothing it back once more. "My man wants to add curls at the ears,
but I have never yet allowed it. Perhaps I should."

Livia wanted to sift her fingers through those abundant locks. A hint
of a curl coiled the ends, tempting her to touch, to wind them around her
fingers and drag him back. What he'd shared with her was explosive, and
if not for the advent of their visitors would have gone much further than it
did. That powerful body, the slight roughness against her palm when she
stroked his jaw, the promise of more…he had beguiled her. She couldn't
call it seduction. She was as much of an active party as he was.

With practiced hands, he grasped his hair in one hand and wound the
ribbon around it with the other. "I will not swear to stick to your script,
though. If embellishments occur, I will use them."

Lady Strenshall grimaced. "Try not to. My daughter's reputation is at stake."

He turned to face her, the skirts of his rich velvet coat swinging against
his thighs. "I am aware, ma'am. I will not damage that."

"Any further than you have already." Lady Strenshall sighed heavily.
"I suppose there is no stopping you."

After a sharp knock on the door, a footman in the Strenshall livery
entered. "My lady?"

"Lady Livia has damaged her ankle. Carry her to the carriage and take
her home. Send it back for me. Ensure she is carried into the house and up

to her room." She fixed Livia with her gimlet gaze. "Go straight to bed, and do not allow anyone other than your maid into your room."

Livia wanted to protest, but what did she have to protest against? She could not go downstairs with Adrian, that would answer everyone's questions and the scandal would spread. She could hold her head high and see the scandal through, but she could not bear to face that.

Not after she had hidden a much greater scandal. Casting about her, she spied the brooch, nestled in the folds of the counterpane. Snatching it up, she gripped it firmly. At least she had that back.

Chapter 8

"Are you sure about this, my dear?" Lady Strenshall was surrounded by the gowns that her daughter had already discarded. The bed was piled high with silk, satin, cotton and velvet.

Livia glanced over her shoulder to where her mother stood, deliberately in the way. Her maid, in the process of pinning a lace cap to her mistress's head, tutted, as well she could with a mouth full of pins. More of a low-throated grunt of protest. "About what?" She plucked the skirts of the gown she had finally settled on, a cream and cherry-red concoction, and flipped the satin bows marching down the front of her stomacher. "Do you think it isn't right?"

"It will do. Your father is closeted with the Duke of Preston."

"He's arrived already?" Goodness, she wasn't prepared. She hadn't considered what she should say, or how, or if she should allow him anywhere closer than a yard to her. Livia had spent last night making her bed into a churned-up mass of sheets.

"An hour ago." Lady Strenshall turned over a gown. "You still have this thing? I told you at the time you should not wear it. I thought you'd passed it on to Drusilla. Apricot is not a color you should even consider wearing. Not with your hair."

The gown had been Livia's small rebellion against blues and greens, together with the peach she had worn the other night. But the apricot had been a mistake. "Do as you wish with it, Mama. It would become you, if you wish to take it." What did gowns matter?

Her ladyship addressed Finch. "Bring the gown to me when you clear this up."

Finch, her mouth full of hairpins, bobbed a curtsy. "Yes, my lady." She thrust in another pin and dropped the rest in the dish on the dressing table. "I suggest you wear the pearls, my lady."

Good woman, doing her job. However, Livia didn't want to discuss anything with the woman present. She would trust her maid, but the fewer people who knew of her dilemma, the better. "You may go, Finch."

The woman bobbed a curtsy and left.

"Good. Now we may speak freely," Lady Strenshall said with satisfaction. Livia didn't like the sound of that. "About last night?"

"Naturally. You cannot marry the Duke of Preston."

Her heart leaped and her stomach screwed itself into a small ball. Hearing that sentence did terrible things to her. Made her want what she couldn't have. But she did not voice those feelings now. "I know."

She picked up her fan and tucked it in her pocket, taking one last look at herself in the mirror before turning away. Finch had drawn her hair back tightly, so the drag was almost painful. Her gown had few embellishments, only a double ruffled cuff. She hadn't allowed her maid to pull her stay laces as tight as usual, so her breasts did not rise under the prim linen fichu wrapped around her chest.

She would not wear the pearls.

"He isn't for me. I'm not for anyone, Mama, I know that."

Her mother nodded. "You must accept his proposal for now, but I trust your father is making clear that this is only a temporary measure."

She shook her head. "If I marry at all, it cannot be to a philandering scoundrel." Recalling Preston's many kindnesses to her, she bit her lip. He had not shown that side of himself, the ruthless, uncaring man who took and discarded women quicker than he used handkerchiefs. "It cannot be to someone at the center of society. I have tried to avoid contact, Mama, I truly have."

Lady Strenshall's eyes showed nothing but sorrow. "Your father is doing his best to find an excuse, a reason to stop him even asking you."

Because now Livia had become an official old maid. On the shelf, unmarried, a spinster. She had longed for this condition, not to have the pressure of marriage any longer. Nobody would eye her as a prospective bride, other than the eternal fortune hunters and old men wanting companionship. Perhaps she should consider them.

A lifetime of being an aunt and cousin, becoming a companion to her mother, who did not truly need one loomed before her. She could pursue studies, paint, spend more time playing music. All the things she enjoyed more than attending balls and having men and mamas judge her for what she was, not who. That ended today. As soon as word got out that she had refused the Duke of Preston, she'd be relegated to the back seats of life.

Just where she had always wanted to be.

Boredom awaited and she couldn't be happier. Except, one thing was for sure—she would never be bored with Adrian.

Except she'd had a taste of what might have been. Those kisses, the caresses had woken her to a world she hadn't believed existed. If she turned her back on all that, she would never know it again. That touch of ecstasy.

Not for her. Never again. She had donned her armor, and she was ready to use it. She had even painted her face, albeit with a little red on her cheeks and a dusting of rice-powder. Not the heavy white cream some of her contemporaries used, but more than usual.

"Will this create a scandal?" Her lip trembled, but she easily controlled it. She'd faced much worse than this.

"Probably, but not much of one. He did the honorable thing by proposing marriage, and you will do the right thing by accepting him, but only for a few months. He is a walking scandal."

"Yes." But he should not be. As she'd come to know him better, she'd understood more about him. He had done no worse than many other members of society. Only his recklessness made him stand out. And his coloring, proclaiming him a living scandal, a constant reminder of what his mother had done. Society would expect her, the daughter of one of the country's most prominent peers, to refuse him.

Her mother dusted her hands briskly, as if the situation was already dealt with. "We can leave for the country as soon as tomorrow, if you wish. As soon as his Parliamentary business is done, your father will follow us. Then the news of the betrothal can die a slow death. There is no reason at all why we should even visit town next season, if you do not wish to." With the practice of years, she glided with unconscious grace to the door. "I will not chaperone you for more than five minutes. I trust you to do what you need to."

She put her hand on the door panel and stood frozen before she turned back. "But if you wish to go ahead with the marriage, we will not cast you off."

Then she left, with a swish of skirts and the gentle tap of her shoes.

Livia had nothing left to do, no more preparations to make. She followed her mother down to the green drawing room.

* * * *

After an excruciatingly tedious meeting with Livia's father, Adrian finally left what was admittedly a comfortable study and a footman escorted him to the green drawing room. For a horrible moment Adrian thought the man was going to announce him but fortunately, after a gentle tap and a "Come!" from inside, he opened the door and allowed Adrian to enter.

His attention went immediately to Livia. If he'd been struck blind he'd still know where she was sitting. He bowed to her first, although he should have offered his first bow to her mother, as the older lady and the superior in rank.

But perhaps not superior in rank for long. His discussion with her father had solidified a few things in Adrian's mind, and the decisions he'd come to were probably not what his lordship had wanted. Served him right, for assuming matters he should not.

Livia sat, white-faced and unsmiling, her hands folded in her lap. Resplendent in a cherry-red and cream gown, she warmed his heart. Enough for him to worry a little. First he had to go through the kind of social niceties he despised and avoided at all costs. When he picked up his tea dish and answered Lady Strenshall's question about the success of the last harvest on his various estates—something he left to his staff—he caught Livia's half-grin before she suppressed it. And damnation, he answered it with a smile of his own, warm and intimate, just between then.

Abruptly, Lady Strenshall put down her tea dish and got to her feet. "If you will excuse me, I will leave you. I need to discuss something with my husband. I am anxious to catch him before he leaves for his club."

If affairs went according to plan, Adrian could be leaving with him, in order to put on a united front. He stood and bowed, going to the door and opening it for her ladyship. Blackamoor or not, Adrian knew his manners.

Although he closed the door quietly, Livia flinched at the small sound. She was nervous. Why, he couldn't imagine. They had struggled through the awkward situation last night. Now all they had to do was arrange the niceties.

Instead of returning to his chair, he sat next to her and reached for her hand. "Now, my sweet. Shall we decide what happens next?"

She snatched her hand back, clasping it in the other protectively, as if he'd burned her. Turning her head, she stared at a spot past his left ear. He would rather she looked at him. "Sir, your grace, I appreciate your kind offer. You got us out of the uncomfortable situation with considerable aplomb." She bit her lip in a way that made him want to do it. Then to soothe it with his tongue before taking the kiss deeper. Even the thought of it made his groin tighten. *Later*, he promised himself. *Let her speak first*. He didn't take her hand again, although he sat close enough to do so.

Adrian knew the value of patience, although he rarely imposed it upon himself. He did so now.

Livia blinked hard, and her throat moved in a swallow before she spoke again. "Indeed, there was little else we could do, given the circumstances. I'm aware that the situation was of my own making, and I owe you an apology."

Adrian could think of many other things they could have done, but he still waited. "You owe me nothing of the kind."

"I appreciate your help. However, I do not assume that your offer had any validity. In time the story will die down, and people will forget."

"What brought this on? Why do you insist on thinking that I'm not sincere?"

Her eyes widened as finally, she settled her gaze on his face. "Of course you are, but I put you in an untenable situation. Everyone knows you do not intend to marry. You are happy as you are. Or am I wrong?"

He allowed a small smile to curl the corners of his mouth. "You are not. Or you were not. However, I got to thinking. Why should we not go ahead with the match? What is stopping us?"

A single tear trickled from the corner of her left eye and began to meander down her cheek. Despite the jerk of her head as she turned away from him, he saw it clearly, gleaming in the bright light of the late-winter's day.

No, she would not cry. That would not happen. Adrian urged her into his arms, although her body stiffened and at first she tried to pull away. But he did not attempt to kiss her.

His impulse took him by surprise. He despised women who used tears to manipulate men, and rarely indulged them, but Livia's demonstration of distress only gave him the urge to hold her and soothe her troubles. These were genuine tears, rare items in his experience. She would not cry while he was there to calm her. "What is it, sweetheart? Why the tears?"

Giving up her attempt to pull away from him, she clutched his waistcoat, tucking two fingers between the buttons closest to his heart. "Because we can't. I have to refuse you."

Now it was Adrian's turn to stiffen. "You have a reason?"

Of course she did. Who would want to marry him, barring an ambitious fortune-hunter?

"Yes, but I cannot tell you. It is impossible, that is all. The reason has nothing to do with you and everything to do with me!"

What on earth did she mean? "Livia there has always been honesty between us. Let that continue now. It is my reputation? Or the history of my family?"

"No!"

Her vehemence made him smile. "You don't want to have anything to do with the Blackamoor Duke?"

She drew back, eyes sparkling with tears and anger. "No. What do you take me for?"

That was better. Her spirit had only disappeared temporarily. He preferred her like this, with anger heating her cheeks and adding sparks to her blue eyes. "A woman of sense," he suggested, watching her closely. He still didn't know her well enough to guess her reaction.

"Thank you." She folded her hands in her lap again, her spine rigid, her appearance perfectly judged. He liked this austere look on her. "But my decision stands. I cannot marry you. I owe you a great deal." She touched the gold brooch, which was pinned to her bodice. "You restored something to me that I hold precious. But I am not grateful enough to marry you for it."

"Good." He almost spat the world. "Gratitude is not what I'm looking for in a wife."

"I didn't think you were looking for anything in a wife." She turned her head, her emotions already neatly tucked away. "You were married before. By all accounts the marriage was tempestuous."

"Yes, it was. I was very young, but my grandfather wished to marry me off before I could blacken my reputation too much." He used the provocative word deliberately, but he evoked no response. If she wanted to talk about Anna, he would indulge her. Nobody had more right. He'd never asked another woman to marry him since her death.

"But you were in love."

A wry grin twisted his lips. "I thought I was, but I learned differently. Did you ever see her?"

"Of course. One could hardly miss her."

He remembered. "Anna appreciated being the center of attention. She had risen from country miss to duchess and she enjoyed every moment of it. Her attitude attracted me."

"It did?"

"Society called her a parvenu, an adventuress, a woman of little taste." He gave a harsh laugh. "She held her head high through it all."

"Because she had nothing to lose," Livia pointed out.

Perspicacious woman. "She could have returned to the country. But why should she? Unfortunately, her attitude and beauty attracted me, and I looked no deeper. My reputation could hardly be worse. We deserved one another, people said, and indeed we did." Perhaps he wouldn't go into details about what they did. Besides, Livia had a cousin who did something similar, married a woman who'd set society on its ear. Except that Lord

Winterton and his first wife had never evoked such condemnation or received the cut direct.

When Anna had done so, society's response had made Adrian furious and vengeful. Perhaps a few less duels, a more circumspect arena of operations might have helped. Because after the fact, after she'd died, he'd realized she wanted acceptance all along. He genuinely didn't care. She had.

"She was a rebellion against my grandfather, a symbol of my growing up. Except neither of us were completely grown up. We were children, playing games." Games that had killed Anna.

"She was very beautiful," Livia said.

Adrian tired of discussing what was gone. *Dead and gone*, he recalled bitterly. "So are you." He laid his hand on top of hers, feeling how tightly she held them, how stiffly she retained her pose. "Livia, why are we discussing Anna?"

"Because you said you would never marry again. You've said it often."

"Yes." Because he never wanted to make the same mistakes again. But he would not, not with Livia. "I have changed since then." Because of her.

He hadn't known how much it mattered to him until just now, when the threat of losing her was presented to him. With Anna, he dared her to do something, and that was enough. Livia would laugh at him and refuse him anyway. Maturity, or just a different attitude? But Livia had more fear, and he didn't know why.

He would find out.

"You can find someone else. Despite your—reputation, you're a duke and you're wealthy. Look about you." Getting up, she crossed to the window, arms folded across her waist. "Many women will welcome your advances."

"Even from the Blackamoor Duke?"

She didn't turn around but stared out of the window. "You rely on that epithet. Abandon it."

"Why should I? It has served me well over the years." He got to his feet and strode over to join her, standing behind her. "What has attracted you out there?"

The square had its usual appearance for this time of day; a few carriages, some pedestrians, one or two street sellers and a couple of chairmen waiting for custom, their sedan chair propped on the pavement before them, effectively blocking the passage of a nanny with her small charges. The woman made a fuss of walking around them, hustling the two children before her and glaring at the men, who leaned against the rails, hands in pockets, watching her.

Vaguely amusing but not enough to hold the kind of concentrated interest Livia was giving it. Gently, he placed his hands on her shoulders, the warmth of her body giving him tacit encouragement.

"Served you well?" She didn't turn around.

"Indeed. Importunate young women anxious to become my second duchess have reconsidered, once reminded of my story." To Livia he could not bring himself to lie. "I am a walking scandal. I should never have inherited the title, people said." Even though they were wrong. Once his father had acknowledged him as his son, nothing could dislodge Adrian short of death. "I can do anything I want, and nothing is as bad as that."

To his shock, she covered one of his hands with hers. He had not expected sympathy, but her warmth soothed him. "How did you bear it when you were a child?"

Recalling times when people had shouted names at him in the street, told him to get to the plantations where he belonged, or worst of all, turned their backs, Adrian closed his eyes. Anger had driven him then, and a sense of injustice that had never left him. Still drove him to perform his most outrageous acts. "I bore it," he said briefly.

"It does you no good. Stop using it. Then other people will."

"It's a familiar stick to thrash me with."

"Don't let it hurt you." The pressure on his hand warmed him far more than it should.

An opening. He wouldn't be the man he was if he didn't press his advantage. "Then stay with me and help me."

"What?"

Releasing his hand, she spun around to face him, a frown between her delicate brows. "What do you mean? You know we cannot marry. I told you as much."

"But if you refuse me after last night, you'll be labeled a flirt and a jilt. And worse."

Her shrug did not disguise the pain in her eyes. "Then that will happen. Since I do not intend to marry, that won't matter."

"That is foolishness. You aren't even thirty yet. You will marry."

She shook her head with a vehemence that told him more than he suspected she meant to. "No, I will not."

"You can hardly hold men off for the rest of your life. You're beautiful, Livia, accomplished and wealthy."

Again, a one-shouldered shrug. "I'm used to fending them off. Besides, if I refuse them all, I won't be trapped, will I?"

Something had happened to hurt her. Deeper than he'd suspected too, because that pain did not indicate the usual turmoil of youthful passion. He had assumed some disappointment had marked her, and she had dwelled on it. He'd assumed too much. She was not the spoiled beauty he had thought her on their first meeting. Though why she'd had such a reaction to the orphanage still eluded him. Violent and unreasonable. She could have waited for her carriage, but she'd run out into the street, endangering herself. From what she'd just said, she knew the dangers of an action. Her hair made her distinctive, easy to spot, as did the richness of her clothes. A fortune hunter could have swept her up in the street, and God knew that had happened more than once. The papers were full of the news, and a law had recently been enacted to prevent the spate of abductions.

Why would she lose her head? Before he left London, he would make more enquiries. Perhaps Mickey could help. It had something to do with that damned brooch, he was sure of it. He had not mentioned it since he'd returned it, but that lock of hair in the compartment at the back was the real treasure, not the brooch itself. Who had it belonged to?

To discover more, he had to keep her close, protect her.

"I have something to tell you," she said hesitantly, fear shadowing her eyes. "Something you'll find shocking. Unacceptable."

What could this sweet woman tell him that would shock him? He doubted anything could. "I swear, anything you say will not deter me. Consider this, sweet Livia. Accept my proposal." When she opened her mouth to protest, he touched her lips with his finger. The softness beguiled him, but he could not let her distract him until he'd had his say. "We know what this is. But for both our sakes, go ahead with it. Your father has invited me to your home for the Christmas season. We present ourselves to society, sign the contract and I will come to Derbyshire. We will let the betrothal continue. Society will see us together, and at the beginning of the season after Easter, we can consider the matter again." If he had to wait for her, then so be it. At least he could gain some time to win her.

She swallowed. Was she thinking the same as him? That their proximity would make endurance harder? If it did, Adrian would not complain.

His cousin had bellyached again about his annual visit to the estate, and Adrian could not blame him. He had his own life and did not wish to inherit the dukedom. "Once the new crop of young ladies enters society and the flurry of come-out balls begins, new scandals will erupt and people will forget us."

"I had not planned to come to town next season."

He took her chin between his thumb and forefinger, smiling down at her. "Then we will not do so."

Before she could protest, he gave in to temptation and kissed her. Her lips softened under his and she opened her mouth. Already she molded to him, bending her body into his, sighing into his mouth as he slipped his arm around her waist to bring her closer.

If he had to marry anyone, this would be the woman he'd choose. Hell, he had chosen her. Now he had to persuade her to choose him. If she agreed to his plan, they were partway there.

He loved kissing her. Usually a kiss softened a woman enough to make her amenable in bed. That was all. But with Livia a kiss was an end in itself. Touching her, holding that slim body next to his tempted him almost beyond bearing. So did the way she'd bundled herself up today. But when he held her tight, her body wasn't as tightly laced as he was used to in her. A delicious give that pressed her closer, her modest hoops bending under his insistent hold. Hunger took him, raging for more. He restrained himself, forcing an unaccustomed brake on his desires.

If he did that, he might tip the balance and she'd refuse his offer outright. Seduction, that was what he needed, not raw passion. This was a lady, a virgin, and he had to go slowly.

Adrian gave himself up to the lushness of her lips and the softness of her skin. He imagined himself in bed with her, stroking her skin, caressing her and talking to her.

Even that did not bring him up short. Fire surged through his veins and desire had its predictable result, hardening him, ready to take her. The thought of never having her, never touching her naked body, never making her his own, maddened him.

Separating their mouths was one of the most difficult tasks he'd ever accomplished.

Her eyes were dark, circled with ethereal blue, her lips reddened and slightly open. She was breathing heavily, her sweet breath touching his chin and the exposed part of his neck.

Smiling came naturally when he was looking at Livia. "So what do you say? Shall we agree to go along with society's plans for us?" He kept his voice low, and any doubt out of his eyes.

"You want me."

He had not expected her to say that, but he knew the answer. "Can you doubt it? Yes."

"After all those women?"

"Yes." Because she had something they did not, and damned if he knew what it was. But she fascinated him, and he hungered for more.

She bit her lip, and that proved enough for him to claim another kiss. This time she pushed her fingers into his hair and gripped his scalp as if holding on for her life as he kissed her. He guided her head to his shoulder, let her rest there while he took her.

Her cheek felt different. Chalkier. She'd worn powder. Alarm arced through him and he broke the kiss but kept her in his arms. "Promise me one thing."

"What?"

"You will not wear ceruse. Ever." That thick, white cream had done enough damage to him and his loved ones. "I have banned the stuff in my house."

She gave him a slumberous smile. "Why is that?"

"Promise me."

At his sharp tone, her smile faded and she blinked, the blue of her eyes returning. "Are you a tyrant, then?"

He shouldn't have mentioned it. He'd made a mistake, letting emotion ride him. "I try not to be." He stroked her cheek, watching her carefully. "I'm sorry." The words choked him, but he had to remember always that Livia was not Anna. Thank God. He must never compare the two.

"I don't wear the stuff anyway." This time he felt rather than saw her shrug because they were entwined, as close as they could be while dressed. "None of my family do. It's poisonous, you know." She gasped and stiffened. "Of course. I'm so sorry, I should not have teased you. I didn't remember—"

He touched his lips to her forehead. "Don't. This is nothing, and I shouldn't have mentioned it."

Ophelia d'Arblay had made copious use of ceruse, but Adrian hadn't cared. The decision belonged to her, and if she believed she needed it, then he would let her. But he wouldn't let the stuff come into contact with him, had always made her wash it off before he touched her. Because Livia was right. The stuff was poison. It had killed Anna.

Women became addicted to ceruse. It caused skin blemishes, so they used more to cover it up, then the blemishes festered. It discolored and destroyed teeth, and made the hair drop out. The notion of Livia using it made his body clench in pain. She would not, and he had yet another reason to hold her close and take care of her.

"Your wife was very beautiful," she said softly. "Everyone remembers her that way."

"She was." He wouldn't mention how hideous she had rendered herself at the end, so much that she retreated to her rooms and had all the mirrors covered. For the last six months she'd worn a veil. And more of the cream that was killing her, even though she knew it would. He'd raged and ripped up at her, but she'd told him not to hurt her so, pouted and cried. He'd withdrawn, vowing he would never care for anyone again.

Until now he'd kept that vow. "But you are here, and alive, and lovely. Let's concentrate on that."

A tremulous smile lit her face. "Very well. But this is a temporary arrangement, is it not? You're doing this for me, which I appreciate."

"It will save you from scandal."

Livia had sense, experience and enough of a fortune of her own to assure him she was not after his wealth. Not to mention her beauty and the devastating sensuality he was sure hid under her demure appearance. He had tasted it and brought her there. And he wanted to be the man who gave her more, who introduced her to the world of sensual intimacy.

When their passion abated they would remain friends, and if fortune smiled on them, they would raise their children together.

Because love was out of the question. Lasting love, the kind the novelists liked to lie about, didn't exist.

* * * *

Livia waited for the condemnation of her mother. Lady Strenshall had come upon her kissing her betrothed, and although they had broken apart, Adrian had kept hold of Livia's hand, and presented her to her mother as his future wife.

Lady Strenshall, her face a mask of pleasure, had congratulated the happy couple and informed them they would be leaving for the country the following week. Adrian had expressed his delight at the prospect and left them.

"I gave you a little longer," her mother had said, watching the maid clear up the tea tray. "I trust you will not allow him to maul you all the time."

Livia's cheeks heated, but she refused to hide away. As part of their arrangement she could claim kisses from Adrian, something she looked forward to with eagerness. But not in public, naturally. "No, Mama."

Livia had every indication that her siblings regularly "mauled" their other halves and enjoyed being mauled in their turn.

Although she would not go as far as they did, because she was not marrying the duke.

"Did you tell him?"

Livia didn't need her mother to explain what she needed to tell Adrian. As the door closed behind the maid, she said, "No. But I will."

"Before you wed, you must tell him everything. You cannot keep him in the dark."

"He will know I'm not a virgin on our wedding night. But I will tell him before then."

If matters ever grew that close, but she doubted they would. He had offered her a way out, and the tactic would work for him too. They would announce that they did not suit, or merely drift apart, and spend less time together. Since the duke was so volatile, he would probably drift off. Livia could use his next mistress, whoever she turned out to be, as an excuse. No doubt society would call her too fussy, since most men of fashion had a woman in keeping. Except that her father did not. She knew that for a fact. She also knew the door between her parents' bedrooms was well-oiled and in frequent use. Servants chattered.

"You must tell him everything." Lady Strenshall laid a hand on Livia's arm, forcing her to meet her mother's eyes. Lady Strenshall's brow was furrowed with concern, her finely drawn mouth flat.

"Yes. Everything. Even though I don't even know if my baby is dead or alive," she concluded bitterly.

"He is dead to you, Livia. We have not come all this way for nothing." This close, Livia saw her mother's distress. The baby was her first grandchild, the one she would never see.

Tears misted Livia's vision. "Can I not even know if he is alive?"

The hand on her arm trembled. Although her mother was too well-practiced to weep, Livia felt her tears. "We cannot know. It's for the best. In any case, the one person who knew where he went died before she could tell us. I'm sorry, my dear, I did not intend matters to fall out the way they did. Sherwood was to find the child a good home and keep me informed of his progress. In time I would tell you. But although she took the baby, she did not survive long enough to tell me anything but the boy was alive and in a good place. That is truly all I know."

"Was it to a local family?" Perhaps she could discover more when they went to the country. She might be able to ask people.

"I do not know. She was away for a week. She could have traveled to the end of the country in that time or passed the baby on to someone to take abroad. She had relatives in the south of England, and she'd worked for three families before she came to us. I am sure she did the best she could for the child."

Livia must keep faith that her baby was alive. She couldn't bear anything else. She had steadfastly refused to tell her parents who the father was, the only way to keep the peace between the families.

She refused to give up. The hole in her heart wasn't as open and raw as it once was, but it would never be healed.

Chapter 9

Adrian enjoyed walking through the streets of London. All life lay there, if one cared to look about. If a man didn't mind brushing shoulders with miscreants, could bear or even enjoy the various scents, and the noise, then the great city was better than the theater. He always kept his belongings buried deep, and more often than not left his sword at home in favor of a tidy little pistol and his fists. Today he wore the weapon as a symbol of his status. He might need it, if he was to face a significant number of the Emperors in one room.

He'd like to know how her family had brought Livia up to scratch, but she had promised to meet him today in a brief note delivered to his house by hand. Mickey trotted at his heels, groaning about the pace Adrian set. Loomis, in full livery today, strode behind.

Adrian rounded on his footman. "Why are you dogging my footsteps?"

Loomis raised a bushy black brow. "I'm your footman, your grace. It's my job."

"Not always. You never did this so much before."

Loomis was what was often known as a family retainer. That was, his family had served Adrian's family for generations. Annoying at times, amusing at others, but Adrian would never forget Loomis. He had done him several favors in his childhood that had made it more bearable.

Still, the man seemed to be a positive magnet these days. Today Adrian could understand the point, but when he went about town, especially the fashionable part, Loomis stuck to him. Adrian had never insisted on strict protocol, so he could not understand why this change had occurred. He certainly hadn't ordered it. The man just appeared and for a big man, Loomis could be quiet as a cat when he wanted.

"You're a duke, your grace."

Had his footman taken the duty on himself? Come to think of it, when Loomis wasn't with him, his groom, another family retainer was. Annoying.

"I know that. But why now?"

"You're taking on new responsibilities, your grace."

He'd give the man that part. Maybe with a duchess imminent, the servants had decided formality was the order of the day. Then they had not visited Livia's family. If he was careless of protocol, they completely ignored it when the whim took them.

Knowing he wouldn't get a straight answer from the taciturn footman, he turned irritably to Mickey, also in livery today. "You're a fit boy. Keep up." However he shortened his stride a fraction. Although twelve, Mickey appeared younger, scrawnier, despite the food Adrian's cook was pouring into him, complaining that the boy had a bottomless stomach.

Adrian glanced down. Mickey should really trot behind him, but he wouldn't scold the boy for that. He looked winsome in his new livery. Green and gold, a suit he could sell to a pawnshop for a tidy sum, but he hadn't done so. Mickey was a bright lad. He knew when he was well off and when short-term gain was better sacrificed for long-term advantage. His dark hair was brushed neatly back into a queue, much like Adrian's own, but his eyes were Irish blue. Innocent-looking, if a man didn't know him better.

Lack of education notwithstanding, Mickey had a native cunning that could blossom into something better, with a little coaching. "The man you stole the brooch from. Do you remember him from anywhere?"

"Yes, y'r grace." At least the boy remembered his honorific, though Adrian usually preferred "sir" when they weren't in a formal situation.

"Was he the same person who came to the orphanage?"

Mickey frowned. "You mean the one who wanted the brooch in the first place?"

"The very same." They passed the old theater. Lincoln's Inn Theater had been a center of excellence in its day, but now it looked almost dilapidated and decidedly shabby. They turned the corner into a square lined with respectable houses in the modern style, tall and neat. Unlike the theater, these had an air of prosperity. As they should. Lawyers lived here.

"I can't say for sure." He scratched his head. "I only got a quick look. But he was the same height, and he wore a wig, like this cove. Didn't see his face proper. But I think it was him." The boy glanced back at Loomis.

Disappointing. Adrian wanted certain identification before he took the action he intended.

Whoever wanted that brooch knew how much it meant to Livia. More than Adrian himself did, that was for sure. The thief might even know why it meant so much to her.

In that mood, he strode up the stairs of the address he'd been given and rapped on the door. A manservant answered immediately and bade him wait.

The hall was spacious, with offices opening either side. Neither had plaques, unlike the discreet one outside that indicated that "Andrew Graham, lawyer and barrister" resided within.

Unusual to have both qualifications, but Andrew Graham was an unusual man. Barristers made little money these days, and very few men took that path, but Graham had dealt with an unusual case. The trial of a peer of the realm for murder. He now lived in illegal bliss with the peer's brother, upstairs in this house. Even more unusual that his clientele had not suffered, in fact, had increased. Instead of dealing with the well-off middling sort, he now handled the business of the company owned by his—lover, an insurance company that was going from strength to strength. They could probably afford to live in something far more extravagant than this house, but by all accounts they lived very happily here. So why change what was perfect?

Adrian wouldn't know. Perfect was something he'd ceased to believe in.

When he entered the office, he had to wait for the others to arrive. That gave him time to become acquainted with Graham, a pleasant man with a sharp mind. "Is Lord Darius attending today?"

"Along with the rest of the clan." Smiling, Graham handed him a glass of port and waved him to a seat. The room was filled with chairs, some that didn't belong here. Because the family was coming today. "Your lawyer is arriving soon?"

"If he doesn't, he is dismissed. Even though he has worked for my family since his grandfather and mine were alive." Why had he thought of his grandfather at a time like this? The old man had brought him up. He'd been a tyrant until his dying day. Adrian had learned a lot from him, most of it of the negative kind.

But his lawyer was a decent man. And honest. How often did a man meet an honest lawyer? It appeared he'd just met another. He couldn't imagine any Emperor taking up with anyone less than honest. Or maybe Livia had charmed him so much he was seeing everything with rosy-pink edges.

Crossing one leg over his knee, he took a sip of the excellent port.

Graham glanced up from the stack of papers on his desk. "Are you sure about this?"

Adrian nodded. "Why would I not be?"

"The clan is close and extended." His gaze flicked to Mickey, standing silently behind Adrian's chair. "Is he trustworthy?"

"Completely." He wouldn't drop the helpful information about Mickey's sticky fingers. The fewer people who knew about that, the better.

Graham raised a dark brow. He wore the conventional white wig, black coat and breeches, but his silver waistcoat showed hints of a flamboyance that might reveal an inner wild man.

With the hint of a smile, Graham leaned back. "I am, as you must know, allied closely to a member of the family. The Emperors can absorb you if you let them."

A friendly warning? Graham would naturally have done basic research into Adrian. Not that he would have to ask far. He had settled the legends circulating about him a long time ago, using stories he preferred to cover the ones he wanted hidden. And the hidden ones would stay that way.

He took another sip of his drink. "I am aware. I have watched them at work. But thank you. I am certain enough to take this step today."

His lawyer arrived as he was speaking and then, in short order, his betrothed and her family. He greeted Livia with a kiss on the hand and a sense of pleasure that took him by surprise. He was expecting to be glad to see her, but not to this extent, not the way she brought lightness to his soul.

Using his privilege as her betrothed, he led her to a seat next to his, after greeting her parents, her oldest brother and Lord Darius. A clan indeed. This close, their similarities were easy to discern. Their collective confidence filled the room, but Adrian doubted they realized how much they could take over a place.

Catching Graham's eye, he gave a barely there nod, acknowledging the truth of what he'd said. If he went ahead with this marriage, Adrian could easily find himself overcome by Emperors.

That would not happen, but he would not set himself against them, either. That would be suicide, even for a duke.

Watching them was akin to observing a flock of birds. Well-ordered birds, with certain characters dominating the proceedings. Or being allowed to by their quieter partners. He had already noted that Lady Strenshall led most of the social interactions, but from the way they exchanged glances and quiet nods, he presumed that if his lordship had wanted, he could have controlled the situation.

Eventually they were all seated, and Graham proceeded to read out the important parts of the contracts they were preparing to sign. Adrian received a nod from his own man of business. Everything was as expected.

Then Livia got to her feet. "I cannot do this." She lifted her chin, stilling the trembling Adrian caught sight of before she controlled it. "This isn't right."

Lady Strenshall got to her feet, a mother hen protecting her chick. "It must be your choice, my dear." She sent a poisonous glare to Adrian, making him want to plead his case, that he had done nothing wrong, more like a boy caught out in a transgression than a grown man.

Perhaps if he'd had a mother like this one, he might have turned out differently. Ah well, too late now.

Rising, he took Livia's hands, turning her to face him. She lowered her head, refusing to meet his eyes. "Why not? Has someone spoken to you?" When Lord Darius took a step toward them, he shot him a warning glare. Nobody had more right than he did now.

"Several," she said. "But despite that I thought I could go ahead with this. It isn't fair." Then she did meet his gaze and the pain in her eyes struck him to his soul. "On you."

His harsh, hard laugh was not planned. "Nothing is fair on me. If you leave now, today, that will only add to the long list. But if you truly cannot sign this contract, then I will not hold you to it. Nor will I say anything to anyone. You have my word on that. This is your decision, Livia and yours only."

The sigh came from Lady Strenshall, standing close to her daughter.

While the Shaws protected each other with a fierceness that emulated a den of wild cats, this was surely too much. What did they know, or was this their natural reaction when looking after one of their own? Adrian had no way of knowing. He had not experienced this kind of family loyalty before. And why was she having second—or third, or fourth—thoughts?

"If I hurt you in any way, or pressed you too hard, then I'm sorry. But I do want you for my wife, Livia. Never doubt that."

And he did. Losing her would hurt. That had not been part of his plan. He had not wanted a wife who would affect him personally. The shock gave him pause. Should he let her go now, when he could recover from his disappointment, or push forward? Take the risk that his feelings would deepen?

He should walk away, he really should, but his senses screamed at him not to, to hold on. He kept her hands in his, trying to impart all the strength he could.

"You do?"

Keeping her hands in his, he said to the room at large, "May we have a moment?" With an exasperated sigh, he continued, "I swear I will not press her. But Livia needs time to compose herself." She was near tears. He would not have her break down in front of her family.

When, finally, they had gone, filing out reluctantly, her mother last of all, he drew her into his arms. Something inside him relaxed, relieved to have her back once more, however temporarily. "Sweetheart, what is wrong?"

Livia held herself stiffly, refusing to relax against him. "I have not told you everything. You have a right to know."

His blood ran cold. What had she done?

"I'm not a virgin, Adrian."

Relief surged through him like a tide, warming the places that had chilled in anticipation of hearing something truly terrible. "Good."

"What?" She jerked her head up, almost meeting his chin. He moved it just in time.

"Do you think I care for that?"

"I'm not pure. I've had—relations with another man."

"Recently?" If she had a secret lover, Adrian would not share her. But he would still fight for her. He hadn't noticed anyone too close to her recently. Perhaps he would fight another duel. One more stain on his record would not make much difference at this stage of his life.

She shook her head, her golden curls catching in his cravat. "No, a long time ago. But I am not pure, Adrian. I'm—"

Rather than hear her call herself one of the foul names preferred by clergymen in the pulpit, Adrian kissed her. Her lips trembled against his until he firmed the kiss and deepened it. But he did not linger, although he would have loved to. "Sweetheart, I have a confession too. I'm not a virgin, either."

Her shaky laugh sounded much better. "Of course you are not."

"I haven't been a virgin for a long time. So we are two of a kind. Except I am probably less of a virgin than you are."

"You are so foolish." But she said it with laughter in her voice.

"Come, that's better. Do you think that would make any difference? In any case, we are signing the contract because your family expects it. Nothing is irreversible until we stand before a vicar and say 'I do.' Let's take this a step at a time. We agreed to a long betrothal, did we not?"

She nodded.

"Then do not concern yourself. We go ahead. Now you've told me, may we sign those damn—blasted papers?"

Another nod.

There was something else, he was sure of it. For someone in her position, with so many powerful relatives, one slip was easily overlooked. If that was the only impediment to a marriage, then men would be lining up for her. But she had deterred everyone who'd come close. He recognized it now. Like called to like. She'd let her twin take control, allowed the flamboyant members of her family to step in front of her.

He would discover everything in time. The brooch, her confession, and her old childhood friend Sir Jeffrey Creasey were all linked somehow. Sir Jeffrey could be the person who'd deflowered her, or he knew who had done it, and held that knowledge over her. Adrian had done his homework, and from the dates Sir Jeffrey had married and left to join the army when he was eighteen, which would have made Livia not yet sixteen. While country girls thought nothing of marrying at fifteen, these days society preferred to wait until the young lady was at least eighteen. If Sir Jeffrey was the one, he'd done Livia no favors. And that was deliberately putting the situation mildly.

He went outside, where, not surprisingly, her family lingered in the hall. "You may come back in. Thank you. Livia has recovered. A temporary attack of nerves, that is all."

It would have to be. Because, virgin or not, he determined to have her.

Since they were so close, he'd make a visit to Doctor's Commons next. He might as well arm himself for any event that came his way.

Chapter 10

Taking five days to travel to their country home tended to be about normal for the Shaws, especially when December had arrived with gray skies and almost constant drizzle. Was cold rain the most miserable weather in the world?

As she stared up with relief at the grand front of Haxby Hall, something inside her fell away. The tension that affected her every time she visited London. This was home. She had expected it to be so for the rest of her life.

Except that she'd actually signed the marriage contract. Persuaded that the document was not a final decision, she'd let her family and most of all, Adrian cajole her into signing. Their constant assurances that she could draw back if she wished proved an incentive, rather than a deterrent.

Ever since she'd had her doubts. Now she was home, that scene in Andrew's office felt like a dream.

She had made one confession, but not the other. His easy acceptance of her non-virgin status came as a relief and a concern. If she'd imagined that fact would deter him, she was sadly mistaken, and now she had to face the possibility that she truly was about to marry. Unless she made that last confession.

But she suspected even that might not put him off. He was right, of course, she'd used that excuse for too long. She could have confessed it before and received absolution, but she had never met a man she'd wanted to tell. And knowing what she had gone through, her parents had not forced the issue. With her money and her powerful network of relatives, a thin piece of skin was no bar to marriage.

However, the story that had seared its way through London the day before they left was certainly a bar to any marriage with the Duke of

Preston. A scurrilous tale of Adrian and his friends in the St. James's Club, roaring drunk with whores on their laps. If Adrian could not refrain even for a day, then she would not go through with this marriage. And so she would tell him.

The skies found the extra impetus to increase the power of the rain, which pattered down on her bare head with the promise of more, so she lifted her skirts and scurried up the stone staircase to the top where the family butler waited for them. "His grace has arrived, your ladyship," he told her, in a voice of doom.

"Which duke?" After all, she knew rather too many. Her sister Drusilla had just married one. And perhaps she did not want the answer to be the one she expected. A few days to collect herself and prepare for the Christmas season would be useful.

"His Grace, the Duke of Preston."

Garland closed the front door behind her since she was the last person to enter. The chill of the Great Hall invaded her. Nobody stayed here for long in the winter. It was situated at the wrong side of the house for the sun to reach it, particularly when the days were short. Already the sky was dimming. Or maybe another rainstorm was on the way.

Her mother was handing her cloak to the maid, but rather than follow suit, Livia gave them a vague wave and scurried up the stone staircase, heading for her room. She did not have to think about where she was going, despite Haxby being such a warren. The stairs up to the second floor were carpeted, so her outdoor shoes puttered up them. Finch might not have arrived yet, having traveled up yesterday when the rain was at its worst. The family had elected to wait another day at the comfortable inn rather than face the floods.

Flinging open the door to her bedroom, she discovered she was right— Finch had not arrived. Either she climbed out of this damp, creased riding habit on her own, or she called for a maid.

Her traveling trunk stood in the center of the room and her dressing case was laid on the table. Her jewelry would be with her maid, but she could manage without it. She touched the brooch pinned to her jacket. She had the piece she cared most about.

"You're here."

Spinning around, she confronted the man leaning against her door jamb, his hands thrust in his breeches pockets. Her heart missed a beat, then throbbed harder as if to catch up. So her reaction to him remained the same. A pity. She'd tried to suppress her foolish emotions where he was concerned. Tossing her head, she tried to appear cooler than she felt. "Indeed. Well observed."

His smile broadened. "I arrived late last night. I tired of the carriage and rode the last twenty miles."

She took a step forward, drawn, as always, by his vitality. "You must have been drenched."

"I was, but fortunately I'm waterproof and this house is very well run. They had a hot bath ready for me within half an hour of my arrival."

The vision that shot to her brain was instant and unstoppable. Adrian naked, in a tub filled with steaming water before the fire. Herself leaning over him, dressed in something diaphanous. His hands on her, drawing her down, a wicked smile on his face.

Hastily she turned away, going to the dressing table and lifting the lid of her dressing case. The gleam of cut, polished crystal and shiny silver greeted her. Finding her hairbrush, she stroked her fingers over the monogram engraved on the back.

"You'll need that re-engraved, will you not? Or perhaps I should buy you a new set."

Of course he would know what she was thinking. "But you won't have to. I'm not changing my name, after all."

"Are you not?" Unbidden, he entered the room. At least he left the door open.

She should be alarmed, but she wasn't. The walking scandal entered her room and approached her, the warmth in his eyes unmistakable.

He took the brush from her unresistant fingers and laid it back in the case, annoyingly finding its slot, although he did not look away from her. That smile would be the death of her.

Taking her hands, he lifted first one to his lips, then the other. "I missed you."

She returned his smile. "Would I could believe that. I heard of your adventure before you left London." She hardened her heart. She could not do this and she had to tell him.

He raised a brow. "Which particular adventure?"

"The one in the St. James's Club. Five nights ago, was it?" She pulled her hands away from him, determining to wash them thoroughly. "You had a whore on your lap."

He tilted his head to one side. "And where did you hear that from?"

"Does it matter?"

"Yes, yes it does. Ask one of your brothers. Lord Malton was there."

She gasped, her hand going to her mouth. "Marcus?" Her oldest brother was deeply in love with his wife. Or so she had thought. Did he, then, engage in this orgy?

"He was engaged in the same activity I was." His mouth thinned into a straight line. "Ask him." He scanned her face, his dark eyes hard. "Come to me when you have satisfied your curiosity. And do not believe everything you hear."

She stared after him, before quietly closing her door and setting her back against it. She sensed hurt in his anger, and she felt in the wrong. But she had only spoken to him about something that had eaten her up since hearing about it.

She had no reason to doubt what she'd heard. But if Marcus had been there—what had happened? And if she confronted Marcus with what she knew about the orgy and Marcus confirmed it, what would she say to Viola?

During a woman's pregnancy, some men would leave their wives alone, and they'd seek out whores to feed their urges without bothering their spouse. Was Marcus one of those?

A knock came on the door. Had he come back? But no, it was Finch, here at last with a harassed expression and the promise of a hot bath. She busied herself lighting the fire laid ready in the hearth, chattering that she had forced the driver to get up at dawn so they would get here in time. Livia hadn't even noticed the chill in the room. She'd thought the chill came from her heart.

A man who thought nothing of consorting with whores would not become part of her life. Ever.

* * * *

Marcus didn't arrive until the next day. During dinner the night before, Livia emulated her mother. She behaved with perfect decorum, smiled politely, but heard very little. Pleasing a headache, she went to bed early, leaving Adrian holding court and charming her whole family.

This would be the worst Christmas she had ever experienced. But she would not allow anyone to see it. If dignity was all she had left, then she would use it for all she was worth. But she could not use it for long. The strain became too much and by the next morning she had a real headache.

Although insisting Finch prepare her clothes for the day, and allowing her maid to give her a wash-down, she had to stop in order to vomit into the slop pail. Finch insisted on putting her back to bed, behaving more like a nurse than a lady's maid.

Livia felt so awful she let Finch do it, and suffered a visit from her mother, assuring her she would be fine. "The journey beat me down," she said.

"And the stress of recent weeks." Lady Strenshall patted her hand. "Don't worry. We'll cope with it. Now relax."

"Is Marcus here yet?" She desperately wanted to get to her brother before Adrian did. Otherwise she wouldn't trust anything Marcus told her. Men stuck together, everyone knew that, and she owed this to herself as well as to Viola.

The story had involved raucous goings-on and a great deal of whoring and drinking. If it was true, her betrothal was at an end. She would not stand that kind of behavior. But Marcus?

That worried her more than anything else. Her own heartache faded into insignificance next to the duty she would have to perform. Because Viola was a friend as much as she was a sister-in-law. Livia could not live knowing that Marcus was consorting with whores. Dangerous too, considering the diseases those women often carried. But to see Viola giving her heart to her husband, knowing otherwise, Livia couldn't bear that. She was no saint. She knew she would slip up one day.

"No, they are taking their time. They set out late because of the rainstorm, but they will be here tomorrow."

Livia sighed with relief. Although tempted to pour out what she had heard to her mother, she decided to keep her secret to herself, until she had spoken to her brother. Perhaps she should speak to another of her siblings. Drusilla would arrive with her new husband in time for Christmas, and Val was already here, with Charlotte. They had settled so well together it was as if they'd been married for years, even though they'd had trouble. Which was putting matters mildly. But while time had healed Val of his greatest excesses, she doubted Adrian would ever find the same thing. His wildness was deep-seated, part of him. "I should be better by tomorrow."

Lady Strenshall got to her feet. "You'll be fine tomorrow. Ready to greet him, I'll wager. Meantime, you've left your duke to his own devices. That might not be wise."

That was so much what Livia was thinking, that she started. "Then keep him away from the maids." She tried for a smile, but she only managed a weak one.

"Be sure," her mother said, her hand on the door. "Be very sure of this step you are taking, Livia. There is no coming back from it. If in six months you discover you have made a mistake, you must deal with it the best you can. Do not come running home with your tail between your legs. Shaws do not behave that way." A ghost of a smile flitted across her features. "However, I have heard no complaints from the housekeeper yet, and believe me, if there were any, I would hear."

So at least Adrian wasn't seeking solace for her absence with the maids. Livia should be thankful for that, but for the life of her she could not.

* * * *

The next day Livia rose bright and early, and hovered at the front of the house, waiting for her brother's arrival. She might have to wait all day. But the sun had come to dry the grounds after the rain of the past few days, and the Home Park looked freshly washed. The ground would be muddy, otherwise she'd don her oldest clothes and boots, and go for a walk. That would shake the cobwebs free.

Slipping into a small room at the front of the house, she found a book and settled for a solitary day. She would not call attention to herself, and Adrian would not find her here, in the parlor that had been laid out as an afterthought. The builders had left the space during some alterations, and her mother had put a chair and table in here. Although the day was chilly, she spread a blanket around her shoulders and she was comfortable enough.

Her book, however, proved less than engrossing.

The sound of someone walking down the hallway reached her ears, and a door opening. Not her door, thankfully. But it would only be a maid, or rather, a footman, because the sounds were somewhat heavy.

Then her door opened and Adrian stood there, gazing at her gravely. He closed the door and stood against it. "Livia."

Livia pulled all her dignity around her as her heart quickened its beat. "Yes?"

"I promised myself I would stay away, but I could not."

"How did you find me? Who told you where to find me?" Only Finch knew. If she had taken a vail from Adrian, Livia would dismiss her immediately.

He shook his head slightly. "Nobody. I have investigated every room on this floor. This is the third corridor I have tried. This place is more confusing than Hampton Court maze."

"I know the key to that," she said, when she should really keep her mouth closed. She didn't want a conversation, for heaven's sake.

"I wanted to assure myself that you were well. I worried for you."

She shrugged, and closed her book, resigned to the loss of her quiet day. "I had a headache. I get them sometimes."

He swallowed. "I see. I have them too, from time to time. They used to worry me. I'm glad to hear you're recovered."

"Why do headaches worry you? Everybody gets them. Especially a man who drinks and whores too much."

He rubbed the back of his neck in a curiously endearing gesture, the lace falling from his wrists, obscuring his features briefly. "I deserved that. But I don't drink and whore as much as you seem to think."

Rage seared her. "How dare you say that when you were caught in the act so recently? Could you not refrain even for a few days? Do you need—*that* so much?"

Even worse, he smiled, that intimate expression that seemed to indicate they were sharing a secret. They shared nothing. Neither would they from now on. Better to make the break now and ask him to leave before the family expected to see her with him. Before he grew too close to her heart. "No, I do not. Livia, I will tell you something you may choose not to believe. It is up to you, but you must choose the person you want to trust."

She frowned and forced her anger down. If she did not listen, she would regret it, because his expression hinted at something deeper, something he would not tell most people. With her society mask firmly in place, she gestured to the other chair in the room. He nodded, flicked the skirts of his coat back—dark green today, wonderful against his bronzed features—and sat. "I find that where I would have left another woman to stew, I cannot with you. I don't know who told you that story about the St. James's Club, but it is only partially true. Perhaps the person who told you had their own reasons. I do not know. But I cannot allow you to create trouble with your brother and sister-in-law." He grimaced. "No, I'm not so noble. I want to tell you for my own sake, because I don't want to lose you."

"When you allowed the whore to sit on your lap, that was when you lost me."

He nodded. "I would not blame you for giving me up then. After all, I appealed to your affections, did I not? However, you did not hear the second half of the story. Usually the St. James is a reasonably sedate place. Gentlemen meet there for conversation, cards, and company. Not for whoring. It's set above the coffeehouse, and the membership is small. I went there in the company of your brother Malton as I am not a member. We sat with a few others at a table and set up a quiet game of whist. Someone was celebrating." He shrugged. "The celebration spilled over and several women approached us. One 'fell' into my lap." He regarded her gravely. "That much is true. But what is also true is that I tipped her off my lap, gave her a guinea, and told her not to come back." He met her gaze, wouldn't allow her to look away. "Livia, I only take one woman at a time. I do not take whores indiscriminately."

"I heard different."

"I'm not surprised. I am the walking scandal. I can't do anything without it being marked down to my bad character." He gave a tight smile. "It has even proved useful on occasion. I have never cared what they said about me, not until now. Who told you this story? Your brother?"

"God, no!"

He touched his finger to his lips. "Think about that too. Your brother does not make any secret of the way he feels about his wife. He adores her, does he not? Do you truly think he would do this to her? Dandle a whore in public, for everyone to see? In truth, he did the same as I did. It was a trivial incident, soon over, but the room was full. Stories circulate, especially when most of the people in the room were blind drunk."

"I see." But she had been so upset, far more than the incident deserved. He was right. Marcus would never have hurt Viola in that way. He had never caused scandal in his single days, always took his role as heir to the marquisate seriously. Why would he suddenly engage in an orgy now?

The Adrian she knew did not compare to the legend. Had he helped create it to provide a useful distance for himself? Livia knew how avidly dukes were pursued, even the older ones, the widowed and the ones with what her mother termed "unfortunate personal habits." The smelly ones, in other words. Adrian was none of these. He was remarkably handsome, in the private life and far more intelligent than she found comfortable. A good thing, to have someone to challenge her.

He leaned forward, resting his arms on his knees, clasping his hands together. "Livia, if you marry me, you'll hear many stories with me set as the villain. Most are not true. I encouraged the stories for many years, or rather, did not care what people said. I do now, because of you but if you cannot come to me and know that I will always tell you the truth, we are finished with one another." He waited for the space of three heartbeats. "You must make your mind up. I promise that I will not lie to you on these matters. But you alone must decide if the truth lies in your heart or not." He lifted his hands to the arms of the chair, as if to get to his feet. "Shall I leave you to decide?"

She swallowed. He had been true to her thus far, answered everything she asked him. She shook her head. "There's no need. You're right."

Unmistakable signs of relief swept through his expression. His mouth relaxed and the tense lines in his forehead smoothed out. "Thank you."

"But, Adrian, this shows how little we know one another. We should wait. Neither of us are pressured to marry, are we? We don't have to rush."

"You're getting cold feet." His smile warmed her now. "Don't. Spend as much time with me as you wish. As far as I'm concerned, we can't spend too much time together. But don't jilt me."

That sounded like a plea. She wanted to test him, and at the same time test her power over him, that power she was barely beginning to understand. "Why not?"

"Because if you do, I can never approach you again," he responded readily. "I cannot come near you. We will never have this chance if you do that. I will not demur, naturally, I will leave immediately." He paused, as if searching for words.

"Then I will not." She hadn't meant to say that, but she couldn't bear the sadness in his eyes. She must be some kind of fool, but she believed his version of the story. He had offered no proof, but she no longer felt the need to talk to Marcus as urgently as she had. "Not jilt you, I mean." Not yet.

"It would probably put the last nail in the coffin of my social acceptance." He spread his hands, palms toward her. "You would be doing me a favor."

"I see. So do you want me to?" The tease was irresistible.

"No." Rising to his feet in a smooth motion, he held out his hands, this time inviting her to take hold. She did, the blanket she wore slipping off her shoulders and falling to the chair behind her. A chill hit her body and she shivered even as he folded his arms around her. "We should get out of this ice pit and find a room with a fire."

She wouldn't argue with that. "I could show you the house."

"When you've warmed up."

He surrounded her, holding her close to his heat. His body was a furnace. Livia nestled in, soaking it up, giving herself the illusion that this man could protect her from everything that troubled her. Used to caring for herself for so long, the notion came to her as a balm. Even if it wasn't true, he gave her a respite from thinking, from a life that occasionally threatened to move out of her control.

"I'm sorry."

"What for?" He sounded surprised. "How do you know I'm not lying to you?" A thread of anxiety worked its way through his words.

"For doubting you."

He laughed gently, the vibrations rumbling through his chest, transmitting themselves to her cheek. "Is that all? People doubt me all the time. You had reason to, sweetheart. I don't know who told you, but they may have done so in good faith. They were wrong, but they might have seen something and misinterpreted it. I swear to you now that while I am with you, I will not seek out another woman." He laughed again. "I take one woman at a time. While I was once not averse to spending time with a whore, I never tupped them."

"What?" She drew back to stare up at his face. "Why not?"

His smile broadened into a grin. "Not many women would ask that. Since you have, the answer is simple. Most whores carry diseases."

"The pox?"

"Precisely. Having seen the consequences at close quarters, I have no desire to take that path. My father died of it, you know."

"Oh."

"Indeed, oh. That was how they knew for sure that I was not his son. My mother showed no signs of the disease and I was a healthy baby."

"I had heard that she had it too." But rumors abounded. She could not be sure of anything anymore.

"She did, but not until after I was born. She still lives with the consequences."

"Ah." She would not ask about the blackamoor page. Refused to question him on that.

"It was obvious that my father would have no more children. He died of the pox and overindulgence in everything. The doctor was not sure of the direct cause of death, so he put it down to drink." He waited, as if expecting her to recoil, but she only felt sorry for him. "I don't remember him. Only my grandfather, who took me away from my mother when I was born and reared me carefully. Too carefully," he added with a wry grin. "He compelled my father to acknowledge me."

"Oh," she said again. Nobody had heard these truths before. And they would not hear them from her. "My brothers are the same. When they were single they employed mistresses and took care to ensure their health."

"It's the scourge of our age. Worse because it's hidden."

She smiled, the comparison too delicious to ignore. "You sound like a clergyman."

"They're not always wrong." He shook his head. "You are the most remarkable woman. You never flinch from the truth, never make excuses. What a subject to be talking about, when you're in my arms!"

"Better now than later."

"Indeed so. But do you mind not talking for a minute or two?" Tilting her chin up, he bent his head to her.

His kiss was as gentle as the touch of a baby, but with far more intent. As he'd taught her, she opened her mouth for him, but he only traced her lips with the tip of his tongue, before holding her close and kissing her again. "Have you eaten?" he said when his lips left hers. His words brushed tantalizingly against her mouth.

She shook her head. "Only a bread roll with my chocolate this morning."

"You like chocolate in the mornings? A decadence I find hard to believe in practical, quiet Lady Livia Shaw. Perhaps there is fire beneath the sensible attitude. Like your hair." Lifting his hand, he stroked her hair back, tucked his fingers between the strands but didn't attempt to dislodge the pins or her cap. "It's the color of angel hair, but it has a touch of the sun. Hidden depths." Humor laced his deep voice. "I'll ensure you have chocolate in the mornings for the rest of your life, if you want it."

No warning bells sounded in her mind, no flashes of self-defense. She badly wanted to give herself to this man. She'd told him the secret she had to, that she was not a virgin, but she was not yet ready to tell him the other. That secret was so deeply locked in her heart she didn't know if she could ever tell anyone who didn't already know. Telling the truth would be pulling her finger out of the dam and letting the sea rush through and drown her.

Another shiver shook her, but this time not from cold.

"Come. Let's get you to breakfast and out of this room."

"Oh, breakfast is well over. Mama has it served much earlier in the country."

"I'm sure we can find something. I regret sleeping too late to join everyone."

She lifted her chin and met his eyes. "You missed it too? Then we should. Men are not allowed to starve."

Smiling, he released her, but linked his fingers through hers, steadying her with his strength. "Only scrawny boys who are sent out on the streets too early in their lives."

"Yes." Thinking of her son, she closed her eyes. But then she recalled Mickey. "You brought your protégé here?"

"Of course. He's probably set the whole kitchen on its ear by now. He's too intelligent for his own good, that child. Knows exactly how to set one person against another." Opening the door, he paused to check the hallway, poking his head out and looking left and right. "Come." He drew her out, and they walked to the end of the corridor as if they'd been strolling around the house all morning. "Mickey is a constant source of amusement. I fear, though I will have to decide what to do with him eventually. He cannot be my page all his life. I'm forever tripping over him, and I swear my patience will run out before long."

"You didn't have to take him."

"Yes, I did. Believe me." He wouldn't expound on that enigmatic statement but walked her briskly around the corner into another corridor, this one lined with cabinets displaying the china Livia's grandmother had adored. These days they were a little dusty, especially this time of year, when the chill invaded the corridors of her home. The staff would get it out soon, wash it and get it ready for the celebrations to come.

She loved this time of year. All the family they could muster arrived at Haxby for the season, and the house grew busy and full. This time an unaccustomed nervousness filled her. Her skittishness where Adrian was concerned overrode every other emotion. And her growing desire for him.

At the end of the corridor, at the juncture with another, he abruptly stopped, and pulled her around to face him. Her cheeks heating, Livia tried to turn away but his hold on her arms was firm, just short of bruising. "We need a date," he said. "You refused to give a date in the contract, just 'the next six months.' What are we to tell your family?"

"Have they spoken to you?"

"Your father has. He wants us to wed as soon as possible, to show the world we are serious. Either that, he said, or not at all. At the end of six months our arrangement is terminated. He had that put in the contract."

"But that is what we want, is it not?" Although she lowered her voice, the sound still echoed in the still, waiting space.

"No. We should be more certain. We are, after all, in love."

"You told them that?" Heedless of her surroundings or who might be listening, her voice rose.

"No, your father says he sees it. He's suffered the throes of his other children doing the same thing, and he can see the same here."

"Then we must be better at dissimulation than he thinks." Surely physical attraction was not the same as a lasting connection? But she had no way of knowing. She had not discussed such matters with her siblings and they had not ventured to confide in her. Even the latest to be married, Drusilla, had kept her own counsel. But Dru was like that, full of secrets.

Chapter 11

Adrian found Livia maddening when she wasn't being adorable. The temptation to go further with her in that little room was close to unbearable, until he felt her shiver against him and knew it was not from passion. She had frozen there, waiting for her brother to arrive. And avoiding him too. She had not appeared at the jovial, bustling breakfast, and he had not managed to get anything out of her tight-lipped maid. In a way he was glad of that because he appreciated a loyal servant, but why now, and why this servant?

Realizing what she was doing, he'd tried every door on that benighted corridor, the one at the front that looked out over the drive. The fear in her eyes when he came in had struck him to the heart. How could he leave her then? He'd known she was afraid, angry, doubtful. Where he would have ordinarily left a woman to stew, knowing she would be more eager to see him when he deigned to present himself, he could not do it in this case. Thinking of Livia distressed, perhaps in tears, struck him to the core.

What was he thinking? Was he turning into the kind of henpecked man he despised? No, because Livia did not do that to him. But his desire to protect her had driven him to deliver the kind of kiss that would reassure her rather than turn her away.

He wanted her, and now that she had awakened his desire he wanted to enter into the next part of his life. Finally, he felt ready to move on. On to what, he wasn't sure, but not what he was leaving behind.

Now he was ready, Livia was not. Her evasions maddened him. As he accompanied her down to the huge painted hall to greet her brother, who had finally arrived with his family, he pondered his change of heart. Inside, he had altered and that was because of Livia. She intrigued him, drew him in with her secrets. That damned brooch had interested him, but she fascinated him far more. He wanted to know all her secrets. Every single one.

In return, he would have to give his own secrets into her keeping. He should do that before they married. And marry they would. Sooner than she thought too.

* * * *

That same evening the family held a dinner for their landed neighbors. Christmas was one of the few times the two factions, Country and County, came together. Each despised the other, and respected them too, recognized the vital places each held. The County men looked after local affairs, took their positions extremely seriously. Country men, on the whole the nobility, ran the country and its position in the world.

The king? He did very little, although he thought he ran everything. County and Country agreed on that.

Adrian was an observer here. His part of the world lay farther north, where he had similar tussles and agreements to cope with. The large dining room, the table opened to its fullest extent in honor of the guests, glittered with candlelight. It made the cut-crystal glasses twinkle and the silverware gleam. A three-course dinner lay ahead, with twenty removes to each course. Adrian settled to watching.

At least he had Livia next to him. The old way of dining, gentlemen on one side of the table and ladies on the other had more or less been abandoned by all but the old-fashioned. They had entered the dining room by rank, but servants had discreetly directed them to different places. Adrian enjoyed not being the only duke present, although as the eighth in direct line, he was the senior.

On her other side, Sir Jeffrey Creasey had secured a seat. "Should you not be sitting at the other end of the table?" he asked smoothly.

No doubt he wanted Livia to himself. Such a shame Adrian had determined that he would not have that signal favor.

"His lordship was kind enough to bid us sit where we chose," he said. Five hours close to one of the prosy bores he'd met tonight would probably kill him. Either that, or he would kill them. "I've never stood on ceremony," he continued, moderating his tone to the smooth, careless one most calculated to irritate the young squire. "Some do. The Duke of Richmond, for instance, a relative newcomer to the ducal rank, detests anyone except the monarch taking precedence over him. Therefore, I delight in doing so."

At least Livia laughed. Sir Jeffrey did not. "You do not believe in adhering to age-old customs and procedures, then?"

Was the man trying to start a fight? Probably. "When it makes sense, yes. But why hold to customs that don't make sense?"

"Because people are comfortable that way."

"Are they? Or is it the people making the customs who are satisfied? I seem to recall that once people did everything by bartering goods. I would hate that restored. If they had not changed, we would still be bringing herds of cows into town to pay for our vegetables."

"Or in my case, sheep," Lady Claudia's husband murmured from the other side of the lady next to Adrian. Sandwiched between the twins, Adrian was struck by their differences, not their similarities. Both preferred not to powder, but that was a fashion spreading among the younger generation. He adopted the new fashion, because it took half a ton of the stuff to cover his dark hair properly, and by then he was wheezing from the clouds of powder in the air.

Their hair glowed in this kindly, warm light, and their eyes sparkled. Claudia's eyes were a touch lighter than Livia's, and she was perhaps a little more rounded. That was most likely caused by her recent confinement.

The thought of Livia rounded in that way, with his child, hit him with shocking intensity. The inner vision had appeared out of the blue, but once he'd seen it, the notion would not go away.

Could he really do this, and sire an heir to the title? That would at least stop his cousin complaining, but more than that, he might actually rid the family of the curse that had dogged them for so long. Since the Restoration no duke had died content with his life. Until now, Adrian had taken for granted that he would go the same way.

"But these changes happen on their own," Sir Jeffrey persisted. "Changing them for their own sake is not to be desired." He stated it as if it was a known fact.

Handsome though he admittedly was, this man had the heart and soul of a squire. Any change, even the moving of a fence post mattered to them. Unless, of course, they had instigated the move, after years of careful consideration. His time in the army must have increased Sir Jeffrey's rigidity of mind. Not an admirable quality, in Adrian's opinion.

"I accept change when it is beneficial," he drawled, deliberately refusing to allow the man to rile him.

He paused to help himself, and offered to help Livia, to the dish to his right, which turned out to be lamb ragout. Haricot beans were set close by. The marquess, at the head of the table, had the roast beef to dispense to his neighbors, but Adrian could hardly demand a slice. That would be the height of bad manners. So he made do with the lamb, which turned out tasty enough.

"Everything changes, whether a man wants it to or not. For instance, after we are wed, I fully expect Livia to move to my houses, as a wife should."

"Where are they?" the baronet demanded testily.

"My main seat is in Northumberland. But it is not a place I'm particularly fond of." To put it mildly. "It is larger than Haxby and far damper. Stone walls do not make for comfort in wintertime." He paused to take a mouthful of food. Perhaps the lamb suited him after all. "I tend to stay in my house in Oxfordshire more often. It's more modern, and neater." And it did not have his mother in it.

"So fortunate. I count myself lucky to have a tidy house and estate close by." Sir Jeffrey found a dish of mushrooms that occupied his attention, and added, as if by accident, "And my army career, of course. I had a share of booty from that, but the main honor was guiding my company to victory."

Someone across the table lifted his head. Lord Brampton, the husband of Livia's twin, also a man who had served in the army. He raised a brow, and met Adrian's gaze briefly, before nodding and turning his attention to Claudia.

Interesting. Brampton obviously had something to say. But Adrian could hardly shout across the table to him.

"A man of substance," he murmured, lifting his glass and glancing at Livia over the rim.

Pink rimmed her cheekbones. She had an adorable blush, and because of her coloring, she treated him to it often. He wanted to lick that delicate heat, to see if it tasted as delicious as it looked.

He turned his thoughts away, back to the man sitting on her other side. Livia was engaged in conversation with him now, reminiscences he had no part in. He had no doubt that Sir Jeffrey had deliberately excluded him. He was not so unsure of her that he felt obliged to interrupt. Let the man have his small triumph. Adrian had the bigger prize.

Before tonight he had not understood how close the Shaws had been to Sir Jeffrey as children. They had not precisely run wild, but their parents hadn't kept them apart from others in the neighborhood. And that had given them opportunities they could have taken advantage of. If Sir Jeffrey had not left to join the army so early, he'd suspect the man of being the one who took Livia's virginity. Whoever had done that, she wasn't saying, and although he'd kept his eyes and ears open, Adrian was none the wiser.

His instinctive dislike of Sir Jeffrey gave the rational side of Adrian, the part he kept well hidden, pause. His prejudice would assume too much. Where Livia was concerned, the fierce protectiveness that took him by surprise drove him to discover everything about her. And then prevent harm coming to her. He would have his work cut out to do that. But he had chosen his path, and the only person who could deter him was Livia.

However she seemed fond of Sir Jeffrey. Childhood sweethearts always had a place in a person's heart. If Adrian'd had one, no doubt he'd feel the same. But Anna didn't count. He'd married her at nineteen. She had been a symbol of his freedom, after his draconian grandfather had finally passed away. Together with the excesses they indulged in.

After three hours the meal eventually ended. The ladies left and the gentlemen settled in for port and gossip. Here, in these gatherings, the true secrets were divulged, the real core of power. Much of one's standing and wealth depended on informal discussions like these, and in this exalted company they would reveal even more.

Adrian heard of a new venture at sea, of which he took careful note. Shipping had become increasingly important to him, since a rich seam of coal had turned up on his land. Transporting it to where it was most needed involved ships, so that he had built up a small fleet of coast-hugging ships. Most interesting. But not as interesting as learning about Sir Jeffrey and his proclivities. He did not hold his drink well. After the ladies left for the rarefied atmosphere of the drawing room, the men moved to the top of the table, filling in spaces.

Adrian did not imagine this was a convivial meeting. The other members of the family were judging him, especially the ones who had not yet met him except in passing. Lord Valentinian eyed him warily when he gave his twin's excuses. "Darius will come up as soon as possible after the new year. He has urgent business in town."

That business being not wanting to rile the sensibilities of the more Catholic of the people present. That would include Sir Jeffrey, who was remarkably silent as the others expressed their regret. Darius would have brought his—partner, people usually referred to Andrew Graham, since they were in business together.

The sticklers here would not have the flexibility of mind necessary to accept such a relationship. They would probably object to a man marrying a woman from the wrong village.

Recalling Livia, Adrian behaved himself remarkably well. At one point Sir Jeffrey, tiring of trying to irritate Adrian enough to force a scene, wandered off to talk to another squire. Lord Brampton chose that moment to slide into the seat next to Adrian. "We are to be brothers-in-law," he said, coming right to the point as military men frequently and tediously chose to do. "Do we yet know the date?"

"Considering your wife is closer to Livia than most, I would think you would know first." Adrian lowered his voice. "To be truthful, she is proving remarkably elusive on that point."

"Ah," said Brampton, as if he understood. "The Shaws are difficult to catch."

"So am I."

"As I was. I wished to continue my military career, and only when I was inveigled to visit the worst whorehouse I've ever had the misfortune to enter, did I meet the woman I was destined to spend the rest of my life with."

"She went there?" The world knew that Lady Claudia had inherited a house in an area once respectable, now thronged with whorehouses and sinister private clubs. But the world assumed she'd sold it without inspecting her property.

"She wanted to see her property. I was in search of someone else entirely." As the port came around, Brampton topped up their glasses and pushed the coaster on. Neither man took more than a cursory glance at the ruby liquid dancing in their glasses.

"You intrigue me," he drawled.

"Mountsorrel was cast as the villain in Lady Drusilla's timeless epic," Brampton reminded him. "The Shaw women tend to take life in both hands."

"And break it."

"Ah yes, if they do not take care."

Adrian turned his glass, watching the candlelight make the surface of the drink glitter and gleam, as if something sinister lurked beneath. A thistle was engraved on the side. "I wonder why I never noticed this. It's a Jacobite symbol, is it not?"

Brampton's laugh sounded forced. Idly, Adrian wondered if Brampton, who, before his father's death had been Lord St. Just, and an officer in his majesty's army, had anything to do with the struggle against the Stuarts. The Cause was all but dead now, but after Culloden the fight had gone on away from the battlefield. "The marquess collects all kinds of oddities. I daresay this is one of them. I wonder how the set arrived here?"

"I can answer that," the marquess told them. "It came into the family recently from a source I cannot reveal, but one very close to us."

"Mysterious," Adrian commented. He'd never taken much interest in the doomed Stuarts, but he was glad they had gone. Romantic but foolish, most of them. Except for his great-grandfather, King Charles II, who had taken a brief but fertile interest in his great-grandmother. Exile had given that monarch a grain of sense.

Brampton fidgeted and Adrian glanced at him again. Getting a man off-balance, for whatever reason, was a good way of discovering more. He lowered his voice and turned away from the men laughing at some sally of Sir Jeffrey's. "I believe Sir Jeffrey was a childhood friend of Livia's. He would have it that he was more than that."

Brampton lowered his voice too. "As to that part, I do not know." Pity. Adrian had thought Claudia might have confided some dire secret in her husband. "I came upon Claudia in London, and we conducted our courtship there. Only when she told me of her neighbor did I recognize him. A very good *office* man, Sir Jeffrey, by all accounts."

"Ah."

"Worked at headquarters, panderi—attending to the generals' needs."

Oh-ho. That slip of the tongue was deliberate. So Sir Jeffrey had spent his war making the generals a little more comfortable? Perhaps obtaining luxuries for them, like, say, good wine and doxies. "I see. Not on the battlefield, then?"

"Few of us had that honor." Brampton shrugged, and by that Adrian knew he had seen action. "But I met him a few times and had to get through him to the other generals occasionally. The French have lords of the pen. He would have worked well there." He had not deliberately shown disrespect to Sir Jeffrey, but he didn't have to. Brampton was warning Adrian that Sir Jeffrey's word was not always sterling.

"He left home very young." After a scandal?

"So I understand, but for that part of his history, you are on your own. He was, for what it is worth, a great administrator. He has the ability to keep any number of people in line with a pen."

Adrian understood. Sir Jeffrey was meticulous when he needed to be so.

Adrian would continue to watch him. He didn't entirely trust Sir Jeffrey, who had appeared remarkably attentive to Livia during dinner and for that matter in London, far more than a childhood friend would be. Because if the man had taken Livia's virginity and then sped out of her life, he would find out.

But why would he? Sir Jeffrey was ambitious. He was jockeying for a place in government, climbing the greasy pole of politics. A wealthy, influential wife of impeccable birth would help him enormously. So why, if he had Livia before, had he not taken advantage of her then? If he'd been the one to take her, he would have held on to her. Everything in Adrian's understanding of the man told him that.

So why didn't he do that?

Chapter 12

The next day being fine, Livia decided to get out into the fresh air. Besides, the constant congratulations and speculations about the wedding day wore on her patience until she was ready to scream.

The rain had eased off enough to make a walk possible. The ground was still soft, but if she kept to the paths, she could breathe the air and not hear the chatter of the guests and her parents. Her mother was beginning to talk about Livia's dowry and the jewels she would bestow on her daughter. Livia didn't want to hear it. Guilt wore her down.

She wore a broad-brimmed hat of waxed straw to help keep the drips off her face and a gown of grass-green woolen cloth that reached her ankles, with a plain dark green cloak over all. Her sturdy leather shoes would keep her feet dry.

Stepping out of a side door onto the path leading to the outside world, she paused to draw in a lungful of the clean, crisp air. The world was newly washed, the sky blue, the clouds pure white, not the gray of the past week or so.

Her feet crunched on the loose stones as she made her way around to the back of the house, and out to the garden. The roses were pruned, their stumps holding the promise of spring, but silent and still. No wind stirred the bushes today, as if today was a respite before more bad weather arrived. A gardener moved in the distance, going out of sight after glancing around and spotting her. Livia didn't mind. She was home, and her restless spirit had stilled. Maybe she wouldn't go to London next year and watch her putative betrothed flirting with other women and taking another mistress. He would not stay celibate for long, for all his protestations. One woman at a time was not no women at all. When he did that, she could jilt him. Or maybe, as he suggested, allow their betrothal to quietly die. The marriage contract had a six-month expiry clause. They should probably wait until it ran out.

But the thought of losing Adrian's vibrancy in her life lowered her mood. She would have to say goodbye to him, but not yet. She could at least have this season.

The air of her home was doing her good. She could think properly again, and take control of her life as she'd always intended to do. Her last season was over. She would not go through another as an eligible young woman, although she would never be without suitors because of her position and her dowry. She might even become "poor Livia."

A smile tightened her lips. Burying her hands under her arms, she continued with her walk. She wore only thin leather gloves. Vanity should have played no part in her outing, but she was so accustomed to considering her appearance, it had become a habit. The thought made her smile. She would not have to do that for much longer. She could become a real old maid, grumpy and eccentric, because she'd have nobody to please but herself. She could knit her own gloves.

"Livia!"

The soft voice heralded the end of her privacy. Fixing a smile to her face, she turned and found Jeffrey waiting for her.

This was not the Jeffrey of her childhood. This Jeffrey had some town polish, his brown coat fashionable and new, his neckcloth carefully folded and tied, instead of carelessly fastened with the ends thrust through a buttonhole to keep them secure. Moreover, he still wore his wig. As a child he'd doffed it at the first opportunity, declaring it got in the way. The thick, dark brown hair beneath had proved more than adequate in the adventures they got up to.

Memories of running her fingers through the dark mass evoked no fond images for her, although she had done so more than once. She had no urge to run to him, and feel his arms closing around her, as she had once. She had never noticed when those impulses had fallen away, but they had. They were gone for good.

But he was still her neighbor and she still liked him. "Sir Jeffrey," she said, deliberately using his honorific. "I felt cooped up indoors, so I decided on a trip out."

"Cooped up?" He sent a smiling glance back to the house. "You could sleep in a different room every night and not use the same one twice in a year."

"Not quite true." Haxby was a monster of a house, but not as big as some she had stayed in. Intrigued, she wondered if anyone had ever counted all the rooms. And did the little, accidental room without a fireplace where she'd met Adrian count? That had only been created because alterations had left the space. A bolt-hole, her brothers had called it once. She'd certainly bolted there enough times herself. "But near enough. I miss this air when I'm in London."

"But the day is not warm. Could you not have walked the Long Gallery?"

That was where they had arranged trysts, back in the old days. The reference did not escape Livia. But she had not thought of it today. It had nooks where a couple might enjoy relative privacy and have some warning of a new arrival. The floorboards creaked and echoed, but Livia and her siblings knew every one, and where to tread without sound.

Livia didn't reply, but turned and continued to stroll along the hard path. Unbidden, Jeffrey joined her. "I wanted to speak with you, Livia. I had word that you were searching for something in London. Someone?"

Her heart leaped. What did he know? "I'm not sure I understand you." She needed to know more. He could be referring to something completely innocuous.

"You lost your grandmother's brooch, did you not?" His gentle tones held a wealth of meaning.

"Yes, yes, I did, but it was restored to me."

"You lost it in that orphanage you visited." Alarm bells rang in her head. Had he been watching her? Having her spied on? "Why did you go there, Livia?"

She tried the excuse she had used with everyone. "I wanted to become more involved with good works. Find a cause to support."

"Why did you leave?"

What, he'd seen that too? Her mind leaped forward. Then he would have seen, or known of, the scandalous kiss she had shared with Adrian in the street later. Obviously she could not tell him the real reason she left the orphanage, but one of the minor concerns. "The children overwhelmed me. They crowded around and confused me."

"You saw the records first, though, did you not?"

Yes, she'd perused them with the rascally owner. "How can you know that?"

"Because I spoke to them later. I wanted to find out what had taken you there."

Discomfort crept up her spine. She didn't like the idea of him following her in that way. "Why didn't you tell me, or ask me? I would have spoken to you, explained."

He shook his head, his mouth straightening. "I was not sure. I wanted to know why you abandoned our child, why you gave him away."

Shock shot through her, a jagged fork of lightning rendering her speechless. She turned, her hand to her mouth, her shoulders shaking. No, she would not cry. This was too important. Eventually her control returned to her, and she forced steel into her body. Swinging back to him, she said, "You knew?"

Hard-faced, he nodded.

"Before you married Maria?"

He sucked in a breath. "No." Coming back to her side, he offered his arm. "Please. Let's walk, as if we're taking the air."

As she had been before he had arrived. Still numb with shock, Livia placed her hand on his arm, her movement born of years of training rather than conscious thought. She had kept the secret to herself for so long that even speaking of it made her rigid with fear. "I saw him briefly before they took him away."

"And you thought he was at that orphanage?"

"Yes. At one point my grandfather had owned the place. I thought the slender clue was worth pursuing."

"Did your grandfather know about the child?"

She laughed shakily. "Of course not. He was long dead." She recalled finding the list when she was going through her father's account of charitable donations. A letter had arrived from a new donor, addressed to her in error. A few guineas were enclosed, and that had sent her hunting for the list.

Had they sent her baby there? She couldn't wait to find out. But no. She'd found her grandfather's concern, but no reference of the baby. No child fitting the description of her son had entered the orphanage during the vital two weeks.

"How do you know?" Four people had known and one of them was dead; Sherwood, the one that had taken the baby. The one they couldn't ask. Had her mother let something slip? Unlikely. Her father? No. Claudia? Had she told her husband? Even if she had, Dominic was an army man, had undertaken covert operations for his country, and held a secret much more explosive than hers. So even if he did know, he wouldn't tell anyone.

"I found out. That is enough. Do you think your sojourn in the cottage went unnoticed?"

"But you were away at the time." Away in the army and married.

He nodded, and abruptly stopped walking, turning to face her before she had time to pull away. "I heard. You know Maria always followed me around like a puppy after its master."

Not the most flattering way to describe his wife. But Livia nodded, wanting to know where he was taking this discussion. If she let him lead, she would learn more than if she demanded answers. Jeffrey had always been that way, arrogantly certain of the superiority of the male sex. Once she'd found his conviction endearing, restful, even. "But you loved her, did you not?" More than he had loved Livia, that was for sure. He had walked away from her. At the time, that had devastated her.

"My parents arranged the match. Once your father sent me away, I couldn't resist the pressure any longer. You know my mother had been at me for years to marry Maria. I could not bear to see you in society, finding yourself a husband. At the time it seemed like the best thing to do."

Livia knew what family pressure felt like. "Did your parents know? Did you tell them what we had done?"

His gaze dropped. "No. But they thought I had no right to court you. They were—against any closer link between us."

Courting? Was that what they called it? To be honest, Livia could rarely remember the fateful time when she'd allowed him to go further than he should have. He'd been asking her for weeks, pointing out that since they wanted to marry, surely it did not matter so much. Then she did, and she hadn't enjoyed it half as much as she'd thought.

That one time had given her the baby she still missed, still frantically sought. But she couldn't let him know that. A quiet conviction that something was not right. She wasn't going back into time, she wouldn't let him weaken her by talking about her baby.

"I lost a child too," he said softly. "I know what that feels like."

"Maria?"

He nodded. "With yours, I have lost two. Perhaps I am fated. I will never have a child, and I long to fill my nursery." He lowered his voice. "Particularly if you were the mother."

At least, that was what she thought he said, but even so close she could not quite make out his words. She guessed she was meant to lean even closer to him, but she wouldn't do that.

Confusion reigned in her heart. What did he want from her? He'd known about their son all this time and he had said nothing, done nothing? Or had he? "How long have you known?"

His mouth twitched, but he said nothing at first. His gaze roamed over her face, as if searching for something. He used to know her so well, but she'd learned a lot since they had parted. Eventually he answered her. "For some time."

Too briefly. She wanted to know more. "When?"

"After I married Maria." He swallowed. "After the deed was done and I could not go back on it."

He turned away, his hands clenched into fists.

She watched him helplessly. Were they both victims, then? She had to speak to her mother, painful though they would both find it. "Thank you for telling me."

About to turn and walk back to the house, she paused when he spun around to confront her. "We could look for him together. You did not find him at the orphanage."

If he'd been watching her, he'd know that. She shook her head. Unable to bear the pain, she'd fled, and then regretted it. But she would not tell him that. Look for their son together? "What do you care?"

"Oh, I care. I always did." His tone was savage. "But what could I do? Your father obtained my commission when my father asked him. He arranged everything after your parents discovered I meant to marry you. But they did not tell me that you'd given birth until after. I left, and I heard you had smallpox and your mother had taken you into confinement. But it wasn't that kind of confinement, was it?"

He slashed his hand through the air, his voice shaking with emotion. "I was worried. I threatened to come home. I paid someone to watch the cottage where you were. That was when I knew."

He faced her, his expression softened. He swallowed, a sure sign of his nervousness. She remembered him doing that when they'd been in trouble, and one or other of their parents had confronted them. "We could start again, Livia. You don't have to become an old maid, a spinster. Marry me. Let us do what we always wanted, and complete our story. Maria is dead, God rest her soul, and you are not."

She'd received more romantic proposals, but never did a marriage proposal pierce her to the heart like this one. Not even Adrian, who had proposed to her out of expediency.

Although the kisses that had accompanied Adrian's words had over-topped anything Jeffrey had offered. Of course, she and Jeffrey had both been so young then. But still she did not feel that same excitement.

Why would she think of such matters now? Jeffrey was offering everything she had ever wanted. But like a modern-day Romeo and Juliet they had been torn apart by their parents' dispute, from no will of their own.

But they had both changed. He had an army career behind him. He was now a Member of Parliament and in control of his own career. She was relegated to the back row of aristocrats and would retreat even further once her betrothal to Adrian collapsed. She had nothing to lose, looking at the situation in those terms.

"I am betrothed to the Duke of Preston," she reminded him.

"Do you truly want that? Are you in love with him as we were in love?" Closing his eyes, Jeffrey shook his head. When he looked at her again, his expression was fierce. "As I am still in love with you?"

His words hung in the air.

He tempted her. Could she do this? Find what she had once had with him? The answer came immediately. "I cannot."

"Not yet, not until you have broken your engagement. Or is this what you want?" His mouth twisted, his tone turning bitter. "Maybe you want wealth and a position in society and you are willing to sacrifice personal happiness for that. But at what cost? The world knows what Preston is, that he is the child of adultery. And with what a vile creature!" He reached for her hands, but she took a step back, anger rising that he should castigate the unfortunate pageboy that way. "Please, Livia. I love you, I always have." He let his hands fall to his sides. "We fell in love at the wrong time for both of us, but we can continue now. Come and live with me at the manor. Forget Preston and his corrupt ways. You will never be happy with him, and you know it. He is not worthy of you." He glanced up at the house and fell silent.

If anything, the page who had fathered Adrian was nothing but a pawn, used by the duchess. How dare Jeffrey castigate a boy he did not know? But as anger rose, she held it back. She needed this man. Jeffrey knew about the baby. His story did not ring entirely true, but she couldn't say why not. It made sense, that he would stay with Maria, but he had not contacted her, not once. "Do you know where he is?"

A voice pierced her consciousness. "Where who is?"

She had been so distressed that she hadn't felt his approach. Adrian came up behind her like a protective wall, his warmth shielding her from the chill that she hadn't noticed until this moment. As she forced back her awareness of her surroundings a breeze swept past the side of her neck. Glancing up, she saw the sky had more cloud than sky. Their respite from the rain was about to end. Or something else, sleet or snow perhaps. After all, December had arrived.

When she shivered, he pulled the edges of her cloak more securely about her, his arms wrapping her in warmth before he drew them away. "Come, sweetheart, the weather is turning. Come indoors before you're caught in a downpour."

"Did you know I was out here?"

"I saw you from the house. I would have joined you but you were—busy." His voice hardened as he stepped to one side of her and glanced at Jeffrey before turning his attention back to Livia.

"I have not seen Livia for some time," Jeffrey said. It did not elude Livia that he had used her first name as if he had a right to. In private it was one thing, but before others implied an intimacy they no longer had.

An intimacy she no longer wanted. For all his faults, for all his problems, she was drawn to Adrian like nobody else. Certainly not Jeffrey. He had an appeal, but of her youth, of memories lost, not of the present. Even if she were not betrothed, she would not accept him now.

But the knowledge that he had known about their son for all this time shook her to the deepest recesses of her soul.

* * * *

Livia and Sir Jeffrey did not look like lovers now. Adrian sensed the distress in her rigid little body before he saw her face. When he touched her, he confirmed it. She was tense, her shoulders raised. He kept his arms around her a fraction longer than he needed to, using arranging her cloak as an excuse. Left to his own devices, he would have held her against him until she stopped trembling. "Is there a problem?"

"I had some news about someone we both knew a long time ago." Sir Jeffrey used his question against him, pointing out that he and Livia shared a life Adrian could never enter. Well, he might have been part of her childhood, but Adrian vowed that Sir Jeffrey would have nothing to do with her future. Not if he could help it.

This man had to have been the one who took Livia's virginity. He'd gone around and around the issue, and this was the only answer that served. Also that her parents did not know, otherwise he would not have been allowed past the elaborate iron gates at the end of the drive.

Why had Livia agreed to meet Sir Jeffrey here? Did she want to hear his declarations? Accept them? Had she ever forgotten him?

A touch of fear breezed along his senses, matching the wind around their heads, which was trying to whip off his hat. He clamped the offending article on firmer with one hand but used the other to link with Livia's. To hell with the society convention of placing her hand on his arm. He wanted her closer than that, and if anyone saw them, well, he didn't give a damn.

But she might. That was all that stopped him claiming her in the most expeditious way. "I'm glad you've had an opportunity to talk about old times," he said through clenched teeth.

"And the future," Sir Jeffrey said, his features smoothing out to an expression of superiority. Or perhaps that was his usual expression. Adrian did not know, but every time he came across the man, he wore that same look. "We will be seeing much of one another."

"Oh? I move between my estates in Cumberland and Oxfordshire. Do you have establishments there?"

"Not yet."

As if Sir Jeffrey would buy a cottage at the gates and pine away there. Even if he did, Adrian would ensure he did not stay there long. He was not one for acting lord of the manor, but if it got him what he wanted, then he would use everything in his power to achieve it. And he wanted Livia more than anything else. Moreover, he wanted her happy. Content.

This man might have been the first to have her, but Adrian fully intended to be the last man in her bed.

If only he was worthy of the honor. But since she had thrown herself away on this scoundrel, Adrian would work to be the best version of himself possible. Until now he had not concerned himself with the petty gossip of society, but for Livia he would reform.

Nodding to Sir Jeffrey, he turned Livia and almost dragged her to the house. Rain began to fall, gently at first, pattering on his hat and skimming off the heavily waxed surface of her straw, creating its own trickle around her face. "At least you remembered to wear something warm, although your hands are cold."

"My gloves are too thin." She sounded listless. Had he interrupted something she wanted to continue? A shame he was not about to allow her to return.

As they approached the rear of the house, she tugged him aside, leading him to a nondescript door that had escaped his notice until now. Lifting the latch, he ushered her in, one hand at her back, urging her into the house and the warmth of the black and white tiled hall. Smaller than the grand entrances at the rest of the house, it was nevertheless welcome and saved them getting wetter. The rain had increased, pelting against the mullioned windows on either side of the door. "We got in just in time." He smiled grimly. "Sir Jeffrey will get soaked." *Good.*

Because he had glanced back to see the squire storming off in the other direction, probably in the direction of his own house. That could not be too close. He probably had a horse tethered nearby, although that would not stop him getting wet.

Served the bastard right.

A door stood at the end of the hall, but Livia led him up the wooden staircase and through a door to a part of the house he knew. He had taken some time exploring the various corridors, getting his bearings so he could find his way around this house. Obviously it was one of those places that had grown from a medieval seed, and gained a unified frontage to cover all the alterations and additions. Much like his house in Cumberland.

A small parlor lay on their left. Grabbing her hand, he tugged her into it, but left the door open. A small fire burned in the grate, a netted guard before it to stop sparks falling on the polished boards. This house was extremely well curated. He didn't release her hand but lifted it and turned it to unfasten the little button at the wrist. Then he tugged it off and followed suit with the other. Taking her hands between his, he rubbed them. "You should wear warm gloves, not these fashionable things. It's nearly Christmas, and there's snow in the air."

"There is?"

"There is." Unfastening the bow under her chin took some effort, since it had tightened, but he managed and pulled her hat off her head, tossing it aside. She'd flattened her hair, but to his eyes she was still lovely. She'd be lovelier if she wasn't shivering.

Without considering possible consequences, he drew her close, wrapping her in his arms. "You should have come in earlier." His anger dissipated as if it had never been in the face of her possible ill-health. "You'll catch your death of cold. As long as you were walking, you were fine. You should not have stayed still for so long."

"I wanted some fresh air."

"And to make your tryst." To his surprise, his anger crested once more. Along with his arousal, which seemed to happen every time he came close to her. He was almost getting used to his lack of control where Livia was concerned. Fortunately, the effect only happened around her.

"I didn't know—"

He broke into her words. "Don't lie to me, Livia." The thought sliced through him, hurt cutting through parts of him he'd imagined nobody could reach again. He'd been wrong. She belonged to him, damn the woman, and he would not allow her to choose anyone else. "Please don't do that."

"I won't." When she looked up, her blue eyes wide and melting with honesty, he believed her. Even though he knew he should not. And that angered him more. But beneath those eyes lay shadows, silent witnesses to a sleepless night.

He knew how she felt. He hadn't slept too well, either. Normally he slept like a baby, but his concerns kept him awake, together with a bed that felt strangely empty.

She nestled into him as if she belonged there, her body slowly warming by the fire and against his body.

"Aren't you going to ask me about Jeffrey?"

Defeated, he shook his head. "If you want me to know, you'll tell me. Is there something I need to know?"

Her breath swelled her bosom against his chest. "Yes." She drew another breath, and a small frown appeared between her brows. "But not here."

He knew. He'd left the door open as a nod to propriety, but also, perhaps, he didn't want to know. Not yet. "Very well." He bent his head to her, unable to resist those cherry lips a moment longer.

Their kiss was tender. Why he enjoyed the soft, affectionate kisses he'd never know. Kisses in his world were a forerunner to purely physical activity, nothing else. But with Livia this was enough, for now. Touching her, having her near and sharing kisses soothed his soul and calmed the restlessness that was his constant companion these days.

Warming her lips with his, tasting her and feeling her response urged him to do more. But he drew back. She blinked, as if as surprised as he felt. Every time he touched her he claimed a little more of her. She would be his, and he would know all her secrets.

Her confiding in him had grown in importance in his mind, and in the way he wanted to claim her.

In return, he would tell her everything. All of the sordid details that had helped to make him the man he'd become, why and how. All that she wanted to know. He would not force painful details on her, but Livia had said she wanted honesty. She would have it.

Was he really thinking of telling her about his mother, and the man who had fathered him? Gazing into her eyes, he knew the answer. But not until he had that ring on her finger. He hadn't gone that far into the vale of the good.

Her trembling wasn't all due to cold, either. Sir Jeffrey had upset her, but Adrian didn't know how.

So as always, he took the offensive. "Don't distress yourself. If you'd prefer to take Sir Jeffrey, then you must tell me. I want no unwilling wife in my bed."

As she jerked back her gasp echoed against the walls of this small room. "No! I mean I did not intend that at all. Please let me explain." A nervous glance at the door followed, before she went on. "But not here."

"And not now," he said firmly. "Let me take you up to your room. Your maid can get you into some dry clothes and find you something hot to drink."

"Tea." She sighed, and the lines around her mouth relaxed. "But I should tell you." She bit her lip, as if doubtful.

Sliding his arm around her waist, Adrian guided her firmly toward the door. "Come."

At least he had the pleasure of her company as far as her bedroom, where he delivered her to her harsh-faced maid who glared at him as if he had kept Livia out too long. "The weather has turned bad again," she said, glancing at where sleet was sliding down the windows. "You should never have gone out, ma'am." She took control of her mistress, guiding her into the room.

Adrian turned away, but halted when he heard her voice calling his name. She came out to him, and led him to the window, where the perceptive maid could not hear them. "Come here tonight," she said. "At midnight. I'll be waiting."

Before he could reply, she scurried back into the room and closed the door.

Of all things, Adrian had not expected a clandestine tryst. He would attend this one in a far different mood to his usual appointments in great country houses with beautiful women.

Chapter 13

If she told him everything, he might insist on going away. Livia strode up and down before the fire, unable to relax. She had been jittery all through dinner, something that had not escaped her mother's notice. Or her twin's. Drusilla would arrive before Christmas and then she would have two sisters on her tail as well as her mother. Her brothers, the two that were here, had noticed something but she had not given them the chance to get close.

She couldn't go on in this way. Two days into her visit to her home, and she was walking on upright pins. Mincing as if any false move would betray her. At least Jeffrey didn't come to dinner tonight, and neither did the local gentry. She could be thankful for that. Last night old Miss Denning had even treated her with kind condescension, welcoming her into the ranks of the unmarried lady. "It is not as thankless as people suppose," she'd confided from behind her fan, her stiffly ordered curls bouncing as she turned to Livia. "We have plenty to keep us amused. My dearest brother has cared for me all his life, and I am sure your family will treasure you too." Miss Denning, who had spent her life caring for children not her own, an unpaid companion and nurse.

At least Livia would not do that. Her dowry would provide her with the means to buy a small house somewhere and live quietly, if she wanted to. Probably with her cousin Poppy, who was heading for such a fate, if her mother was to be believed.

A lonely existence. Clasping her cream silk robe around her Livia took another turn on the Persian carpet. It was a wonder she had not worn a track in it by now.

Jeffrey would give her the life she'd always thought she wanted. Contentment, living with a husband she'd known most of her life, who she could discuss local affairs with. High society had never suited her. All those balls, and extravagant clothes, all the discussions on the affairs of the day wearied her. Or so she'd always thought.

Although Jeffrey had entered Parliament, he did not have a parliamentary turn of mind. He would do what the local grandee, in this case her father, told him to. The appointment came as prestige to him and his family, making his mother proud, and giving him a reason to visit London when he wished. If she married him, Livia would bear him children, and make her life in a part of the world that she loved and knew well.

Her life would be set on a course she had longed for ten years ago. Before the baby. Before the man who said he adored her had abandoned her for another woman and a life in the army.

Then there was Adrian. Livia halted and closed her eyes, feeling again his arms around her, his mouth on hers, the gentle kisses she hadn't believed a man like that was even capable of delivering. And the passionate ones that exposed his vast experience. The stories about him grew fiercer and more scandalous every year, and yet he could still enter any ballroom in London.

A man set in the mold of her brothers, who loved with all their hearts and souls. But Adrian had not offered her that. He'd given her a way out of a scandal she would never recover from. That was all. She doubted he wanted to go ahead with the wedding, and she certainly should not. How could she?

But she could not marry him. She had a son somewhere in the world, if he had not perished. Not knowing was its own particular torture, but she felt, in her heart, that the boy lived.

Livia wrung her hands and forced back her tears. She could not think of the child's death without that happening. Ten years had not dulled her grief. She could not lose another child like that, could not feel so helpless ever again. And if she allowed Adrian access to her body, surely he would know she had given birth.

And yet every part of her yearned for more. Wanted to feel him against her without the encumbrance of clothes, to experience his kisses all over her body, to have some of that legendary loving for herself. Before she reconciled herself to the life of a loveless spinster, which she had always known would belong to her.

Someone scratched at her door. Servants often did that, rather than knock, as the sound was deemed less intrusive. Picking up the skirts of her robe she positively ran there and lifted the latch.

Outside, dressed in a banyan easily as magnificent as a Turkish robe, stood the Duke of Preston.

Hastily, stumbling on the fabric trailing under her feet, she stepped back and let him in. He entered, strolling in as if entering a society gathering. "You've done this before," she said, unable to control her wayward tongue.

"Indeed I have." He turned, closing the door so softly nobody could possibly hear it. "More times than I care to remember." He spoke in a quiet, intimate murmur as he turned back to her, his gentle smile firmly in place. But his eyes blazed. "Would you like me to tell you about them?"

"No." Most assuredly she did not. "But this is new to me."

"Not entirely." Without hesitation, as if used to seeing her with her hair down and her body unburdened by stays and hoops, he took her hands and drew her forward. As if they were married in truth. But he did not tug her into his arms, merely secured her so she could not turn away from him. "Would you like to tell me about it?"

That was why she had asked him. Strangely grateful to him for approaching the truth without equivocation, she nodded. "Shall we sit?"

Releasing one of his hands, she led him to the window seat. When they were settled, she folded her hands in her lap, staring at them. "We were very young."

"Your parents should not have allowed Sir Jeffrey such access to you."

She started, her eyes widening as she lifted her gaze to his face. "You know who did it?"

"It would be hard for me not to. He has behaved toward you as if he owns you. Standing over you as if he had a right to do so. He has taunted me since he knew I had an interest in you."

"Oh!" Except for the duel that had forced their betrothal she hadn't known that, but yes, she could imagine Jeffrey doing such a thing. "He was always competitive." In truth, she was not surprised Adrian had worked out who had taken her virginity all those years ago.

"Marriage is not a competition." He leaned against the window frame, his arms folded over his multicolored, flamboyant robe.

Suspicion edged into her mind. "Did anyone see you come here?"

Supremely confident, he shook his head. "Of course not. As I told you, I'm used to such trysts. Where is your maid?" He glanced at the door leading to the powder room. Maids generally slept near their mistress, in case she should want them. And to keep her safe.

"I sent her to bed. She does not sleep near me in the country. I prefer to have my solitude."

"You do not have it now." He raised his voice to a normal pitch. "I shall leave you if you wish."

"No, I need to tell you. You know I am not a virgin. That is why I have never married."

"Just that?" His incredulity was emphasized when he raised both brows. A smile flirted with his mouth.

Could she tell him about the baby? Her heart failed her. If she let him do what she longed for him to do, if they made love, he'd see the marks childbirth had left on her body. Then he'd know. So many years of not telling anyone had built a barrier around her. She didn't know how to tell anyone, or where to begin. If he saw, and yet said nothing, perhaps she could accept that he understood.

For all her longing to see her child, all her searches had led to nothing. One way or another, the boy had gone, and she had to find a way to accept that. Let him assume the baby had died, once he saw the marks.

"It may be nothing to you, but it is vitally important to me."

He brushed her concerns aside with an elegant sweep of one hand. "Your position in society makes that a trivial matter. I suspect you have allowed your single state to become a habit. You are already making plans for your life as a spinster. Are you not?"

Damn him, yes. "What other choice do I have?"

"You have a choice now." Leaning forward, he caught her hands in his before she could pull them back. He moved so quickly and silently when he wanted to. "You can marry me."

"But that was a mere subterfuge. You were kindly helping me escape total social ostracism."

"Was I?" He smiled. Too warmly, too intimately. When she tried to draw her hands away, he tightened his hold. "Are you sure?"

The air around them pulled tight. Of course she was. If she had thought otherwise, she wouldn't have invited him here tonight. Would she? She didn't know what to say, so she said nothing.

"You're not, are you?" If he'd sounded in the least triumphant she would have asked him to leave. But he was too old a hand at this game. He kept his voice low and unthreatening. Although she knew what he was doing, talking to her as if she were a scared kitten, she found his approach irresistible.

He watched her when she wet her lips, his eyes those of a predator waiting to pounce. Observant, desire banked but definitely there. "Of course not," she said crossly. "You're one of the best lovers in London. Everybody says so."

"Do they now?" A smile creased the corners of his eyes. "Now why would you say that?"

"I only say what everybody else does. Even—single ladies, even if they are not virgins, hear gossip." This was far too comfortable. She didn't want to sink into this discussion. Wrenching her hands away from him, she stood and took a few paces into the room. The candlelight from the two sconces on the wall and the two set on the bedhead glowed brightly, making the silk of her robe glimmer as she moved. "I have the most notorious man in London in my bedroom." Turning, she let her skirts swish around her before she spoke again. "In his undress."

Although that magnificent banyan, a rich blue embellished with heavy gold thread embroidery could hardly be described as such. But it wasn't the formal coat men had to wear. Under it, his legs were bare, his feet shoved into soft leather slippers. Was he naked? Men frequently changed into the softer banyans in their homes, but they only took off their coats to do so, not everything.

He crossed his legs, letting the garment fall open from his knees. He knew she was watching. Hairy, powerful, his calves taut with muscle. The thought of rubbing her legs against them made her lose concentration. Tonight she meant to have everything she shouldn't have. He was experienced, so he would know these things.

"Adrian..."

His eyes sparkled when she said his name and his expression softened. "Ask me." He spoke so quietly, but in a low tone that rumbled through her.

"Do you know how to make love without—consequences?"

"Without the deed resulting in a pregnancy, you mean?"

Unable to speak, she nodded.

"Yes, but there is always a risk. It's possible to reduce it, but not to eliminate it completely." Smoothly he got to his feet and came to her, towering over her. "Tell me why you want to know, Livia."

She sucked in a breath and used it to steel herself. If she did not ask she would regret the opportunity for the rest of her life. She knew so much about making love, had even done it, but she had never understood what it was that enticed people to risk their reputations, their lives, everything they had to get it.

No hiding now. No equivocation. "Because I want to know what it's like. I want to know what it feels like when an experienced man makes love to a woman. But I can't risk children."

That wasn't all she wanted. If he made love to her, he'd see the evidence of childbirth. Perhaps he'd feel it. Did a woman who had borne a child feel different inside? She'd always assumed so, though she could hardly ask anyone.

Then she wouldn't have to tell him. He would know, and he could make his decision. She still couldn't work out how to tell him in words. This was the best way.

He gazed down at her, his expression unreadable. But he didn't appear angry. Then he spoke. "A man can withdraw and spend his seed outside the woman's body. In that case, the risk is that he does not do it in time, or that he releases early. The lady may insert a small sponge into her body, soaked with something like lemon juice or brandy. Something acidic. Nobody knows why that works, but if she leaves it in place until the next day, it is reasonably effective. She may insert half a lemon, the insides scooped out, and cover the tiny opening inside with it. There are other methods, herbs and such, but I wouldn't recommend those. Some are ineffective, some can cause damage to the body. You will not do that."

"Oh." Her body heated. She had never discussed anything so—personal with anyone before, much less someone of the male sex. "I—I wanted to be sure. It sounds so—cold, so calculated." But he knew how to prevent conception. That was good enough for her.

"It is anything but that."

Her hasty nod loosened one of the ties fastening her nighttime braids. She'd coiled them up on top of her head, trying for something less—young, but now they came loose and swung around her face.

"You look adorably confused." Amusement colored his voice.

"I am. I have never…"

"But you had the courage to ask. The least I could do is answer you straightly. Are you satisfied?"

"Yes."

"And, Livia, if you want to do this, I have two conditions," he continued. She swallowed, her throat dry. "What are those?"

He clasped her upper arms, holding her in place. "That you do this with nobody else but me."

Her answer came before she thought it through. "I don't want to do it with anybody else but you."

Tilting his chin, he raised a brow. "You don't?"

When she shook her head something changed in his expression, his eyes warming once more and his mouth losing that tight look. "I'm glad to hear it. Very glad." That didn't sound like the cynical Duke of Preston at all. But she had not thought of him like that in some time. She'd discovered a man of far more integrity than she had expected. At several points in their relationship he could have taken her, seduced or even taken her by force, and he would have faced few consequences. Once she had all but offered herself, and he'd refused her.

"I don't mean to trap you," she said. "I just wanted to know. I won't tell anyone, and I sent Finch away. She said she should stay tonight to ensure I had not taken a chill, but I assured her I had not."

His hold on her softened, his hands moving up her arms to cup her shoulders gently. "Were you telling the truth?"

She nodded. "I was cold and wet, but I have taken no lasting damage." She gave a shaky laugh. "I'm not made of paper. I can stand a little rain without collapsing."

That smile should be outlawed. "Good. Because I would probably call your maid myself if that were the case." Moving to her braids, he took the end of one between his thumb and forefinger. The twist of thread fastening it came loose and fell away. The braid began to unravel. He helped it.

"But then they'd know, if you called Finch. About you being here, I mean." She would never move again if only he left his hands on her, warming her all the way through. He finished unfastening one braid and moved to the other. She'd rarely had her hair loose. It was the regulation length of three fingers, perhaps a little more since Finch had not trimmed it lately. He sifted his fingers through the mass as he undid it, concentrating on his self-imposed task. The action felt more intimate than it should.

"Better that than have you suffer," he said. "Are you sure you're all right?"

Touched by his concern, she nodded. She had more to discuss with him but having him so close scattered her wits. She had not meant to ask him so soon. And he'd said two conditions?

He kept his attention on her braid. "Are you sure you want me to make love to you?" At last she heard something. A slight tremor in his voice, soon suppressed.

"I want it, yes."

"And the consequences?" He touched her chin with his thumb.

"You said you could…" She didn't have the courage to say it again. She had shot her bolt, as the saying went, and she could not say more.

"Yes, I did, but I also warned you that nothing is certain."

"Then yes, I can take the consequences. Whatever they are." She had been through that before, but this time she was in a position to care for her child herself, to ensure it had a good upbringing. She had heard of ladies adopting "foster children." She could do that, and damn the people who speculated. If she was past marriageable age, why should she care?

And she wanted this too much to go back now. "I'm only asking for this once. I won't force you into anything. And if anyone sees you, feel free to deny everything."

A gleam of amusement lit his eyes. "Nobody will see me."

When she opened her mouth again, it was to feel his lips against hers. He was clearly done with discussion. That solution worked well for her too. Curling her arm around his neck, she responded enthusiastically. She already knew how he liked to kiss, but he had given her several different kinds, from tender to passionate. This one was different again. It was as if he'd unleashed the hounds. He positively devoured her.

Plunging his tongue into her mouth, he treated her to a blatant display of what was to come, thrusting in, tasting and claiming with a masterful finesse Livia found irresistible. She responded eagerly, holding on to him as if he was her only lifeline. If he moved away she'd fall to the floor in a messy heap. Her legs shook as she groaned into his mouth.

He tore his lips away from hers, his gaze hot, and glanced over her head to the bed. Finch had already drawn the covers down to reveal the inviting, smooth white sheets, it stood, a silent witness to what she was about to do.

Joyfully and willingly. She initiated the second kiss, eager for more. He tasted of man, deliciously different, a touch of spirits, maybe brandy, still lingering to inflame her desire even further. Had he taken a drink for courage before he'd come to her? Surely not. She'd rarely met a man so confident, so sure of himself.

He slid his hands around her waist, over her gown, and a streak of cold air slid down her side. When she tried to pull away to find out what had happened, he dragged her back, kissing her feverishly, returning what she had initiated. He finished the kiss only to glance at her, and then kiss his way to her ear, exploring the rim with his tongue. Who knew her ear was so sensitive? She certainly had not. He kissed down her throat, finding new spots that ratcheted her arousal. She moaned, and he sighed a hot breath over her skin in response, raising the tiny hairs, making her shiver.

When he touched her bare skin she understood what he'd done. He'd unfastened the sash fastening her gown and it was loose. He'd pushed it aside to find her skin. Fear tickled her senses before he stroked, and sent her into new transports of delight.

Nobody had touched her bare waist other than her maid and, presumably, her nurse. No man, that was for sure. And now a man was taking possession of her. All of her. Leaning back into his touch, she gave a small "Oh!" of shock and pleasure.

"Sweetheart, let me see you."

With a catch in her breath, she stepped back, automatically pulling her gown together once more. The sash was lost somewhere on the floor. His eyes were all black, no brown showing, his mouth reddened with kisses, his olive skin flushed with arousal. "You want to stop?"

She shook her head and found her voice. "No. I'm just—no man has seen me..."

"Naked?" A smile curved his mouth and put tiny lines at the corners of his eyes. "That pleases me, Livia. Trust me enough to let me see and touch."

"You've touched dozens of women. I'm not too special. Just ordinary." She could not compare to beauties like Ophelia d'Arblay, that was for sure.

"May I be the judge of that? I do not compare women, neither do I think of other women when I'm with the one of my choice. You are my choice, Livia. Nobody else."

His words gave her the courage to open the robe and shrug it off her shoulders. Yards of silk slithered to the floor with a swish. A desperate urge took her to cover herself, but she bunched her hands and left them by her sides. If he didn't like what he saw, then at least she would know. And surely, despite the dim light, he'd see those thin, distinctive lines on her stomach and thighs.

Silence. He scanned her once, from her head to her feet and back again. She felt as if he'd just claimed her. His eyes burned with an inner heat, his chest moved as he took a breath.

Then, with deliberation he lifted his hands and pushed the silk toggle fastening the top of his robe through its corresponding loop.

She just stood there.

He put his hands to his waist and slipped the two fastenings there undone with sharp, quick motions.

Her skin prickled.

He pulled back the garment and let it fall to the floor. He was as naked as she.

Not cool enough to serve him the way he had served her, she stared, greedily taking him in. A patch of dark hair marked his chest, filing into a neat line between his slim hips and down to what reared below.

Livia had never seen an erect male before. Not on a man, at any rate. When she'd done it before, the encounters had been feverish and hurried. She'd felt rather than seen. Adrian's erection was angry, red, the slick cap gaining a purplish hue. And it was fleshy, human, every bit of it made for sin. She swallowed.

Before she could back away he stepped forward and took her in his arms. Without clothes, his body was hotter than ever, a veritable furnace of hard, hot male. Muscles swelled under her hands when she dared touch him, curving her palms over his upper arms, as much to keep herself steady as to feel him. Then she only wanted to keep hold. His member pressed into her stomach, imprinting its shape there, the damp tip kissing her bare skin.

"Adrian?" She had not meant her voice to come out so small and scared, but this experience was beyond her understanding. She'd expected a fumble and some caressing. Not that deliberate, open display. The candles shed enough light to reveal every smooth line of his body. She'd stood with her back to the candles, throwing her body into shadow, so perhaps he could not see as much. If he had seen the telltale marks, he said nothing. But she had seen all of him; the small scars from who knew what accidents and perhaps physical confrontations, the powerful shoulders, the slabs of muscle delineating his chest. Even now his chest hair provided a new texture for her to rub her body against. Which, she discovered, she was doing quite shamelessly.

"What is it?" The tremor in his voice told her he was also affected by their undressing.

"Am I enough?" She hated to feel needy, but before all that magnificence, she did.

"More than enough. I have never seen anything so lovely. No." He put a finger over her lips when she would protest. "I mean it. You are singularly beautiful, Livia." He kissed her nose, softly. "I hardly dare touch you."

"I'm not special." Although Adrian was the first man she had seen naked, she had naturally seen plenty of women. Her sisters, her maid, when they shared a room when traveling, people too poor to care about displaying themselves. Enough to know she had an average body.

"You feel wonderful." He cupped her shoulder, then slid his hand down to her waist and around, over her buttocks. "Like the finest silk under my palms. I have never experienced anything quite like this. And your breasts are beautiful. Such pale nipples are a challenge."

"To what?" His response startled how. How could nipples be a challenge?

"To kiss them from pale rose to raspberry pink." He pressed her into his body, and she finally had her wish to discover what his legs felt like against hers. Strong enough to support them both. "Which I will shortly be doing. You're as pale as milk."

She laughed. "Mama used to make Claudia and I bathe in it. And we were always ordered to keep out of the sun because we might develop freckles."

"I think I see one or two." He gazed down his nose at her, concentrating on her face.

"Oh dear. Mama will be mortified."

Swooping down, he kissed the side of her nose, then the bridge. "There, that's those taken care of. Never listen to anyone but me, Livia. You're beautiful."

"Everything? All of me?"

"Every bit," he said firmly, sweeping his hand over her body. He stroked her lower belly, where one of the marks of childbirth remained. Oh he knew. He'd seen. If he asked her where the baby was, she'd tell him the truth. Otherwise, what was the point of telling him? Let him think the baby was dead.

Her heart sank, but she pushed her sorrow away. Later, when she was alone again, she'd mourn, as she had done so many times before. Not now. Relish the moment, because it would never come again.

She glanced down, to where her hand rested on his arm. The startling contrast between his skin and hers made her look almost dead. But the fashion was for pale skin. She preferred bronzed, now that she had seen all of him.

"Better now?"

Jerking her chin up, she met his eyes. Amused, yes, but still that glow banked down deep inside, and the rod pressing into her stomach told her his desire had not abated one whit by the sight of her. Biting her lip, she nodded. "Yes, I think so."

"Good. Here we are, Livia. I should tell you that it is far too late for you to back down. You are mine now, and I intend to make good use of you before I leave."

"Oh." Use of her? What did that mean?

"And you, sweetheart, will be making use of me. At least, I fervently pray that you will."

His kiss came as a shock. She had not been expecting such an all-out attack, but perhaps she should have, because that hand, still pressed to her backside, pressed even farther. Did he mean to enter her directly through her stomach wall?

As his tongue entered her mouth, licking sensuously inside, softly taking her will and her mind, his finger slid between her legs, gently caressing what it found there.

Her gasp sucked his tongue in, but he gentled his kiss, stroking her lips and tongue, as if soothing her before the assault to come. "You're wet," he said when he drew back enough to speak. But not enough to allow his lips to leave hers, so he caressed her with every word.

"Yes." The tops of her thighs had dampened with the welcome she was showing him. Although she wanted to squirm, he held her too firmly for that, one arm around her waist, the other between her legs.

"You're soft, wet and I don't know how much longer I can wait." He glanced down to where her breasts were squashed against his chest. "I want to play first, but I do not think I have the control. Because above all else, I want to see you come."

That word, forbidden but not unknown in this context, his breath warm against her lips, his mouth touching hers meant as much as what he was doing with his finger.

"Turn around."

Her eyes widened. "What?"

"Do as I say."

As he withdrew his finger, she did as he asked, but she had no idea what he wanted her to do that for. With his hands circling her waist he guided her to the side of the bed so she was facing it. Ah, he wanted her to climb in. She lifted her leg.

"No. Stay there." He pressed his hand between her shoulder blades, urging her to bend over the bed.

Livia had a modern canopy bed, not one of the old-fashioned four-posters that had the high frames, but one with a lower mattress. Still she had to go on tiptoe until he found the footstool and helped her to stand on it.

"Prop yourself up on your elbows and open your legs."

The soft commands sent thrills through her. She had a vague idea of what he was about to do, but she was by no means certain. Where she had expected some familiarity, she found none. She was entering unknown country.

Sliding his arms around her body, he found her breasts. They hung into his hands like ripe fruit. "So soft," he murmured, moving closer. His shaft slid naturally between her thighs.

"Adrian?" This was so intimate, so visceral she did not know how to process his actions. And yet the lack of anything but themselves, no subterfuge, no carefully calculated manners, no thought for anything except pleasure drove her to an unbearable level of arousal. She moaned. "Do it."

"Well, I've heard more gracious invitations." Removing one hand, he caressed her, stroking down to her bottom and back between her legs. This time he inserted a finger into her, pushing firmly but without undue pressure until she sighed. "Good." His voice was tight. "That feels wonderful." Drawing his finger out, he rubbed her, gently encouraging her natural response to him. "Better."

Pulling away slightly, he urged his shaft closer, so it pressed against her entrance. "You can take me more easily this way. You're wet enough, sweetheart. Relax, let me do it all. When I push, push back."

What could she do? In this position she could do nothing but take him. And take him she did. Slowly, steadily, he introduced his body to hers. One hand clasping her hip, he held her steady, helping her push back. He paused, and she sighed in relief. She'd done it.

Except she hadn't. There was, it appeared, more, because he pressed in farther, and farther. Could she do this? Take this man who was big in every sense of the word?

He filled her then, when she thought she had no more to give, filled her some more. His lips grazed her spine and he kissed her up to the nape of her neck, rubbing his face against her, a trace of stubble creating a marvelous friction. "So good. Oh, Livia, you are a revelation."

He didn't ask her how she was. If she wanted him to stop, she could do it, she realized. She could pull the covers and escape across the bed. But why in heaven would she want to do that? He felt so good, his shaft deep inside her body, his hands gentle on her body.

A slight breeze hit her skin as he stood. Clasping her hips with both hands, he held her steady while he withdrew. Then he powered back inside her.

Livia lost her breath. Sensations rippled up the spine he'd just kissed, right to the top of her head.

Partially withdrawing, he did it again. And again.

Every time he moved he took a slightly different angle until he stroked a spot inside her that sent tingles through every part of her body. "Ah! Oh, what did you do!"

"Good," he said. "There it is. Every woman has a secret place and this is yours. I can find it better this way. Now that I know where it is—" He lowered his voice. "You won't be able to stop me."

A promise or a threat? Livia didn't care so long as he carried on doing this. He thrust, finding that spot repeatedly, until she lost count of his strokes, until she slid inside her easily, each drive increasing the wetness inside and outside that part of her body. He collided with her, masculine grunts punctuating his progress, marking his success.

The tingles turned into bolts of lightning, but the kind that filled her body with awareness of itself and of him. Her senses heightened and she no longer cared what sounds she made, crying out. Until she cried his name and he gave a shaky laugh, and warned her, "Hush, darling. Not so loud."

Oh God. Claudia's old room was next door, but she and Dominic had moved to a room a floor above, so they could be close to their baby. But for that, Livia's twin would have come running to see what was the matter. But somebody else might hear. Fear froze her, but only for a moment as Adrian continued his relentless drive, mercilessly urging her toward a place she had never been to before.

His strokes mattered more than anything else in the world. "If you stop now, I'll *kill* you," she muttered, making him laugh, hastily muffling the sound before he drove against her. Her bottom and breasts quivered with each stroke, her skin so sensitive that every time he caressed her with his hand, he added to the torment inside her, every part of her as one, powering up to that final...plunge.

Livia dropped like a stone as ecstasy blossomed around her, flowing through her. His hold on her tightened as she buried her face in the bedcover and shouted, unable to control herself in the throes of this—experience.

She didn't even have a name for it. But she knew she wanted it again.

With a sharp sound, he pulled out of her, his hand on her hip clenching tight and releasing, clenching once more before he groaned, soft and long. Wetness splashed her spine. His seed, hot and potent.

"Wait." She was glad to hear the shakiness in his voice, because that meant he was as affected as she was by this experience.

He returned, swiping a towel across her back, before he looped an arm under her and lifted her, letting her slump onto the bed. She could happily stay there, sprawled over the covers sideways all night, but the mattress dipped as he climbed up and lifted her again, turning her to nestle against his body. He drew the covers over them.

"Sleep now, sweet Livia. I'll watch over you."

All awareness gone, only filled with a joy she had never felt before, she closed her eyes. Just for a minute.

Chapter 14

Adrian lay on his back, one arm holding a slumbering Livia close, the other tucked under his head. Livia snuffled and moved, sliding her leg over his to tuck it between them. He smiled. This woman was not getting away.

Her glorious hair lay over his chest in tousled disarray, driving him half-crazy with its silky sensuousness. He wanted her again and again, but while no virgin, Livia was far from experienced. He didn't want to hurt her, which was a novel idea in itself.

Usually he paid women to become his mistress. They had a contract, and a guarantee. When a woman such as Ophelia broke those rules, he walked away. That was how he preferred to conduct his private life. The stories about him were mostly fabricated by a greedy press, but because he never bothered to refute them, they were accepted as the truth.

But if Livia broke his rules, he wouldn't walk away, and that bothered him.

Only a little, though. The bliss that invaded his senses left him swamped in happiness, such an unaccustomed and fleeting emotion that he didn't know what to do with it. Unexpected too. He'd had to take her the way he had because he wasn't sure he could control himself much longer. In an impulse he had not known since the early days of his adventures with women, he knew he had to take her fast, and without her watching him with that dreamy, aroused expression. She had expected a slow seduction, probably lying on her back, but he had no time for that. He wanted in, as deeply as he could go, but he wouldn't come until she had given up her joy. Which she did, thank the Lord, before he had given up the delightful fight. That act was all he needed to know that his search had ended. Began and ended with the same person. Livia.

Separating his intellect from his body, he tried to think his decision through. Rationality never worked well in these situations, but he had to do his best, because she would wake soon, and then he'd be lost again.

He'd decided that Livia would make him a good duchess. She knew her place in society, the marriage would give him useful connections, and she was lovely to look at. Even though he chanted his list in his head, it felt hollow. If Livia had been an actress off the London stage he would be in deep trouble. Because he'd devote his passion to her anyway and no doubt make a complete fool of himself.

Her body, silhouetted by the candlelight behind her had frozen him to the spot. The anxious expression in her eyes made him vow never to give her cause to look at him like that again. He wanted trust between them, so she felt safe with him. But not too safe, he recalled with a low growl, stroking her beautiful skin.

Every woman had at least one outstanding feature, but Livia's had not become apparent until he'd touched her naked body. Her skin was soft and silky, warm and inviting. The milky paleness so valued by society did not particularly appeal, or had not in the past, but when he saw the contrast between them, it gave him a sense of the forbidden, which, of course, pushed his desire up to unbearable levels. He adored touching her.

Their marriage contract had not demanded fidelity, but he would do his best to ensure neither of them strayed.

And he determined one other thing. They would marry long before the contract ran out. Next week wasn't out of the question. Neither was tomorrow, come to that. He couldn't let her sleep alone any longer.

All he had to do was persuade her. Anyone else he could seduce into doing it, or cow them by appearing at his most ducal, but not this woman. Too used to moving in high circles, and he would not reduce what they had just shared into a tactic in what promised to be an interesting and at times difficult marriage. In a few days the house would fill up with siblings and relatives, and he could not risk creeping along the corridors between their rooms. Even less the job-doors that led into narrow servants' passages, places he'd mastered years ago. But not here, not in this house.

She stirred, her little grunt making him smile. When she opened her eyes, she blinked them clear. He watched the sleep disappear. "Oh. I thought you would go."

"Not yet." Propped on one elbow, he gazed down at her, smiling. "How could I leave when you sleep so sweetly?"

"Ah." She blinked rapidly. "I'm not used to this."

"Neither am I."

That made her laugh. "Yes, you are. Don't lie."

"I'm not lying. I do not linger in my mistress's bed. I don't sleep with them." That was true enough. He preferred to sleep in his own bed. Once he had satisfied his desires, he saw no reason to stay. This time he had, and since he had not slept, he wasn't sure why. He could have thought through his position in his own bed easily enough. Except leaving appeared a dispiriting prospect.

"Is that what I am now? Your mistress?" Her lips curved into a smile. She liked the idea.

He liked it too. "For a short time, yes you are." He touched her mouth and curved his hand around her cheek. The texture of her skin affected him every time and arousal stirred. Her hair didn't help him to keep control, trailing bright red-gold silk. "But not for long. Soon you'll be my wife."

A flush ran along her cheekbones and she opened her mouth in an O before she found her voice. "This was a farewell. You don't want to marry me, not now you know everything."

He growled low, stroking her skin. "Everything, yes." She really thought she was nothing special? He planned to spend a very long time showing her how wrong she was about that. Livia Shaw had a spectacular body.

"You only said we were betrothed to help me out of a scandalous situation."

"Do you not think this is *scandalous?*" He couldn't resist the gentle tease.

"Yes, but nobody will see us tonight."

"What if they do?" The notion aroused rather than appalled him. Then she would have no choice. There would be no getting out of this. He could contrive to be seen going back to his room or leaving her chamber. But no, he would not stoop to such tactics. Because that would hurt her. For himself he cared not, but he hated to see Livia distressed.

Another reaction he needed to ponder.

"If people see you here? You know what would happen." She grasped his arm, curling her small fingers around his wrist. But she could not encircle even that part of him. Nevertheless, he didn't resist her loose hold. "Please, can you be careful?"

"I swear I will. But that does not change my mind. Don't you worry about me and my reputation?" He had to ask. He would do his best not to bring trouble to her, but with his reputation, they would have a lot to live down.

"No. My family has its own scandals." She bit her lip. "I have scandals of my own." She gazed up at him as if she could rival him in scandal.

He sensed the precariousness of his position. He could not begin to tell her that story. She had accepted that he was the son of his mother and her black page, like all London. She'd called the boy Marsala, but Adrian could not bring himself to call the unfortunate boy by the name of a fortified wine. He never knew the boy's real name, except, in the way of these things, he'd borne Adrian's own surname, Sterling. "You will meet my mother, by and by." Because he could not avoid that. She would learn the truth then.

"Will I?"

"After the wedding."

"But we are not marrying." She tightened her hold on his wrist. "We agreed to part, you know we did!"

He shook his head, still smiling. "*You* did, sweet Livia. I did not. If there is any jilting to be done, you must do it." Resting his hand on her shoulder, he gazed at her. Her blue eyes glittered in the golden light. "I will not do it. And if you want me in your bed again, we will agree to marry before any possible consequences occur."

"But you—you took care of that." Her eyes widened, and her throat tightened. He had her.

Ruthlessly, he went in for the kill. "Nothing is certain, sweet Livia. No method is completely without risk. I told you that before we made love."

"Fucked," she said, short and succinctly.

The word on her lips shocked him so much he burst into laughter. "Such a word to come from a lady!"

"I have brothers," she said, reddening.

He gave up resisting the siren lure of that blush and moved down, kissing her cheeks, then her mouth, but softly. "Whatever you did, I made love," he said firmly. He guessed she had used the word to shock him. She would have to do much better than that. And that word never used in polite society, but everywhere else, including the clubs of St. James and Pall Mall, sounded sweetly innocent on her lips.

Truth, he was still speaking the truth. He had made love to her. That was why he was still here. That was no swift, necessary coupling, leaving both parties satisfied but separate. The act had joined them in a way he found unfamiliar. And addictive. He wanted more of what she had given him, and by God, he'd take it. "However," he said, kissing down her face to her throat, "if you wish to continue using such language when we're alone, please take the liberty of doing so. I find those words falling from your sweet lips stimulating in the extreme."

"No," she moaned, "you cannot think so."

"If you don't think so, then you do not know men as well as you think." He glanced up at her face. That pink glow remained, but embarrassment was no longer the sole cause. Her nipples were hard, grazing his chest, little points of desire. Bending his head, he took one into his mouth, sucking it to render it harder. Delicious. Her moans drove him to do more. Restlessly shifting, she pushed her fingers into his hair, which had come undone hours ago, pressing her fingers against his skull.

The other nipple tasted just as good, if not better. Releasing it, he admired the result before he kissed around the rosy circle, working his way out to the flushed skin, softly inviting. His cock had hardened, almost painful in its intensity. This time he would pleasure her the way she had evidently expected. And it would be as good as putting her on all fours. Better, because he learned more about her body every time he touched her. She was a library after a lifetime of single books.

He dipped his tongue into her navel, then explored her hips. Few people knew how sensitive the pocket of flesh inside the cup of the hip could be, but Adrian played and explored there, chuckling when she tried to push him away or move from his attentions. But when he heeded her wishes and put space between them, she whimpered. She'd enjoyed it, but perhaps the sensation was too insensitive for a woman as aroused as she was. He nuzzled into the soft nest of red-gold curls at her groin. The hair here was a shade darker than that on her head, and it smelled, well, delicious. Sharp, less musky than he'd expected. And, as he'd anticipated, delicious.

"No, you can't," she murmured, her voice hoarse.

"Watch me." He propped his chin on the prominent bone on her mound of Venus, flipped the sheets back and gazed up at her. "I can, sweetheart, and I have every intention of doing so."

"But I…" She licked her lips.

With a groan, he separated the hair, finding her center, and parted her lips delicately. The scent of her arousal increased and his mouth watered. That little pearl of desire peeked mischievously at him. That belonged to him. "Have you ever played with yourself here?" He touched it with the tip of his tongue.

"No!" She sounded scandalized.

He should be the scandalized one, to hear she had not even experienced self-pleasure, but he could only be glad he was the one who would introduce her to it. Another time. Tonight, this belonged to him. And for a long time to come, if he had anything to do with it.

He sucked, savoring and memorizing her taste. He would never eat tart apples without thinking of Livia from now on. Already wet, she gave him more as he explored her. Her hand still gripped his scalp. She could rip his hair out for all he cared, as long as she kept giving those little moans.

"Oh nonononono!" she said, writhing to one side, pulling away from him.

He put his hand on her thigh, halting her retreat. "You want me to stop?"

"No!" That was more emphatic and said with a certain enunciation that made him smile. "It's just—oh, Lord, what do I mean?"

"Wait and see." He moved her back so he could taste her some more. Increasing the suction, he found her deliciously responsive, especially when he pushed a finger inside her, to the place he wanted to be. He knew where her special spot was now, the place that enhanced all sensation, and he used it mercilessly.

Arching her back, she cried out, and her passage clamped down on his finger in a series of flutters that he loved. Already he was at the level of arousal he'd felt before. Would that ever pass? He wasn't sure he wanted it to.

Surging up the bed, flinging the covers aside, he nudged her legs apart and settled between them. Her hands rose to cup his shoulders as if she'd done it for years, so natural did it feel.

"Kiss me," she said, her voice all breath and little sound.

He didn't need the sound. Guiding his cock with one hand, he slid inside her as he fastened his lips to hers, letting her taste herself on him. The remains of her arousal still quivered along his length as he entered her, pushing him up too far. He sensed all his body, every knob of his spine, every rib, every breath he took, the total awareness too much. Almost too much. Because he would feel her convulse around him before they were done.

In this state she would not care what he did. He could release inside her and she would not object. That would force her to marry him soon. But she had accepted him, her generosity as great as her arousal. She trusted him.

When was the last time anyone had trusted him?

Livia humbled him, particularly when he'd discussed an early marriage with her. For that reason he would not give in to his baser urges but would force himself to spend on her belly. Last time he had nearly left it too late, but one final withdrawal when all his body screamed at him to plunge deep and the gust of cool air when he'd pulled out had proved enough.

It had to be so this time.

Pulling back from the kiss, he watched her, and her reaction to his lovemaking. He held nothing back but let her see the fierce determination in his face, the way he was sinking into her. She kept her eyes open, watching him.

He'd never made love to anyone with such expressive responses. Her openness enchanted him; the way she pressed on his shoulders for more, trying to guide him, and then slid her hand down his body to rest it on his buttock. He loved that.

She responded so well with her body too, lifting to meet his thrusts, holding her body open to receive him, then angling her lower body to achieve greater penetration. "Lift your legs," he murmured to her, and she did so, gripping his flanks with her thighs as he plunged deep, then withdrew, working to hit her special spot with every thrust.

Fever mounted in him, driving him hard, until he had to strain every nerve to hold back, to keep himself from spending inside her. But until she came again—ah yes, there it was, that first twitch of her passage around him.

With a cry, Livia arched up, almost turning her body into an inverted C shape, and she gripped his cock with an intensity he didn't think he could escape. But her violence grew less pronounced, until, while she was still suffering her little death, he pulled out and pressed into her stomach, feeling the wetness of his seed between them. Each spurt took him to another place, into her, with her.

Panting, they stared at each other. "And that," he said softly, "is why we are getting married as soon as it can be arranged."

Chapter 15

Livia woke, as she nearly always did, alone. But she was hugging a pillow, which was something she never did.

Her maid bustled around, getting her clothes ready for the day. A deep red today, Livia noted. Unless she demurred, Finch generally selected her clothes.

Sighing, she rolled over and reached for her hot chocolate.

Adrian waited for her in the breakfast parlor. He had made himself at home, as if he'd always lived here, and Livia's mama had declared him a delightful guest, telling Livia's papa that she was sure his reputation was mainly because of his birth and not his actions.

Livia wasn't so sure. If the marchioness had known what they'd done last night, she wouldn't be so sure either.

Adrian gave her a look that told her if nobody else was present, he would be kissing her right now. She gave him a tremulous smile in return, despite not being a tremulous kind of woman. He made her shake, he made her want. And now, she knew exactly what she wanted.

Getting to his feet, he kissed her hand—the palm—and led her to a seat next to him. Then he went to the sideboard and loaded a plate for her. Her mother gave her a most unladylike wink and a smile, while pouring Livia a dish of tea.

Sighing, Livia gave in to the inevitable. He wanted to spoil her, so she would let him do so. It was rather sweet, actually.

But she nearly choked on her first mouthful of egg when Adrian announced, "Livia and I would like to wed before Christmas. The contract is signed, and there is no necessity to wait."

Lady Strenshall was the first to regain her breath. While Livia was coping with her food and reaching for the tea, she said, "Indeed? But we will need to have the banns read. And marrying in Lent isn't something the vicar of our parish allows."

Adrian shrugged, and Livia breathed a sigh of relief. Despite last night, she couldn't imagine being ready. Although…

Adrian reached into his pocket. "I have a special license. I procured it after we signed the contract and before I left London."

"Goodness!" Livia's mama pressed her hand to her bosom. "You have come prepared. Nevertheless—"

Before she could register her protest, Livia's papa interrupted her. "My brother should be arriving today." He bestowed a smile on the happy couple. "He's the Bishop of Scarborough. He can visit the vicar in the village, obtain the parish register and we can do the deed here in the chapel."

Livia could hardly believe what was happening. Had her father and her husband concocted this plan to rush her to the altar? From the conspiratorial glance the men exchanged, she could believe that.

Lady Strenshall's perceptive gaze went from Livia's heated cheeks to Adrian's fond smile. "I can see that he makes you happy, my dear. I am surprised, but after all it is high time. I'm so glad you are putting the past behind you."

Perhaps she should. Perhaps, after all, it was time she put the future first. Adrian had helped her past one hurdle. The next was a high one, but she might do it. But so soon?

After a flurry of congratulations from everyone present, including her sister Claudia, Livia finally left the breakfast parlor and leaned closer to Adrian. "A word," she said.

"Of course, my love."

Being a nearly married couple gave them privileges even a betrothed pair could not command. This time when he led her to a parlor, her mother merely told her to leave the door open. But she did not station a servant outside it, giving them a degree of privacy.

Livia needed it.

But anticipating her protests, Adrian caught her in his arms and gave her a kiss that took her breath away. "Listen," he said firmly, when finally he came up for air. "Last night we turned our betrothal into something we will not retreat from. I told you I didn't want to spend another night away from you, and I meant it."

"Jeffrey said he wanted to court me," she said numbly. Strange that he hadn't crossed her mind until now. Once she'd spent days dreaming about him, but another face occupied that part of her mind now.

"Jeffrey can want," Adrian said. "You're mine now. You gave yourself to me, and I to you. Why not marry quietly? We will marry, Livia, don't doubt that. So let's get the deed done, and you can save me from stubbing my toe on my stealthy way back to my room from yours. And freezing to death in those corridors."

"Is that why you want to marry me?" She couldn't help smiling.

He kissed her again, rougher this time. "You know perfectly well it isn't. We'll marry as soon as the ceremony can be arranged."

What he said made sense. After all, he knew everything now. She'd asked him after they'd made love that first time and he'd said yes. He had not asked about the baby, though, and she had told him no more, not wanting to mar her perfect night. She still found herself unable to talk about the events of that time to anyone else. How could she when she had kept the secret for so long, holding her tongue against every provocation she'd received in ten years?

But he had seen it. That must be enough. And painful though it was, she had to put the past behind her. After ten years, she would never find her son, if he was still alive. He was gone, and she must learn to live with it.

One day she would tell Adrian the whole story. Perhaps she could gain the courage later today. "Will you come to my room tonight?"

He groaned. "The temptation is unbearable, but no, sweetheart. Not now I know I can claim you as my own legitimately. We will behave properly. To damage your reputation at this late date would be foolish. In any case, I found it unimaginably difficult leaving you last night. I want to wake with you in my arms, not sneak away like a thief in the night."

* * * *

The only concession Adrian gave was to wait until Livia's family had all arrived. They sent word to London. Society be damned, Darius should be here to see his sister wed.

Livia spent the next few days in a constant state of nerves, while her maid, thrilled that her mistress was about to become a duchess, made herself busy sorting Livia's wardrobe and making a flurry of lists.

Her sister Drusilla arrived with her new husband a week before Christmas. While ordinarily Livia would be delighted to see Dru after a few months' absence, she wished her gone because she took the suite of rooms next to Livia's and she no longer had that part of the house to herself. That meant Adrian couldn't visit her at night even if she could persuade him to. Which she had not succeeded in doing.

She hadn't known anything like what she'd shared with him, and she wanted more. Longed for more. But did that just happen with him because he was experienced, or would it be the same with anyone? True, she'd had a hurried, fumbling experience with Jeffrey, but they had never had time to explore that part of their lives. Or, she realized with growing knowledge, he had not allowed it to happen.

Once Finch had helped her dress, she did the only thing she could think of doing. She went upstairs to find Claudia.

She found her twin in the midst of domestic bliss. From her state of undress, she had just fed her baby. Livia claimed the tiny boy while Claudia put herself to rights, and then handed the sweetly slumbering child to the nurse, leaving her sister to take her into the adjoining bedroom. "It seems strange to see you like this. My sister, a mother!"

Claudia laughed. "And so happy. Who would have thought it? I certainly didn't." She glanced at the door her nurse had just used. "And you too. Mama is so glad to be rid of us all."

Livia joined in the laughter, but she didn't feel like laughing.

"What is it?" As usual, Claudia had noticed Livia's disquietude. "What's wrong? Do you not wish to marry him? Are they making you do it? You know you can always make your home with us if you wish."

While Livia warmed to her sister's concern, Claudia's words brought her dilemma into perspective. Looking at her sister was like consulting a mirror. Claudia was more reckless than Livia, or at least, her first attempts at recklessness had not had such far-reaching and devastating effects. That was true. Claudia's eyes were a shade darker than Livia, but they both possessed that unusual hair color. They were of a height, and their taste in dress was similar. But more than that, they had shared the same bedroom until Claudia's marriage, they had exchanged opinions and expressions daily. They knew each other as they knew nobody else.

Claudia's leaving had come as a shock, even though Livia was glad for her sister. But now, facing her again, Livia realized how they had grown apart. Not completely so, they would never do that, but each had their own identity. "No, they aren't making me do anything. Adrian—Preston—is insistent that we marry soon." She bit her lip. "At first it wasn't a serious betrothal. We signed the contract for six months, and we planned to let it expire along with society's interest." Except that Adrian had told her she would have to break the betrothal, because he would not. Had he planned his campaign?

Claudia shrugged. "That's true. The king is in frail health, we've just declared war on Austria and Lady Davies is marrying a man old enough to be her grandfather and declaring it a love match."

"You're well informed. I imagined you tucked up with your baby and your husband, shutting the world out." How could Livia have imagined for one moment that Claudia would not keep herself abreast of affairs?

"Letters, journals, and a husband who was closely involved in covert matters on behalf of the Crown," Claudia said carelessly, as if everyone could discover for themselves both the salacious gossip and the political detail. Which was far from the truth. "Don't tell me you haven't noticed."

"Only to wonder what the unmarried daughter of a marquess wears at a coronation."

Claudia groaned. "Whatever it is, it will cost a fortune and then be relegated to an attic. Our attics are full enough already. Until the death of my dear father-in-law, we assumed we would be somewhere else, but now Dominic is the hope of his house, he has to take these things seriously. We receive regular reports on the health of the king. Covertly, of course."

"Of course," Livia answered just as dryly as her sister. Dominic was much more than a peer of the realm, but he was happy to remain that way. But very few people knew that and worked hard to ensure it remained that way. The information he still received helped him and the others in the same situation maintain their silence.

"I planned to buy a small house somewhere and live as a widow with my child," she said wistfully.

That brought Claudia's head up. "You've found the baby? No, wait, he would be nearly ten by now. Where is he?"

Livia shook her head helplessly. "I tried. How can I find him after ten years?"

"And what does Jeffrey think about all this?" Claudia was the one person who knew the identity of her baby's father.

Tears filled Livia's eyes. The hurt Jeffrey could have assuaged, just by telling her. She'd fought so hard to keep the truth from him, thinking the information wouldn't help Jeffrey's new life with the woman he'd married. "He knew, Claudia. He knew about the baby, and he didn't tell me that he knew."

From the cold, hard expression on Claudia's face now, she had not relented in her opinion of the man who had fathered her child. "What did he do then?"

"He's been trying to find the boy. He wants to court me, and marry me." Claudia set to refilling the tea dishes. Not a tremor marred the smooth stream of tea from the pot. "I daresay he wanted to get out of the arrangement with poor Maria once he'd snared a better prospect. But his father always hated us. A diehard Tory, that man. If Jeffrey knew about the child, or the possibility of one, he should have acted like a man and stood up to his parents."

Claudia put the pot down on its stand and reached for the milk jug. "So what do you want, Livia? The man you once loved? A man who you cannot trust? Or the man who has helped you hunt for what you lost? The one who looks at you with desire? The man who will never be described as comfortable and quiet, however long he lives? You've lived your life for the last ten years as a quiet, unassuming woman. But you and I know better. You're as wild as me, given the opportunity. Going to that foundling hospital on your own? Did you even tell our mother?" Her mouth curved slightly when Livia didn't reply. "I thought not. I'm proud of you, Livia."

She refilled Livia's tea dish and pushed it over to her. "Choose, and hold to your course. The neighbor who let you down once before, or the man who wants you so badly he can't hide it? The man who would get anything for you that you wished for?"

"Oh my goodness!" Realization hit Livia with the power of a hammer. "He gave me my brooch back. I lost it on the day I visited the orphanage. It was stolen from me. Mickey, the duel, the story that nearly broke us up..." All of them Jeffrey's doing. He had stolen the brooch that Adrian restored to her, he'd provoked the duel and spread the tale about Adrian and Marcus at the St. James's Club.

Only then did the seesaw hit the ground and Livia knew the answer.

* * * *

Doubts assailed Livia again on the morning of her wedding, but she ignored them. She was right, and so was Claudia. Love was worth fighting for, and she would fight if she had to. Her husband-to-be was not an easy man. Even now, after she had given in to his demands to marry soon, he surrounded himself with an invisible shield she had only seen dropped once—when they made love.

Examining her appearance in the mirror, she decided she would do and brushed Finch's efforts to get her to the pounce-pot aside. "No, no powder today." The wedding was to be a quiet one, family only. And early. They would inform people after the fact. Even the bishop had been reluctant to marry them during Lent so they were doing it now, on the day after Christmas.

Livia was to become Duchess of Preston in a small ceremony at nine o'clock in the morning on the twenty-sixth of December. Her uncle the bishop waited for them in the family chapel. Livia was glad they could use the chapel at Haxby, the place she had used for her worship all her life. The pews were scarred with the names of past Shaws, carved by children, and occasionally by adults, during tedious sermons. Hers lay at the very bottom of the front pew, scratched with a pin, but deeply enough that she knew it was there, and would be for many years to come.

All her family had arrived, even Darius, who had arrived late last night with his business partner, Andrew Graham. Andrew had brought the copy of the marriage contract up for the family records in the Muniments Room downstairs, in the oldest part of the house.

After today, Haxby would no longer be her home. She had not yet seen her new homes. Her only truth remained—she loved the man she was about to marry.

The shock of that realization remained with her. But her twin had brought her to it, forcing her to face reality. If Livia did not marry Adrian, she would regret it for the rest of her life.

In the meantime, her courses had come and gone, late but copious and painful. However, when she had discreetly told Adrian, he'd reacted with dismay rather than the relief she'd expected. In a quiet moment, he'd taken her shoulders and kissed her. "Then we will have to keep trying, will we not?" Then he'd brought her a pot of tea and bade her sit before the fire. His knowledge of precisely what she had wanted affected her almost as much as his bald declaration that they would marry before Christmas. Almost, but nothing could conquer that.

When she'd told her mother she was abandoning her search for her child, Lady Strenshall had beamed with relief. "I'm so pleased, my dear! I thought you would never get over your sad loss, but you are right. You have been grieving for too long and it is time to look forward, not back."

Grieving. Yes, that made so much sense. She had grieved for that baby, and refused to accept any other suitor, or any possibility at a new life. Jeffrey had continued with his life, even though his first steps had been forced on him. Now was her time. And not with Jeffrey.

He still wanted her; he'd made that clear by seeking her out when he'd come to dinner last week, but she'd made sure not to be alone with him. Finally her mother had named the emotion that had made Livia lose interest in everything except the baby and the loss of the man she had considered her love.

Finch opened the door for Livia and she stepped out of her room. She would not return to it alone. Already her mother had facilitated a discreet shuffling of rooms, so that Adrian occupied the one next door. He could easily get to her bed now, and she couldn't wait.

Wearing her best ivory gown, printed and embroidered with red and blue sprays of flowers, and the matching petticoat, she felt very grand. White powder would not have suited this gown. The heavy sacque-back clung to her shape to the waist and flared out below. It made that sound that only expensive, heavy silk made, a kind of hushed swish. Shaking her ruffles into place, she made her way down to the chapel.

Everybody was waiting. Her siblings and their spouses. Even Darius and Andrew, who would leave immediately after the ceremony. Nobody could change their minds about that, although they'd tried. Marcus, her oldest brother, the future marquess, and his wife Viola, Valentinian with Charlotte, Darius and Andrew, Dru and Oliver, Claudia and Dominic. Outside this place they all had impressive-sounding titles, but here, they were family, and they needed no other names.

The chapel was old, always faintly smelling of damp. The oak pews, high-backed, were almost black with age, and the black-and-white diamond-patterned tiled floor bore the impressions of generations of feet passing over them.

The smell of damp laid under the stronger smells of lavender furniture polish and beeswax, but the overwhelming perfume came from the flowers that festooned the chapel. Not for her, but to mark the end of Advent and the celebrations of the festive season. They had gone to the village to join their neighbors for the Christmas service yesterday morning but had gathered here last night for prayers. Hothouse flowers decorated the rest of the house in glorious abundance. Here, white roses were wound around the pews and on the altar.

Her father waited for her. Dressed in his favorite brown velvet, his reassuringly familiar smile brought tears to her eyes. Her stomach tightened, but with excitement. He nodded and she smiled back, placing her hand on his arm.

No music heralded her arrival, where her betrothed waited for her. His hair was smoothly combed back, gleaming like a raven's wing in the muted light of an overcast day. They'd had a sprinkling of snow, but for the most part it had gone now. Most likely they would see rain before nightfall.

Livia didn't care. There, in dark green velvet, his waistcoat resplendent with gold jewelry, the man who represented the rest of her life waited for her.

He didn't look around until she reached him. His dark eyes gazed into hers, as if trying to reassure himself about something. Livia floated serenely from her father to him, a smile flirting with her lips.

Together they turned to face the bishop.

In a remarkably short length of time she became the Duchess of Preston, and more importantly, the wife of Adrian Sterling. She learned that Adrian had only one name, that he could stand proud before the formidable personages behind him and that she loved him. She tried to tell him, lingering on the "love" part of the oaths, but he appeared oblivious, repeating his words as if by rote.

They had no separate vestry, so they moved to a table to one side, where the bishop had set the parish register for them to sign.

And that was it, done.

* * * *

Adrian tried not to panic, and then he discovered he did not panic at all. Seeing Livia settled him. She was radiant, happy, the woman he wanted, the *only* woman he wanted. That had come as a shock when he'd realized that. He wanted to get the ceremony over with as quickly as possible, so she could appear by his side.

Now he had a duchess to care for, one he could be proud of and show off to society. Of course he loved her. As they left the chapel he spared a thought for Anna, and a silent prayer that at last she could rest in peace. The constant effort to retain her unofficial title of "Most Beautiful Woman in England" had eventually killed her.

Livia was beautiful without putting in hours of effort. She was not afraid to display her true self. She had the background for that, with a supporting, loving family. Adrian had felt deeply alone, standing at the altar waiting for her, especially with the growing storm of the whole of the male Shaws glowering at his back. No doubt they would all warn him to take the greatest care of her. He could assure them all that he had every intention of doing so. But he would not allow them too close. Livia was his now, a Sterling, and his to care for.

Disappointment shaded his discovery that she was not enceinte, but they would deal with that soon enough. The marquess led the small procession to a room on the second floor, in the more modern part of the house. A breakfast parlor. Like the chapel this room had been decked out in festive glory. All the guests were assembled, not just the family, and they watched with wonder as Adrian entered, proudly escorting his new wife, her wedding ring on proud display.

* * * *

Livia's life had changed forever in less than two hours. The thought made her shaky, even though part of her had suspected this might happen, whatever she thought about it.

Before the "What have I done?" panic set in, she forced her emotions down. She had made the right choice. With her hand hooked around her husband's arm, she walked into the room, smiling. He tightened his hold, hugging her arm to his side, and leaned toward her to murmur, "Don't look so worried."

She dropped her attempt at a smile and let her face fall into a more natural expression. The breakfast was reassuringly informal. Adrian and Livia sat at a round table, introduced by her father years ago as the "Arthur" table. Nobody could be at the head. Actually oval, because the maids had put in the extra leaves to expand its size. But they had provided the usual feast, instead of a formal repast. Two sideboards groaned with good things. The scents the dishes released made Livia's stomach growl.

She hadn't realized she was hungry until now. But she had to take her seat next to Adrian and suffer a series of toasts. Fortunately, her father, a man of few words, led them.

First he toasted the bride and groom. "We were not expecting this to happen so quickly, but that does not diminish our pleasure." He took his time sweeping his gaze around the room. "You are all here. This will not be the last time we gather, but with the lives we lead, I fear it will not be often. All my children, happy and fulfilled."

Despite their protestations, Livia had insisted that Darius and Andrew remain for the breakfast. They were as much part of the family as anyone else and Livia could only be happy that Darius had found what he needed.

"I am a grandfather several times over now. I expect that happy fate to occur again," the marquess continued. Her father turned his attention to her. "And my lovely girl, my little Livia, is now with her new husband."

A scraping sound drew everyone's attention to the part of the room Livia had been studiously ignoring.

Shoving back his chair, Sir Jeffrey Creasey sprang to his feet and stormed from the room, followed swiftly by his mother. Livia wasn't sure who had invited him. Maybe he'd invited himself.

She found a singular lack of interest, even that she might have hurt him. Although she doubted that. She'd frustrated his ambition.

They set to eating, moving to the sideboards to help themselves in an informal wedding breakfast. But then, the Shaws rarely did anything in a conventional way.

They sat, and consumed in a convivial way, catching up on one another's business and discussing various public business they were involved in. Adrian mostly listened, but murmured the occasional comment to Livia, and added a few, salient points aloud. In this at least, he fitted. This was why the family would stay together. Together, with the knowledge exchanged in quiet, friendly meetings like this, they achieved a great deal for themselves and for their country.

The contrast with the way Adrian quietly fitted in against Jeffrey's often disruptive, attention-seeking presence confirmed her decision. She would test the waters.

"He will make you very happy," Claudia said, toasting the pair. Since Livia had been thinking of their night together, her face heated.

Beside her, Val laughed softly. "You are too easy to read, sister. You should use more paint on your face."

"Livia has promised me never to do that," Adrian said, equally quietly.

Silence fell at the reminder of Adrian's first wife.

Conversation began again on a different topic.

Chapter 16

"Did you do as I said?" Adrian asked Mickey. He'd called him to his room that evening, when he'd finally persuaded his wife to retire. He would join her in a matter of minutes, but he needed to see his page first.

"Yes, y'r grace. I went over to the 'ouse. House." He made a point of pronouncing the h. Mickey was quick. He'd be sounding like a lord in no time. Adrian wasn't sure he wanted the clever, wily child to leave his sight. Heaven knew what mischief the lad would get up to without his guidance.

He dropped his nail-buffer on the dressing table and got up, facing Mickey. "Don't leave me in suspense, boy. I have to go."

"Aye." With the nerve he was born with, Mickey eyed Adrian's banyan and bare legs. "I can see that."

"Enough." But he spoke gently.

"I talked to the men in Sir Jeffrey's stables. I like horses. Never knew that before. The only ones I used to see were the skinny ones the hackney drivers use, and the tricked-up ones the nobs have. Never spent much time around horses."

"I daresay. What did the men say?"

Mickey poked a finger under his neat wig and scratched his head. "He's looking around him to make money, fast. That's a comfortable place he's got there. He shouldn't force it."

"He's ambitious."

"Aye, I got that too. He's not well liked."

Adrian folded his arms across his chest. "You surprise me," he drawled.

"No I don't. Anyway, that makes my job easier. You told me to arsk around, so I went sweet on one of the maids. They got used to seeing me in the last few days."

Adrian should feel guilt about sending a boy of twelve to spy for him, but he did not. Mickey hadn't survived that long in the busiest, largest city in the world without learning a few things. "Don't do anything else with the maid. You're too young for that."

Mickey sniggered. "Never too young, guv'nor. But some think I'm ten or younger. I tell 'em I make up for being short in other ways. Then they're keen to see. Anyhow, the maid hasn't fallen for it, yet, so you don't have to worry." He grinned. "Captain Sir Jeffrey Creasey wants lots of things, including your wife. He wanted to marry her."

"I didn't need to send you over there to find that out. I knew that already."

"Aye." Mickey nodded vigorously. Adrian feared he would never make a suitable servant. He was too quick to answer back, and totally lacking in subservience, which a good servant should cultivate, whether he liked it or not. But he would keep his promise. Mickey would never return to the teeming streets he came from.

"He wants money fast," the boy went on. "But he's not into the sharpers or the loaners. He wants to buy his way up. He's going to London in the new year so he can make some more, find some schemes. And he wants to pester his lordship for sponsorship. He's not at home right now, left right after his last visit here. He left in a hurry and he didn't take anybody with him, which they say he doesn't usually do. But he told them he'd be back soon."

"Hmm." Adrian tapped his lip with one finger. "Thank you, Mickey. I want to know when he gets home. I don't want him bothering my wife. Understand?"

"Yes, sir. It's a pleasure to do this job. I don't like that man and that's a fact. Something about him, you know?"

Adrian knew. He could no longer ascribe his suspicions to jealousy. He had the prize, after all. Mickey's enquiries had confirmed Adrian's suspicions. Sir Jeffrey was fiercely ambitious, and he would do anything to achieve his aim. If Adrian's guess was right, Sir Jeffrey's intelligence was more of the native cunning variety. And despite his military career, the man had little loyalty outside himself and his own needs.

But now Adrian had far more pleasant duties to perform and he didn't intend to wait a moment longer. Striding to the job-door, he paused, and then laughed, going to the outer door instead. He didn't care who saw him now. He was going into his wife's room and he would be there for some time. Until morning, probably.

* * * *

Livia discovered one good thing about not being a virgin on her wedding night; she was excited rather than nervous, eagerly anticipating the hours ahead. Finch had gone to extinguish the candles over the bed but Livia had stopped her. She'd laid out a virginal night rail, thick white linen, but as soon as her maid had left the room, Livia had stripped off her robe and discarded it, together with her nightcap and her braids. Now her hair flowed over her shoulders and the only garment she wore was the cream silk robe, fastened only with a sash that wrapped around her waist.

She paced, then paused before the dressing table, touching its clean linen cloth with the tip of her finger, deciding not to brush her hair yet again. In the mirror, her face was pale, her eyes large, but darker than usual. She should casually read a book, provide a picture for him, but she was too agitated for that.

The day had dragged on. When the other guests returned from the Boxing Day Hunt, the house had filled up once more. Even the formal announcement of the marriage that Lord Strenshall made at dinner had not affected her too much. The company, thirty strong now, had unanimously proclaimed its delight in the match, even though much surprise was exhibited.

But she had to stay and behave like a lady, even though she longed to be a hoyden, dragging her new husband off to bed, so she could have him to herself and run her hands all over his delicious body. Which she intended to do as soon as she could.

Where was he? Was he coming at all? She picked up the book she'd taken from the library downstairs a full week ago and checked the leather bookmark. She wasn't even twenty pages into it. Not the book's fault. She dropped it back on the daybed.

He'd shown her gentle but insistent attention all day. He hadn't uttered a word of disparagement or disagreement. He'd been so agreeable Livia had started to suspect that Adrian had an identical twin, and he was making his appearance today. This kind, courteous man was nothing like the one she'd thought she was marrying. The man she'd reluctantly fallen in love with. She hadn't meant to, she'd worked hard not to, but here she was, waiting for the man who legally ruled her world and emotionally ruled her heart.

He was taking too long. She wouldn't wait any longer. Either she went to bed or found out what was keeping him. Flinging open her door, she strode out into the corridor and collided with a solid body. If he hadn't caught her, she'd have bounced off him. As he swung her up into his arms, she caught sight of the page scuttling down the corridor. "You were with him?"

Adrian didn't look around. "Mickey had news for me. I really need to get him to use the job-door. He only remembers to use it when it suits him."

"Humph." She wasn't happy that a pageboy had kept her waiting for her husband's company. "You can put me down. I can walk."

"So can I." His arms full of cream frills and lace, he nudged the door open with his foot and carried her through it, shouldering it closed. Still he didn't put her down, but went to the bed, dropping her on the mattress.

Livia put her hands down to stop her bouncing, but before she could recover, he was with her. Naked. He'd stripped off his robe and dropped it God knew where. She gasped, and then his mouth was on hers and he was kissing the sense out of her.

Moaning, she clutched him, felt her voice reverberate around his mouth and experienced his responding groan. She should be—what, overwhelmed, shocked?—she was neither.

With that masterful act he had aroused her instantly.

He lifted his head and gazed down at her. "You were saying?"

"I—I can't remember. Kiss me again."

"All night, sweetheart. As often as you want." He rubbed his smooth chin against hers. "I've even shaved. Again. Three times today." He said the last with a disgusted tone. "I'm glad today is over."

"I enjoyed it."

He touched his lips to hers, but when she would have dragged him back down, he held steady. "So did I. I didn't expect to. Weddings seem to be more for the spectators than the participants. So now we can have our own celebration, the part I've really been looking forward to." His mouth curved into a slow smile. "Tell me what you want."

"You know what I want."

"Tell me."

She blinked. Did he mean that? "I don't know what you mean."

He rolled over, taking her with him, knocking the breath from her. Now she lay on top of him. She glanced down. His chest moved easily when he breathed. He overwhelmed her and she loved it. "How is it you look bigger naked than you do dressed?"

His laugh jolted her. "A good tailor. How is it you're not naked yet?"

"I'm nearly naked."

Taking one of her curls, he twisted it around his finger, creating a natural ringlet. He stared at it. "So you are. Your hair fascinates me, you know. It has since the first time I saw it. It has all the colors of gold and red in it, combining to create warm sunshine. I could bathe in you, Livia."

"That's the loveliest thing anybody has ever said to me!" Startled by his poetic turn of phrase, she turned a beaming smile onto him.

"Sit up."

The command was so abrupt, it stopped her train of thought.

"Sit up. I want to see you." He choked a laugh. "You would think, after my vast and varied experience, I'd do this better. But all day I've been watching you, and wanting you. Each time I catch your scent, or the way you turn your wrist, or that little twist of your mouth when you're trying not to laugh I want you more. I'm going mad here, Livia. Have mercy."

He certainly sounded desperate.

Startled, she stared at him, before propping her hands on his shoulders and pushing herself up. She sat upright, straddling him, her knees tucked under. Her skirts flowed around them, but underneath she was bare. Somehow she'd managed to avoid the folds of silk in her most intimate parts. They touched, skin to skin, her most intimate part against the rough hair of his thighs.

She lost her breath.

He stayed completely still. "Let me see you. Unfasten your robe."

"I...I..." She goggled like an idiot. But yes, she wanted him, she wanted this. She'd been thinking of it all day. His straightforwardness, his honesty in the bedroom had astonished her before. Used to subterfuge, people never saying what they truly meant, she felt born anew. Years in the ballroom, minutes in the bedroom.

"Livia." He caught her hands in his. "Your arousal is kissing my thighs. If I move, I'll take you because you are still killing me here. But I want you to understand your power here, when there are the two of us. I want you confident here." He growled low in his throat. "I want you to take me as often as I take you."

"Why?" She couldn't quite work out what he meant.

"Because I enjoy it."

"Oh. I see." Nothing had prepared her for that. Drawing her hands back, she fumbled with the sash at her waist. Exposing herself to him did not seem as worrisome now. He wanted her to—what?

She dragged the sash free and tossed it aside. He watched her eagerly, his attention absolute. Forcing herself not to think, she slipped the robe off her shoulders.

Her senses roared back in full force, punching into her under his avid gaze. She wanted to be beautiful for him. Taunt him with it. Because he was right—she loved the idea of taking him. The robe fell around her body, the full skirts billowing around them, a sea of cream. Her shoulders went back, thrusting her breasts proudly at him. His soft groan of appreciation rewarded her. Shoving her hand into the gap at the front, she found his member, hard and strong. When she skimmed her thumb across the soft tip she found it damp and waiting.

If he had tasted her, could she do the same to him? What was stopping her? He would not. He lay on his back, his head propped up on the pillows, his arms spread out across the mattress. Totally still, waiting for her next move, his eyes sparkling with dark arousal.

Ensuring no fabric lay between her and her goal, she swept the silk aside and bent her head, claiming him quickly. As her lips closed around the head, his body tightened. The muscles in his groin pulled tight, and the sac beneath bulged into her hand.

"Dear God, Livia!"

Good or bad, she didn't care. Avidly she tasted him, discovered his texture with her tongue. The tip was delightfully silky, but even though he was hard, her fingers detected wrinkles. Fascinated, she experimented and discovered what he liked. He responded generously, threading his fingers through her hair and whispering encouragement. "Yes, that's it. Just there. Run your tongue…oh!" That last as she twisted her tongue around the tip and sucked at the same time.

His hand tightened on her skull. "Come away now, love. Put me into you."

Those words thrilled Livia to the bone. Yes, yes, she would do that. Lifting her head reluctantly, she sat up, the silk rustling around her. It made her feel more in control, having some means of retreat if she needed it. Tension rippled up her spine but she wanted to do this more than she feared it.

The fear came from entering a new world. She'd experienced that emotion many times before. When leaving the schoolroom, attending her first ball, holding a gun against a man who threatened her twin. All of these and more.

Yes, she knew that emotion and recognized it for what it was. Together with excitement and almost unbearable arousal.

His eyes burned into her as he scanned her body when she sat upright. Proud of herself, she watched him, never took her eyes off him as she guided him to that part of her that wanted him most.

Going up slightly, she hovered over him. When he closed his eyes, his jaw tightened and he swallowed. Opening them again, he gazed at her as if everything he wanted was there. "Do it, Livia. Or I will not wait any longer." His voice was strained.

She knew how he felt. After notching his member at the entrance to her body, she bore down. He slid inside her as if she'd been made for him, fitting him closely and securely.

Keeping her movements slow, she absorbed him, took him in, not stopping until his thighs met her backside. With renewed focus, she met his gaze. "Now what do you want me to do?"

His face relaxed into a wicked smile. "Whatever you want to do, sweet one. Show me what you like."

She didn't know what she liked. Except that she enjoyed this control. She tried lifting so she could join them again, but she didn't get very far. Her balance wavered, and she had to shift her legs a little to find it again.

"Here." Taking her hands, he guided them to his shoulders. Hot, hard muscle met her palms. "Now you can move." He caressed her, stroking his hands up from her waist to her breasts.

Livia lifted again, using her hands as leverage. When she sank back down, thrills chased each other around her body. "Oh, I like that."

"Then keep doing it." Cupping her breasts, he lifted his gaze to hers. "I like it too." His voice deepened.

He helped her, thrusting up as she came down, like a kind of primitive dance, one she preferred to any other. Small sounds of surprise and arousal escaped her mouth involuntarily.

Adrian murmured words of encouragement and praise. "Oh yes, that is so good. You are a constant surprise, so beautiful, so clever. Your skin is better than silk to my hands. Come, love, keep working. Can you feel it rising inside you? You couldn't stop now if I asked you to, could you?"

No she couldn't. Involved in the rhythm of their joining, her motions instinctive, Livia rose up and plunged down, slammed her body onto his. Everything in her rose and exploded.

He stopped playing with her breasts and gripped her waist, lifting her and continuing the dance as she lost control. He drove hard up into her, prolonging her ecstasy until, with a cry, he found his.

Flooding her with his tribute, he dragged her close against him. Yards of silk crushed between them, but she found his lips and sealed them together, as he kissed her lavishly, his body still jerking inside hers.

He rolled so she lay by his side, and gently withdrew, but stayed close. When he finished the kiss, he glanced down and laughed. "All that to make an heir."

She stiffened, but forced herself to relax. She had promised herself this was a new start, and that involved children. She'd welcome a baby from this man. Despite his reputation he'd shown her nothing but consideration and kindness. Now he'd introduced her to passion and she was grateful for that too. Another thought occurred to her, a new notion. "How do you know we will make a child? You have made none before." She bit her lip. Unless— "Mickey?"

"An urchin, my love, but nothing to do with me. I merely recognized his intelligence and he amused me." He kissed her again, then sat up. "We are not sleeping with your robe. There must be hundreds of yards of silk in this thing."

"Twelve," she said without thinking. "When I like a fabric, I usually buy twelve yards of it. Or sixteen."

"Hmm." He tugged silk from under her and she obligingly lifted up for him. Silk slithered from under her. Crumpled silk now, probably marked by what they'd just done. Perhaps Finch could restore it. Her maid could work wonders on delicate fabric.

"In answer to your question, no, I have no children. But I have taken great care not to make any." Glancing up, he favored her with a wink. "Unlike just now with you. Coming inside you is glorious. I will never have the strength of will to pull out of you again. Not now I know what delights await me inside your body."

"Oh." He'd done it again. Covered her with confusion but thrilled her at the same time. She wasn't that good, she couldn't be. She'd only known this kind of pleasure briefly. Her time with Jeffrey could be discounted, because that had been nothing. Not compared to what she was discovering with Adrian.

Circling her waist with one arm, he lifted her to pull the remaining silk from under her body, making her giggle and lose her balance. When she fell backward, he released her. As he came over her, he kicked the robe off the bed, and grinned down at her, as he studied her love-soaked body.

His gaze paused at her stomach and lower. When he lifted his eyes to her face he was frowning. "What is this?"

Softly, he traced a line on her lower belly, one she had followed herself, that he had absently traced the first time they'd made love. Then he found another.

"You've seen the marks before. You said you'd seen everything. I asked you."

"Not these. Tell me what caused these." His voice was steady but cold.

Her heart sank. She could not lie to him. If he had not marked their significance before—and the lines were faint, silvery, easily missed in dim lighting—then he needed to know now. Not telling him gave Jeffrey a power over her she refused to allow. If he discovered that she was keeping it from Adrian, Jeffrey would exploit it for all he was worth.

"They're marks left by childbirth."

Carefully, quietly, he rolled to one side of her. The side away from the light, so the candles above and by the side of the bed left her fully illuminated. He swept his gaze over her body but didn't meet her eyes. "You gave birth? Did the child live?" His voice was steady.

She nodded. "As far as I know." Tears filled her eyes. She let them fall, trickle down her face, roll above her ear and into her hair. "They took him away."

"Him?"

"I'm sorry." Unable to hide her distress, she turned to him. Silently he gathered her in. She let him turn her, so they were lying against the pillows, and pulled the sheets up to cover her. He held her against his hard, naked body as she sobbed helplessly.

"I didn't mean to tell you this way."

"Did you mean to tell me at all?"

"I thought you knew. You touched one of the marks and I asked you if you had seen it all, and you said yes."

She would tell him the truth, all of it, and let him decide her fate. "It's in my past. He's gone. I looked for him for years, and I had no success. It was as if he had never existed at all."

"You had a son," he said dully.

"Yes." And it all came pouring out, easier now she'd started. "You knew I was not a virgin, and you knew who did it. When I found I was expecting Jeffrey had already married Maria and was due to leave for the continent with the army. What good would telling him do?"

She stopped to catch her breath. "My mother knew, my old nurse, and my father, and my sister Claudia. That was all. Nobody else. I couldn't tell anybody else, and everybody agreed the whole unfortunate incident was best forgotten." Except her. "When I could not hide the pregnancy any longer, my mother took me to the cottage in the grounds, and told people that I had smallpox. It's normal to isolate the sufferer, and we knew that. And to keep them separated for a time after, so that nobody caught it. I gave birth."

She refused to stop, although everything inside her screamed to stop, to end this. "It was a boy. Sherwood—the nurse—was to take the child to relatives of hers, who had been paid to care for the baby. When I was older, we would bring the boy back and find him a position with us, or so my mother promised. But Sherwood disappeared. We tried to find them, we truly did, but we could find no account of where Sherwood had gone or what she'd done with the boy. Even if he was alive or dead." Then she had to stop.

He held her, listening, saying nothing. Until she stopped, hiccupping against his shoulder. She was wrung out. Whatever happened next, she didn't care.

"So that was why you went to the orphanage," he murmured, his lips against her hair.

She forced the breath back into her body enough to speak again. "Yes. I never stopped looking for him. I'd had information—vague, but it was worth a try. I promised myself I would forget him. But I saw him after he was born, and I heard him. They wouldn't let me hold him, Adrian."

"I see." He sounded angry. He had every right to be. She'd effectively tricked him into marriage.

"I'm sorry. I should have told you."

"Is that why you refused to marry?" he said softly.

She nodded. "I was frozen in the past. A few days ago Claudia told me it was time I stopped mourning. And she was right. I hadn't wanted to get on with my life. Not until that day in the street when you kissed me. That was when the thaw started."

The day her life had taken a totally unexpected turn. The day an accredited rake had kissed her in the street and forced her to think about what she really wanted out of life. But she had wrecked that now. "I should have told you," she repeated. "No secrets, you said." She spoke dully now, unable to muster any emotion. "But I couldn't. I had never told anyone before. Those who knew didn't need to be told. I didn't know where to begin. I'm sorry Adrian, I'm so very sorry. I thought once you saw the marks, you would understand. Once I realized you didn't know, I had to honor my promise to you and tell you the truth." There could be no lies between them. She refused to live a lie for the rest of her married life, or to allow herself to be held to ransom. Rather than that, she would risk losing Adrian, to live apart from her husband if he required it. Why would he want her anymore, knowing she had kept such a secret from him?

"I see. Do you trust your mother?" His voice was steady, without expression.

"Completely." Livia didn't hesitate. She had not forgotten her mother's distress when she confessed the baby couldn't be found.

Fatigue swept over her in a great wave. The lids drooped over her eyes. Held close to the body of the man she loved, she found herself drifting into nothingness. Exhaustion took her under.

The last words she heard were, "Sleep now. We'll talk about this another time."

"You won't leave me?"

She didn't hear the reply. She was already asleep.

Chapter 17

After spending a long time staring at the canopy above them, holding his wife until the candles guttered in their sockets and went out, leaving just the fire in the grate to illuminate the room, Adrian heaved one huge sigh.

She had borne a child when she was sixteen. The baby had been torn away from her at birth.

Fury had chased his astonishment away, and then horror, that Livia had suffered all this without telling a soul. Of course she'd been stuck in grief. How could she not be?

Adrian clenched his teeth. This matter did not end here.

He wanted to damage someone for this, and he had a good idea who.

He hadn't needed to ask the name of the father. That bastard Jeffrey Creasey had abandoned her to marry someone else. She'd said that he hadn't known about the baby, but he'd bet his last guinea that he had known all along. Sir Jeffrey was the kind of person to run when faced with responsibility. Although, in the face of his ambition now, he should have married her. Adrian was thankful that he had not.

Sir Jeffrey's parents had not appreciated the Shaws. Perhaps they had instigated Sir Jeffrey's hurried marriage. Every bit as hurried as his own, Adrian reflected with a wry smile. He'd wanted to secure Livia before Jeffrey had a chance. Well, he'd done that. It mattered nothing to him that Sir Jeffrey'd had her first, only that he did not repeat that boast to anyone.

When he was sure Livia was sound asleep, Adrian slid out of bed. At first, when he tried to extricate his body from hers, she whimpered and moved closer. The task took him much longer than he'd imagined. Dawn was feathering its fingers into the room by the time he'd managed to slide away.

He nearly slipped on her damned robe as he was leaving too, but he righted himself. Grabbing his banyan, he shrugged into it as he left her room and strode up the corridor to his own apartments.

His man came in from the powder room, blinking and rubbing his eyes. Still in nightshirt and cap, his valet shook his head and waited for his master. "Riding clothes," Adrian snapped. "I want a message sent to Lady Strenshall. I will meet with her at her earliest convenience."

The man nodded, leaving the room to dress while Adrian found a pen and scrawled a message on the paper left on the small table by the window. Impatiently he scattered sand over the missive, and tipped it back into the pot when the ink had dried. Pausing, he wrote another. He did not know what his plans were, not until he'd spoken to her ladyship, and then to one other. But he wanted Livia cared for.

Confusion and anger warred in his head. Hearing her story had sent him into a numb world of his own at first, but then everything had slid into place. She'd given birth, and been unable to keep the baby. No respectable woman would have been allowed to do that. Indeed some had "pages" or treasured servants. They sent the child away to be brought up quietly, or they gave it away, and found it later. Had Livia intended to do that?

He would listen to her, but he no longer knew how he felt. Prepared to tell her of his love for her, she had knocked the wind out of his sails when he'd discovered the marks. He'd seen that type of line before. Even if he had not fathered children on his past mistresses, other lovers had not been so careful.

Time to act.

He was up and about now, and the sun was rising. After sending a quiet message via his valet, he received the reply that her ladyship would receive him in her boudoir. In the past, with other women, that had meant an assignation. Today it meant business.

She was waiting for him, hair tucked up into a lace cap, and a voluminous robe enveloping her slight form. She watched him enter, her face stony. "You are dressed."

"I have an errand," he said. "I think you can guess what it is."

She said nothing at first, but her complexion blanched. She sighed. "I told Livia to tell you before the wedding."

"I knew some of it."

"And now you are leaving her."

"Not precisely. I'm going to find what you have lost. But I need clarity first. She had a son by Sir Jeffrey Creasey, I know that much."

"Sir Jeffrey? You're sure?" Her voice rang with shock.

Ah, so her mother had not known the father. That filled a space in his reasoning. If the Strenshalls had known who was the father, why did they still receive him in their home? The answer was that they had not known. Livia had not told them. His admiration for his wife increased. By the laws of society, he should condemn her for what she had done, but with everything he discovered, his regard for her only increased. She'd accepted her fault in the unfortunate affair, she had borne a child and never ceased to search for it. Most women he knew would have given up years ago. And she had continued with her life, refusing to become what people expected of her; a dried-up spinster.

He nodded. "I am sure."

"I suspected, but she always refused to tell me. I never asked her directly, because she would not allow it." The narrowing of the marchioness's eyes told him what he needed to know. She didn't like him any more than Adrian did.

"I don't trust that man. I understand he is away from home," he said.

"He left when he heard that Livia and I were to marry."

"His mother is there. She was at the Christmas Day dinner."

He nodded. "I noticed." Even though he had been deeply obsessed with Livia, and teasing her about their wedding, he made a note of every guest there. "She seemed none too pleased with the news of our marriage. Will she tell her son?"

"Probably."

He grimaced. "I feared as much."

She waved at a chair set opposite hers. "Stop pacing, boy. Do sit down."

So said a tiny woman used to obedience. He didn't disappoint her this time, either, but flipped back the skirts of his riding coat and sat on the spindly legged, gold upholstered chair. "I fear for the boy."

Her hand went to her throat, and her bosom heaved under the confines of her silk gown. "You know where he is?"

He shook his head grimly. "Not yet. But I will."

"Why do you think such a thing? Jeffrey doesn't even know the child exists." She hovered her hand over the decanter by her side, but he shook his head. He'd drink nothing stronger than beer today. He needed a clear head, not Dutch courage. From experience, he knew strong drink would only exacerbate his temper.

"He knows." He recounted the full story of the brooch and what he had found. "Sir Jeffrey wanted that brooch to taunt Livia, maybe to draw her back to him. He's hell-bent on bettering himself in society, and Livia would be a considerable asset to him. But their child—I don't know how he views the boy."

"You think he has him?"

Adrian bit his lip. "I'm not sure. But if he does, the boy is in danger. Sir Jeffrey won't want a hint of scandal to surround him. With my marriage to Livia the child is surplus to his needs. He can no longer use the boy to draw her back to him. The boy becomes a threat, in fact, something that could tarnish his reputation."

He had realized the added danger as soon as she'd fallen asleep. The boy was no longer a trump card. He was a low-value suit, and needed to be discarded, as far as Sir Jeffrey was concerned.

Her lips tightened but she nodded. "I have also observed. He was eager to play with my children when he was a child. He had ambition, but not the kind that his father had. For his faults, his father was a good man, although he was often at outs with my husband. But he kept to his word and he meant what he said. His son is another kind of man entirely. He wanted success and riches. His army career did not bring that to him, despite his comfortable posting. Neither did his marriage. He made Maria pregnant too, you know, and his father, not knowing about Livia, made him marry her. Otherwise he would have come for my daughter, and I doubt I could have refused him. My husband bought his commission after his marriage as a wedding gift."

"Ah." Adrian crossed one ankle over his knee. "And what did you plan for the baby?"

She swallowed. "The usual. We would farm out the child to a respectable household, and later adopt him as a foundling. Charitable work, people would say. We had a family in place, an agreeable couple with children of their own, relatives of the nurse who cared for my children. I trusted Sherwood with the lives of my children and she never let me down." She shook her head. "But Sherwood took the baby and never had a chance to tell us what had happened. She was delirious when we got to her. Do you know who took her in when she fell ill on the way back?"

Adrian's heart sank. Everything fell into place. "The Creasey mansion."

"Yes. Sherwood took shelter there and died. The baby never reached Sherwood's relatives. My husband and I searched for the boy, but he had disappeared. The Creaseys denied everything, even denying their son's involvement. I believe the news came as a shock to Jeffrey's mother, but I was in no mind to comfort her." Her eyes gleamed, but her tears remained unshed. "John and I searched everywhere for the baby, but we had no success. We had to tell Livia when she had recovered from the birth. She could not even have a proper confinement, and she was never churched."

Uncrossing his legs, Adrian leaned forward and put his hand over hers. "I will ensure she's churched, ma'am, I promise."

Lady Strenshall dropped her chin and closed her eyes. "Thank you. I know that was bearing on her. She never shows it." She lifted her head and met his gaze. Her tone firmed. "Look after her, or I will see you in hell, Adrian Sterling."

Finally he understood why Lady Strenshall was so adored by her children. "I know." He gave a wry smile and leaned back. The chair creaked threateningly, forcing him upright once more. "I will treat her with the greatest of care." A vision came to him, the sight of his wife straddling him, breasts bare, silk pooled around them. And she was laughing.

Pain wrenched at him. He could not think of that now. "I cannot tell her I'm going after the boy in case I'm wrong. I might not succeed. This might be a wild goose chase. I intend to visit Sir Jeffrey. From there, I don't know. I will follow the thread until the bitter end."

"Don't kill him."

"I can't promise that."

"He isn't worth dying for."

He could agree with that, so he gave her a reluctant nod. "Not unless his death becomes an absolute necessity." He would go no further, but she was right. He didn't want that death on his conscience, and he would not hang for the blackguard. He got to his feet. "I will take my leave. I will find out what happened to the boy, and follow whatever I find to the end. I have left Livia a note, merely telling her not to expect me back soon. But I didn't know what to tell her. Take care of her, if you please." After bowing, he turned and went to the door, where he hesitated. "I'll write when I know more."

Her faint, "God speed" reached him just before he closed the bedroom door.

He did not tell her his worst fears. After all, they might not be true. But he would return with news for his wife, one way or the other.

* * * *

Livia blinked awake, alone in a wrecked bed. The sheets were tangled around her, the cover tossed over her with more regard to warmth than to order. Her hair streamed over her shoulders as she sat up, dragging the covers with her.

All cried out, no more tears left to shed, she faced the rest of her life.

The door opened and her maid came in. "Your grace." Finch dropped a curtsy.

"Call me ma'am when we're private, as always," Livia said by rote. She didn't want any reminder of her new status. The status she'd stolen by keeping the most important facts of her life from her husband.

"Your husband left early this morning. He sent you this note, ma'am. Will you come down to breakfast?"

Ignoring the last question, Livia tore open the note. He hadn't even bothered to seal it, just tucked one end into the other.

My dear duchess,

I regret I have to leave you so soon, but urgent business has called me away. Pray remain there until I return. I should not be above a week.

When she'd read the few formal, stiff lines, she crumpled the paper in her hand, despair filling her heart.

She was alone. He had gone. Would he ever return?

Chapter 18

Adrian arrived at the manor as morning light was gleaming over the frost-whitened lawns, the birds. The sun sent a deceptively warm glow over the tranquil countryside. The neat manor fitted into the landscape as if it had always been there, the stones settled into the dip below a hill. Formal gardens surrounded it, the squared-off arrangements neatly pruned and tied off, the hedges clipped into balls and cones, silently waiting for spring before fighting the shapes the gardeners had carefully imposed on them.

He gave only slight heed to his surroundings, but rode up to the front door and, seeing nobody ready to take his horse, patted the beast and threw the reins to Loomis, who had insisted on attending him. The footman, already in riding gear, had brought his horse to him in Haxby. Recognizing when he was beaten, Adrian allowed the man to come with him.

Pulling the cord would have amused him if he were not intent on his mission. The old-fashioned bell worked well enough, though, setting a chime loud enough to set the dogs barking.

When a manservant shot back the bolts and swung the door wide, Adrian tossed his hat at the man and demanded to see the master of the house. "There's only the m-mistress," the man replied, gazing at Adrian as if at a vision sent from afar. "Sir Jeffrey isn't at home."

"Where is he?"

"Gone, my lord."

Well, the man wasn't to know he knew that already, but it gave him the open door. Visiting a woman alone wasn't the done thing. Adrian handed him his card. "You address me as your grace," he said kindly. "Now don't keep me waiting."

He didn't. The servant returned as Adrian was warming his hands by the fire, having thrust his gloves in his pocket. He'd tossed his cloak onto a nearby chair. "If you'll come with me, sir, your grace."

He led Adrian to an oak-paneled room on the first floor. The fire had evidently just been lit, crackling and popping as it settled down. A definite chill permeated the air. This would be the best parlor, then. Despite his reservations about the owner, Adrian liked this house. A comfortable size, instead of the palaces he'd grown up in.

Lady Creasey stood to greet him. She was a tall woman with graying brown hair and an anxious expression. With a son like hers, that could be permanent. He bowed over her hand but did not apologize for his early arrival, or for his lack of finesse. "May I offer you refreshment, your grace?" Snatching back her hand, she folded it tightly against the other, gripping them hard.

And suffer more delay? Hunger gnawed at his stomach, but he had sent a servant to the inn to bespeak breakfast. He wouldn't eat here. "No, I thank you. My visit is not of a social nature, I'm afraid. I need to speak to your son."

If Adrian had not been a strong man he might have tumbled to the floor when she threw herself into his arms. The force was such that he was obliged to take a step backward. Worse, the woman burst into noisy tears, burying her face against his riding coat. "So would I!" she wailed and that was all he could get out of her for some time.

Adrian had to guide her to a settle and pad her with some of the cushions that festooned it. Lady Creasey obviously knew how to make herself busy with her needle, for each cushion bore a different design. He needed to ensure she stayed upright and told him what he needed to know.

Half an hour he wasted, while the lady sipped first tea, then brandy, before he got the story out of her. Then it came out in a great torrent.

"Oh, sir, my son has always been an ambitious man. We thought it a good thing." She sniffed and raised a cloth to her nose. She had run out of handkerchiefs some time ago, but fortunately Adrian had discovered a stack of embroidered fabric in her work-basket.

On and on the narrative went in horrifying detail. What an ungrateful son he was, how she feared for her health and her home, all the risks he'd taken to get what he wanted. Adrian couldn't hurry her. If he tried, she'd refuse to say anything.

Finally they got to the point. "He says now you have married Livia, he has no use for the child. I don't know what is wrong with him, sir, I truly don't. I brought him up to respect people, but he won't have any of it."

And she went off again while Adrian's stomach clenched in fear. From what he'd heard and observed, Sir Jeffrey had no conscience. He would do whatever he thought right to protect himself, and damn everyone else.

He was not sure when her ladyship knew about the existence of the child. Perhaps, like her son, she'd always known.

That child was not safe in his hands. "Where has he gone?" he asked calmly.

Lady Creasey clutched his arm in a death grip. "Will you bring him back?"

"One way or another." He would make no promises. He had allowed the man to walk free once. That would not happen again.

"Please, find him! He left in such a temper!" She was holding him tight enough to bruise, her grip surprisingly strong, but Adrian did not budge. If she refused to tell him, he would search the house for an answer. "He's most likely gone to our manor in Yorkshire. It's a little place, and too old to be comfortable, but it has some land attached. Jeffrey likes to go there sometimes. I believe he keeps his mistresses there. Not that I blame him, a man needs diversion, and he is not creating scandal here."

Adrian didn't care about the man's affairs, except that if he did have a mistress, then she might prevent Sir Jeffrey from committing something drastic. However, those words, "no use for the child," reverberated in his head.

He had to go there as quickly as possible. If he could believe her ladyship. If her son had told her the truth. But he had no other clues, so he had to follow this one. He had no choice. And Lady Creasey was either a better actress than Peg Woffington, or she was truly distressed. "When did he leave?"

"When we returned home from the wedding breakfast, in the early afternoon. He took the c-carriage."

So Adrian was several hours behind. More, now Lady Creasey had delayed him. "If you give me the direction of the manor, I will undertake to go there directly."

"Oh yes! Bring him back to me."

He wouldn't promise that, but he accepted the scrawled address from her. He had to use every ounce of finesse to extricate himself from her grasp, but he managed it, though without much grace. "If I am to find him, I must leave," he said firmly, and finally she subsided, sniffing into her square of linen.

Before she could revive her spirits and start again, Adrian made good on his departure.

He spent a bare hour with his groom and Mickey at the inn, enough to make a hasty breakfast and write a letter to his wife. Not to explain in full, but to tell her where he would be. He added a note at the bottom, just for her.

He didn't mince his words with the two sitting with him. "The man is dangerous, I'm sure of it. He has nothing beyond himself, his world only encompasses one person. I watched him in London and that is what my opinion amounts to. Therefore, we could put ourselves in danger pursuing him. You know that a gentleman can influence most matters in his favor. Including sudden, unexpected deaths."

Mickey and Loomis grimaced. If Adrian had to take anyone with him, and he did, it would be Loomis.

"We go now and we go fast. The child I am interested in is in danger. Deadly danger. I have no doubt that Sir Jeffrey will make away with the boy, if it is in his interests. And it is. He is aiming for high office, and to do that, he wants no impediment such as a child born to someone—inconvenient."

Not even to these people would he vouchsafe the secret. Even if they had guessed her secret, he would not confirm it. His wife would remain above reproach. "We have about fifty miles to traverse. That will take us two days, if we're lucky, considering the time of year and the condition of the roads. Frost is making the going hard, but that is better than the rain we've had recently."

He would barely notice the cold. His anger would keep him warm. Traveling unknown roads on horseback in the dark would be too dangerous, so it was up at dawn for them.

He placed his hands on the table, preparing to get to his feet, but a sudden thought made him change his mind. A solution to a puzzle. "Loomis, tell me something. Is Sir Jeffrey Creasey the reason you dogged my footsteps in London?"

Loomis grimaced and ducked his head. "Yes, yer grace."

"Why?"

"We heard rumors. The staff, I mean. When we talked to Sir Jeffrey's people, we couldn't find anybody who liked him. That's never a good sign. Then we heard he was beating people. No reason, just took a whip to them if he was in a bad mood."

Adrian winced. "Why didn't you tell me?"

"Because we didn't have proof, your grace. Servants are dismissed for spreading gossip. Nobody showed us, they just told us. There were all kinds of rumors, and some of them couldn't have been true. But we heard from Miss d'Arblay."

"Ophelia? She didn't write to me." Or if she did, he hadn't opened the letters. Ophelia used to send him several letters a day during their affair, proclaiming her devotion and asking for new purchases. After he'd dismissed her, he stopped opening them. "What did she say?"

"Sir Jeffrey came to her house, you know, the one in King Street, and asked her how much. She told him and he sneered at her, but said he'd pay. Then he hurt her, or so she said. So she threw him out. And he came back and smashed the windows. Every one."

Guilt suffused Adrian. Perhaps he should have opened the letters, after all. But how was he to know? "I see. I'll pay for their replacement."

Ophelia would have done so already, but it would have cost her. Glass wasn't cheap. He had no animosity toward her. After all, she had to make a living. "He hurt her?"

"Aye, took a whip to her. But she recovered."

"Good. I'll still pay for the glass." If he knew Ophelia, she'd have a new protector by now, and he would ensure her safety. Pulling his watch out of his waistcoat pocket, he checked the time. "Come on. It'll get dark early, so we don't have much time. That's if you want to come." He wouldn't put either of these men in danger. Well, man and boy. Another pang of conscience hit him. "Mickey, you go back to the house and look after her grace."

"But, sir—"

Adrian cut him off. "No. You don't ride well enough for one thing. Loomis and I will go faster without you. And if her grace is in any danger, I want someone I trust with her."

That did the trick. Mickey nodded. "Yes, your grace."

"And don't tell her what we're doing. Not unless you have to. You can take the note for her. I'm saying I'm going north because my mother has been taken ill. I told her I'd contact her as soon as I can. Now go." He thrust the paper into Mickey's hands.

Mickey left, and Adrian and Loomis soon followed on his heels.

Chapter 19

My Dearest Wife;
A messenger arrived early. My mother has been taken ill. Please wait at
Haxby for me, where you will be warm and safe. I will send word as soon
as I can. I still wish us to travel to Oxfordshire, but while the weather is
so cold, there is no need for you to put yourself to any trouble.
I will think of you often. Our wedding night will remain a treasured memory.

That was so different to the note he'd left behind a few hours earlier
that it might almost have come from a different person. The first note had
been hastily scrawled, informing her that he would return when he could.
No fond words, no intimation that her confession to him had not pushed
him away. Livia had feared the worst. Been terrified of it, in fact. She
had thought he knew about the baby, but he had not. That was more than
enough to drive a man away.

But if his mother was ill, shouldn't he have her with him? Wasn't her
wifely duty to attend him?

Livia laid the letter gently down on the table. "Where did he give
you this message?"

"At the inn, your grace. He left with Loomis."

The burly footman with the black eyebrows that met in the middle.
She recalled the way the man hovered around Adrian as if his master was
delicate. "I see. On horseback?"

"Yes, your grace. Not long after daybreak."

So, around seven. And Mickey had not brought her the letter until ten.
The boy had waited.

"There's no reply, Mickey. He just told me where he would be."

At least he hadn't left her, as she feared. Unless this was a polite ploy, to prevent society talking. Fear gripped her again. Fear that they would never be as close as they'd been last night. The "treasured memory" part seemed to show it. That part of their marriage was done, the loving, intimate part. He wouldn't come near a woman who'd lied to him.

For two hours she'd thought their marriage was essentially over. Now this new missive reinforced it. Not if she could help it.

Mickey turned to go.

"Wait."

The boy turned around.

"Is his mother really ill?"

Mickey said nothing. Her heart dropped. She would miss Adrian, his amusement, his care of her, his lovemaking. Oh, he would probably come to her bed, but not with the intimacy they'd shared last night.

He was backing away just when she had fallen deeply in love with him.

The knowledge brought tears, but she refused to shed them. So he had gone, and sent her an excuse. Would she let him do it? Wait like an obedient spouse for him to make another appearance? Be damned to that!

"Finch!" She called for her maid without turning around. The opening of the powder room door told her that her maid had obeyed her summons. "Pack. I want enough clothes for at least a week. And I want to leave today, as soon as possible."

"May I ask where we are going, your grace?"

"To Northumberland. My husband's house. I do not want to wait, Finch. You may leave orders to have the other items packed and be waiting for my order to send them. Clear?"

Finch's eyes widened slightly, then she glanced at Mickey. "Yes, your grace." The maid bobbed a curtsy and hurried off.

Mickey was halfway to the door. "You are coming with us," she said to the boy. "Now, are you ready to tell me the truth?"

* * * *

Two hours later they were away. Two hours was far too long, but she'd had Adrian's traveling coach made ready in the time allowed. Finch accompanied her, as did Mickey, but instead of the plethora of outriders, she'd reduced the people accompanying them to the driver, his relief driver and two footmen. Not in livery. She did not intend to travel in pomp. The footmen loaded the trunks Finch had packed into the boot, and her parents waved them off.

"You may say Adrian's mother has been taken ill," she told her mama. "I will write, I promise. But if I am to support him, I have to start now."

Mickey had still not told them where he was going, insisting the story about his mother was true, but she would wear him down. At the worst, she'd end up at the family seat of the Dukes of Preston and meet his mother.

She started by speculating aloud about the places they were to visit, and where they could stop on the way. His cagey responses made Livia positive that Mickey knew what was going on. She had started this journey to call his bluff, but he was still holding strong.

Not until the end of the day, when they were about to rack up at an inn did he relent. After Finch had left the coach to attend to the unloading of the luggage her mistress would need, he closed his eyes and shook his head. "You're not going to give up, are you?"

"No," she said cheerfully. "And we have three more days."

"One," he said. "One." And he drew a piece of paper out of his pocket. "Here."

She took the paper but kept her attention on him. "You can read?"

He shrugged. "My ma taught me. She wanted me to go to the charity school at the docks, but she died." He said it without emotion, but turned his head to glance out of the window. His mother's death affected him, but he didn't want people to know it.

"How long ago did she die?"

"Five years."

"And you're twelve."

He turned back to face her, cocky grin firmly in place. "Thirteen now. I had a birthday."

Thirteen. He'd been on his own since he was seven years old. No child deserved that. And if he'd learned to read by then without anyone's tuition except for his mother, he was a bright boy.

She recognized the address on the paper as an old house that was part of Jeffrey's estate. She hadn't thought of it until this moment, though. It had nothing of note, and Jeffrey had left the house to deal with another time. As far as she knew, it was a ruin.

Except that it couldn't be.

It didn't take long for Livia to work out what was happening. *Oh God, he'd gone after Jeffrey.* There could be only one reason. She'd told him of her baby, and he'd gone to discover more about the lad. Either that, or he knew where her son was.

And Jeffrey, seeing the loss of his expectations when she married Adrian, would not want the boy any longer. He would hide him, send him where nobody would ever find him. Rather than that, Adrian had gone after him. Finch returned and Livia informed her, and the coachman that their route would deviate a little. The man didn't grumble to her face but did inform her they would have to take a side road when she gave him the address. "And in this weather, your grace, it's likely to slow us down."

"As quick as you can," she said. "Time is very important."

Every mile that passed, she gnawed at her nails, but they had another day to travel before they reached their destination. She hardly slept that night, though the inn was good and the beds comfortable. The more she tried, the more sleep escaped her.

Her husband wouldn't be pleased to see her, that was for sure.

* * * *

Having a horse go lame after the first station and then finding the next steed he hired was no better than a slug had not improved Adrian's temper. The journey had taken much longer than he'd planned. The inn they'd stayed at, chosen from necessity, proved rowdy, the beds lumpy. Adrian chose to sleep on top and use his greatcoat for cover against the freezing night. He paid for extra logs for the fire, and probably managed two or three hours of sleep. He'd managed on much less.

The going proved harder. They passed through a wood that had collected the rain of the last few days and stored it, churning the path into mud under their hooves. The frost was better. Loomis never complained, merely got out the map book they had brought to check they were on the right route.

Except then they got lost. By the time they regained their path, they'd traveled ten miles in the wrong direction. Loomis apologized until Adrian snapped, "Enough, man!" at him, and then felt bad because the fault lay with him as much as it did the footman.

And all the time anxiety gnawed at his stomach.

Finally, as dusk was falling on the second day after they'd left Haxby, they arrived at a pair of gates. They lay open, one lurching to the side, an overgrown drive beyond. Their horses traversed the rough, rabbit-holed path with great care. If they had to leave, they would need to lead their mounts back up because darkness would have fallen. They couldn't risk laming the animals. The nearest inn was five miles away, and it was only a small place. Doubtful they had any decent horses for hire.

Adrian did everything he could to quell his growing ire. His temper had let him down before. Over the years he'd learned how to harness it, wait until the icy blast arrived and he could think again. But now, with the weather doing its best to snow, and failing because the cold had overwhelmed it, Adrian couldn't find that core he needed. Only red, flaming fury drove him to get to the house and rescue the boy.

Sir Jeffrey meant to kill him, Adrian was sure of it. With the boy out of the way, youthful indiscretions were done away with. Sir Jeffrey was a tragic widower with a wife who died in childbirth, a war hero, if one didn't know better. Constructing his own past, turning his sordid doings into positive actions. Only Adrian stood between him and a child's life.

He hated politicians. Oily bunch of self-serving acolytes. He'd had a few trying to climb into his backside before, an experience that was as uncomfortable as it sounded.

He forced his mind on the practicalities. They had to deal with the situation and leave, most likely with a child who hadn't ridden a horse. A frightened child.

The front of the house appeared dispiritingly shabby. At first glance it presented as a modest Jacobean mansion, but on closer inspection slates were missing off the roof and the paint on the woodwork was peeling and shabby. A beam on the first floor had a disturbingly deep crack in it, and green, slimy algae concealed much of the wood. Since the place was Jacobean, that added up to a lot of wood. A lot of rotten wood.

The knocker on the front door was rusty, so it was just as well Adrian had no intention of using it. While Loomis found somewhere to tether the horses, he nudged the slab of planked wood, ready for it to resist him.

It didn't. Instead, the door swung inward. Not silently, which was a shame, but the creak echoed through an empty hall. Their boots echoed on the floor. No servant came to greet them. No sound of life. Why bother to lock the door when there was nothing to steal?

Adrian's stomach plummeted. Had Lady Creasey fooled him? Sent him on a wild goose chase? He could have wasted days getting here, only for—

A sound came from above, accompanied by a sprinkling of dust. Someone was upstairs. Glancing at Loomis, Adrian jerked his head. Loomis nodded. Adrian didn't have to tell him to draw a pistol. He pulled out his own, checked it, even though he'd loaded it himself, and walked toward the staircase.

They had no chance of walking quietly, but they went as quietly as they could, and at a gesture from Adrian, placed their feet at the same time. Whoever was upstairs would think only one person was here. At the top of the stairs, Adrian made another gesture. Loomis understood. He would not make himself known.

Adrian placed his gloved hand on the dirty latch and opened the door.

The room was large, and empty but for a few sticks of furniture. A man stood facing him with weapons drawn. A sword, of all things. And he had a small boy in front of him.

Adrian's attention went immediately to the child. Skinny, dressed warmly but plainly, he was about the same height as Mickey—but with a head of flaming red-gold hair.

He'd know that shade anywhere. Slightly darker than his wife's but to compound the issue, the lad had deep blue eyes. This was his wife's child. Ten years old.

The boy stared at him, his mouth open.

Grabbing his shoulder, his fingers digging into the lad's flesh, Sir Jeffrey dragged him to stand by his side. "His name is John. He is my son."

Adrian gave a bitter laugh. "Oh, now you acknowledge him?"

The boy was shivering. His clothes were adequate, and a fire burned, or rather smoked, in the grate. It was not cold that caused that trembling. It was fear.

"Let him go," Adrian said.

"You'd like that, wouldn't you? He's mine. As is Livia."

"I married her," Adrian said bluntly.

"I married her first."

Cold swept through him, raising the hairs on the back of his neck and tightening his grip on his pistol. But that could not be true. Could it? Three years ago Parliament passed a law regulating marriage. Before that, the ceremony had been a casual affair. In some places all it took was a mutual vow, said in a holy place.

Livia had loved this man, or thought she had. Once, she might have stood in a place with him and exchanged vows. Could it be true?

It didn't matter. "I married her in front of witnesses. We satisfied every legal requirement. If you went through anything with her, it was not real. She is not your wife." And he loved her. He would not let Livia go, not to anyone. Least of all to this man.

"Any children you bear will be bastards."

Considering his own origins, Adrian had little concern for these threats.

"You will have to pay a great deal of money to prove that."

Sir Jeffrey studied Adrian closely. "You'd like that, would you not? This is my son and my house. You may leave now."

Adrian let a corner of his mouth curl in a wry smile. "And let you have your will with the boy? Without him, you have scrubbed the slate clean. Did you not think I had worked that out?"

His opponent's eyes widened. Just a little, but enough to let Adrian know he had struck on the truth. "How could I do such a thing?"

"Easily, I imagine, taking into account the way you treat other people. You do not really see them as separate beings, do you? They are there to serve your needs, nothing more." His mouth flattened into a tight line.

"You appear to assume so much about me. How can you know that?" The pitch of his voice rose.

Oh yes, Adrian was certainly on the right track. "Because I have known one like you before." More than one, but one in particular.

"Who?"

"My father." He remembered well enough, though he would not discuss it with this toad.

"Both your fathers died—the natural one and the cuckold." Sir Jeffrey's lips lifted in a sneer. "History repeats itself, does it not? Since I have cuckolded you. Or is it the other way around? You have helped a number of wives deceive their husbands in the worst possible way. Now you have helped another one."

Adrian didn't bother to reply to that accusation. Why should he care what this idiot thought? "You are welcome to try the case in the courts. But today I have come for the boy."

For the first time he met the direct blue gaze of the child. And almost reared back. The boy was terrified. He lowered his tone, softened his words for the lad. "Would you prefer to come with me?"

The boy nodded eagerly and Adrian's heart broke. This child was willing to go with a stranger, rather than stay with the man claiming to be his father. Fathers didn't behave like that. They cared for their children. Or they *should*. He knew all about that too. He would not leave without the boy.

A disturbance sounded below and he smiled. Loomis would stop anyone coming in here. There were bound to be a few servants around. Even though the place stank of damp and mildew, it still had a roof. Just. Someone was still living here, God help them.

"Your caretakers seem to have returned. Now hand the boy over. You heard him. He wants to come with me."

"Whoever gave children the right to decide?" Sir Jeffrey dropped the sword. It clattered to the floor, the only shiny object for miles, apart from the cut-steel buttons on Adrian's coat and waistcoat.

Adrian took a step forward, intending to snatch the boy away from his tormentor. He wanted none of this. If they had to walk the five miles in the freezing cold, they were leaving this place.

Sir Jeffrey tightened his hold. His other hand held a gleaming pistol. The click signaled the cocking of it. "Don't do it," Sir Jeffrey warned as Adrian readied his own weapon. "Let the hammer down. Gently. Then drop it." He turned the flintlock, and pressed the barrel against the boy's head.

* * * *

"Hurry, oh, hurry!" Gazing out of the coach window, Livia could only see trees and hills, with sheep scattered over the frost-sprinkled landscape. Nothing else.

The coach drew to a halt. The footman swung down, opened the door and let down the steps, together with a blast of chilly air.

"We're here, your grace."

"Are we?"

"You mean those?" Finch pointed to a pair of gates on her side of the coach. One swung drunkenly from a single hinge.

"I asked at the inn in the village. They said here." Pushing his wig aside, the coachman scratched his head. "I can't see how somebody could live here. There's a house up there. I saw it, but the trees around it are overgrown. Must have been a tidy manor once."

Stunned, Livia took the footman's hand and allowed him to help her to alight. Just as well she wore her sturdy ankle boots because the ground was hard and uneven. No sign of a gracious path, or any tended greenery. Hedges encroached so far there was hardly room to pass by them. Lifting the skirts of her riding habit, heedless of gentility and grace, Livia prepared to edge her way around them.

"Wait!"

Mickey rushed up to her, brandishing a pair of pistols. The ones they kept inside the coach in case of trouble. They were always loaded. Livia took them both. "Yes, I might need these." She shoved them into the capacious pockets of her cloak.

"Can you use them?"

Blue eyes met gray. "Yes," she said.

Mickey nodded. "Any more around?"

"Coachman has a pair, as well as his shotgun."

Mickey turned back. "Gimme one."

In other circumstances Livia might have found amusement in the way the burly coachman, made even bulkier by his layers of clothing, handed the boy a pistol. He didn't even ask if Mickey could use it. Somehow, Livia assumed that would be a redundant question.

Even Finch found a small pistol. Armed to the teeth, Livia, Mickey, her maid, her coachman, his relief driver and the footman stepped forward. A veritable army. "Stay behind," she said to the footman. "Somebody needs to look after the vehicle."

"There's nobody for miles, your grace."

"There's somebody in there." She nodded in the direction of the yet-unseen house. "And I don't trust them one bit."

Dilapidated or not, the house was a fair size, which indicated a fair number of servants. She wouldn't put it past Jeffrey to order one of them to take the coach, or at least raid it to see what they could find. Or to set the horses free to delay them.

Grumbling, the footman remained behind, going to the horses' heads to placate the animals. He'd walk them if they took too long.

The decision to leave the coach in the road had been a good one. They were bound to have lost a wheel at the very least in one of the holes that riddled the drive. Despite that, it didn't take long for them to reach the house.

"The door's open, your grace," the coachman said.

"I can see that."

"We need to keep quiet," Mickey put in.

Two horses stood, gently steaming, although someone had thrown blankets over their backs. They were loosely tethered to the overhanging branches of an oak tree, a little distance from the house.

The place was filthy, neglected, some of the windows smashed. *Not a place to bring up a small boy*, Livia thought indignantly. "Why do we need to keep quiet?" she asked Mickey, turning back to him.

"Because if he hears us coming..." Mickey drew his finger across his throat in a dramatic gesture.

Alarmed, Livia agreed. "You're right." She paused to tuck her skirts up so they wouldn't make too much noise. "Everyone, no talking inside the house. I want to find the child and leave. If he is on his own, we can do that easily. If not, we'll need all our wits about us." If he was here at all. Jeffrey had described this place as "neat." It looked far from neat to her.

A flight of crumbling stone steps led to the open door. Livia followed John Coachman through. Her gown made the tiniest sound as she pushed past, and she paused to catch her breath.

Then she wished she had not. Damp permeated this place like a shroud around a slowly rotting corpse. Too much wood for a worm to resist. And the place was all but empty. This could not be the house. It just couldn't.

But as she turned to gesture everyone outside, a sound came from the floor above. A child, crying.

Either this place was haunted, or it held what she had come for. That and her husband.

Men's voices sounded, angry tones coming down to them. She recognized them both.

And at the top of the stairs stood a man Livia had come to know quite well, although she couldn't recall his name. Her husband's favorite footman. Loomis held his finger to his lips. She acknowledged his warning with a nod.

Livia led the way up the stairs, which creaked and groaned in protest, but only a little. Fortunately the wind was getting up, and outside the leafless trees were rattling their branches and groaning in their turn.

At the top of the stairs, Livia sighed with relief. Soundlessly. She moved close enough to the footman to murmur softly in his ear. "Does my husband have the boy?"

Loomis gestured to a room with open doors and shook his head. "Not yet," he mouthed back.

Livia heard Adrian's voice.

"I knew you wanted to—hurt the boy. But now there's a witness. Me."

"Drop your pistol. Both of them." That was Jeffrey. "Do as you're told, or the boy dies."

The child cried out again and Livia had to stop herself rushing forward to claim him. Adrian didn't care for his own safety, she knew that, but he would not harm a child. She knew that too.

She crept forward, Mickey by her side.

Two thumps told her Adrian had done as Jeffrey had bidden him. "And how do I know you won't kill me as well, then claim that I killed the boy?" Adrian was speaking rather loudly now.

Livia knew why. Loomis would bear witness if the worst happened.

The worst would *not* happen.

Gun in hand, she stepped through the door.

Adrian, standing with his back to the door, whipped around, too far away from her to do anything but stare.

Livia took in the situation at a glance. When she stared into Jeffrey's eyes she saw nothing but death. This man, the one who had used and manipulated her, had nothing else in his eyes. Only the light reflected from the fire in the grate gave them any kind of life.

Without hesitation, she lifted her pistol and fired at the man holding a gun against her son's head.

Chapter 20

"Two blasted days," Adrian growled, pacing around the small room. The small bed in the equally small inn parlor held the clothes they had worn that day to dazzle the magistrate. The man had arrived, full of pomposity and barely concealed excitement at the inn to declare they could go.

After Livia had shot Jeffrey, Loomis had raced forward and picked up the boy, pressing the lad's face against his waistcoat and taking him from the room. Adrian had rushed to Livia and found her calmly lowering the weapon to the floor and putting another back in her pocket. She'd looked at him then, her eyes clear, heavenly blue, and said, "Well, somebody had to stop him."

After that she hadn't said much. Adrian cared for her, found a room at the village inn she could have to herself if she wanted it. He brought food to her, fed her himself, coaxing her into taking a few bites.

Then he understood what she really needed. He ordered port and brandy. Vicious stuff, harsh enough to burn, but he gave her that, and she took it. Drank herself into oblivion and then she slept.

The next day she had a searing hangover, but she had recovered from the initial shock. "I might be a good shot," she said as she lay in bed, a damp cloth over her eyes, "but I have never shot a person before." She paused. "I nearly did. The person who refused to give Dru her manuscript."

He didn't have a clue what she was talking about until he recalled her sister, now the Duchess of Mountsorrel, was an authoress. A scandalous one. Aided and abetted by her husband, she published the second in her series recently, and her husband, already a dyed-in-the-wool villain from the first book, grew even worse. If it weren't for the evident love between the two, one would imagine she hated him.

Drusilla hated the duke as much as he hated Livia. Which was to say, not at all.

"Where did you learn to shoot?" He kept his voice low, because the last time he'd spoke, to ask her if she needed anything, she'd winced and demanded that he keep quiet. He understood, having been in that situation more than once himself.

"When we were small. My brothers helped, because they practiced. I hated dolls and baby houses, so I went out with them."

"In breeches?" he asked, fascinated.

"Lord, no. Papa would have locked me up if I'd done that. I'm not insane."

He winced, glad she couldn't see it, and changed the subject. "When you're ready to leave, I'll take you to Northumberland. We should be there in a day or two."

"I thought you didn't like your house there?"

He paused before speaking. "I want you to meet my mother. Just once, I swear. But I swore we would have no secrets. You've entrusted me with your most precious confidence, and I will not let you down. I have one more and then we're done with the past."

She sighed. "How is he? My son?"

She had not seen a smile like the one on her face now. Simple, sweet and joyful. A child's smile.

"He's quiet, but eating the innkeeper out of house and home. Mickey is with him constantly."

"Good."

Although he waited for her to speak again, her slight snore gave the game away. Smiling, he went to the basin to wring out a fresh cloth in cold water and went downstairs to meet the constable, who had called.

They had made their way to the inn and ordered food, shelter and the local constable. For two nights he'd held his distressed wife, lying together on a lumpy, but blessedly clean mattress in the inn, waiting for the local magistrate to come to his ponderous conclusion.

Finally he'd returned, together with his officials, all dressed in their camphor-stinking best, and asked to see the duke and duchess.

"It's a clear case of self-defense, your grace, and that's a fact."

Adrian had given him a gracious nod and the promise to visit the village again when he was passing. He would take great care to pass as quickly as possible, but he would send them a generous donation for—something.

Livia sat in the only comfortable chair in the whole inn, her hands neatly folded together in her lap. The two boys sat in a corner of the room, Mickey proving a useful asset as far as John was concerned.

The magistrate nodded affably to her. "And your wife is not to blame for missing her aim. In that situation, I'm surprised she hit anything at all."

Adrian swallowed his words. When her sister had gaily informed him that Livia was an excellent shot, he had brushed it away with a mild disclaimer. But hell, if she wasn't right. That had been the coolest shot he'd ever witnessed. She'd blown Sir Jeffrey's head clean off.

Good God, what a prize he had in her!

With Adrian's guineas greasing his palm, the constable had reacted remarkably quickly, for the country. Not quickly enough for Adrian.

"Two blasted days," Adrian growled, pacing around the small room.

The small bed in the equally small inn parlor held the clothes they had worn that day to dazzle the magistrate but now they were packing, ready to leave.

* * * *

Loomis had procured two decent riding horses, and four carriage horses, but they would only have to take them as far as the next coaching-inn on the main road. Adrian carried her down to the coach and tucked her tenderly into a corner of it, with a blanket and a hot box, promising her they would arrive soon.

Livia didn't care very much. Fortunately she traveled well. Even better, so did the two boys sitting opposite her. She spent most of the first day staring at him and trying not to, pretending to be asleep.

John was quiet, and he could not read. Later, when he'd accustomed himself to her presence, she asked him, "Where have you been until now, John?" Because he could not have lived in that house.

"With Aunt Fanny and Uncle Bill," the boy said, as if that was something everyone knew.

The names meant nothing to Livia. "Were they kind to you?"

"Hush!" That came from Mickey. "He's been going on about them. Crying his little heart out."

Ah, so he wanted to go back to them. That was promising, showing he had been shown care and affection. Livia vowed to find those people and reward them. If she could find them. "Who did you see there? Did anyone come to visit you?"

"Well, yes, the man came. That one who took me away. He said he was my papa, but I didn't believe him. He took me. He said he could make my mama come. He wasn't my papa, was he?"

Livia shook her head. She felt quite confident in doing so. Jeffrey had kept his distance from this boy. How would John take to her as his mother? Would he believe her? Probably not, because in his young eyes, where had she been?

Seeing the child was so different to dreaming and wondering about him. Although thin, her son had the bloom of health, and although not chatty, he talked readily enough. But he couldn't read, Mickey said. These days almost everyone could read to some extent. That was why journals and novels were selling in such large numbers.

Her son. Watching and dreaming, Livia passed her day. That night, in a far more comfortable inn, she slept, but not until she'd asked Adrian about Jeffrey. "Am I a murderess?" Already in her night rail and with a nightcap firmly tied under her chin, she watched him undress. Almost like an old couple. His body gleamed in the firelight, the glow licking his bronzed skin lovingly.

"No, you are not." Tossing his nightshirt over his head, he thrust his hands through the sleeves and came over to her, sitting on the side of the bed. It creaked under his weight. No doubt ropes held it together under the feather mattress.

She threw back the covers. "Get in. You're too big to put all your weight on one part of this bed."

With a laugh, he obeyed her, and tugged her into his arms. She sighed and placed her palm on his chest. They still had a way to go, but they were getting there. To the place her siblings had found with their spouses—and she counted Darius in that number.

He tucked his free arm under his head and gazed at her. "You look good there," he said gruffly. "You will stay?"

"Of course I will. I have to," she added, reminding him of the legal contract between them.

"You don't have to sleep in my arms every night. But I want you to."

"I can't imagine not wanting to." She smiled, and the look they exchanged was as intimate as anything she'd shared with him. A different kind of intimacy, but one that would last. He kissed the top of her head.

"If my family hear of the details, they'll know I shot to kill." She paused, then met his gaze once more. "Why don't I feel sorry? Why am I not full of shame and regret?"

He made a purring, smoothing sound at the back of his throat. "Because you knew he would have killed John. You made the right choice. That was the only way to stop him. He meant to kill the boy, to clear his way to high political office."

"The people in power aren't exactly pure." Scandal dogged the most brilliant, the most effective ministers they had.

"But they have something to build on. Sir Jeffrey was coming up from nothing, and that made him vulnerable, until he could build his own foundation. He had to enter the governing circle with an impeccable reputation." He tugged up the soft blanket that Finch had the perspicacity to pack, tucking it around her. Thanks to the fire in the grate, this room was warm enough, but the fire wouldn't last all night. "Power is largely a game of who-knows-what. If they had discovered his youthful indiscretion, they would have made him pay for it with favors. He had to get to the boy and rid himself of him. At least, he did in his own eyes."

She pressed her hand against his rib cage, feeling his heart beat, strong and steady. "John might not believe I am his mother."

Smoothly, he went up on one elbow, leaning over her, framing her face with his hands. "I have a proposal for you. Will you listen?"

"Yes."

"I've been thinking about this, and I have the answer, but only if you will accept it. If society knows he is your son, you will be excoriated."

"I know." She would gladly face the opprobrium for the sake of John.

"What if we say he is *my* son? My by-blow? If you accepted him as mine, you would be the saintly one, the wife who graciously overlooked her husband's previous discretions? In that case, we could keep him with us. You would not be the first wife to accept that."

She gasped. "I had planned something more complicated. Would you do that?"

"You would not object?"

She loved that her reaction mattered so much to him, that he thought of her first, and society afterward. So many men would have been the other way about. "If it meant I could keep him close, then no I would not. But why should you do it?"

His mouth twisted. "You know why. Nobody will think any the worse of me."

Another difficulty occurred to her. "What about his hair?"

"It's darker than yours. It will probably darken more over the years. If we cut it short and give him a wig to wear on formal occasions, that will help even more."

Exhilaration filled her. Yes, they could do that. And she'd learned that anything the Emperors of London declared to be the truth, became so.

Very few people knew that her cousin, Alexander, had met his wife in a brothel, where she'd been abducted. If they had, they would have been appalled. Even more that Alex had shared her bed before they married. Just as she, Livia had with the man she adored. The family even held the key to a secret that would truly rock society and probably the rest of the world, to the core if they discovered it.

Next to that, hiding the identity of her son was a small matter. "Yes," she said, letting the word go in one long breath.

"Besides," he said, lowering himself to lie on his back once more. "At last I get to put my appalling reputation to good use. A reputation, I might add, that I intend to leave well and truly behind me."

Livia could have everything she wanted. It hardly seemed real.

Chapter 21

This house was not the one she had expected. When she'd imagined the North of England, Livia had thought of rough seas, towering cliffs and gloomy, old houses.

Not this veritable palace. A mansion in the style of the last century sat in the lee of a rolling hill that would be lushly green in the summer. The gardens surrounding it were, it was true, old-fashioned, formal and neat rather than wild and natural. Snow had come last night, but not much, so the green lawns were sprinkled with white. The light was already fading, at four in the afternoon. They had reached the house in time to prevent a slow, tortuous journey through falling snow in the dark. The coach was equipped with carriage lights of course, but with snow falling they would not be able to see holes in the road.

"This is lovely," she said. Why was this house not part of the circuit that the fashionable used every year? Adrian said he preferred to live in Oxfordshire. She had never visited that house, either, but since Adrian had been a bachelor, that was not remarkable.

His mother lived here. Perhaps they were so deeply estranged that he considered giving her this house was for the best. Perhaps she was so deeply disfigured by her illness that he could not bear to look at her, or maybe her behavior had disgusted him. Livia would not argue with that. She had left him a poisoned legacy to bear, because of her thoughtlessness.

She waited until Adrian had dismounted and handed the reins of his horse to a waiting groom. The man bowed and led the horse away. Adrian came to the coach and opened the door. She shivered. "Come, sweetheart, you will be warmer inside."

He led her away, giving instructions for the boys to be taken to a parlor, and a room to be made ready for them. "John will not care to spend the night apart from Mickey," he said, smiling.

He appeared more relaxed than Livia was, but on closer inspection, the lines at the corners of his mouth had tightened. He wasn't relaxed at all.

"Is this home?"

He led her through a pair of double doors, nodding to a footman. "Not my home, though it once was. I will take you to my home when we are done here." He glanced back, at the white sky beyond. "Or when the weather allows."

They had entered into a hall decorated traditionally, with displays of swords and shields, armor made into art, but ready at a moment's notice to fight off the fearsome Scots. For this was Border country. For centuries the English and Scots had fought here, over sheep and cattle rather than countries. They didn't care who the monarch was, but they would fight to the death if a fence was moved a couple of feet the wrong way.

"I expected a fortress at the very least," she remarked.

Adrian gave a short laugh. "Indeed, one once stood here. Remnants of the original house remain, but my great-grandfather rebuilt it. He used to entertain here on a grand scale. So did my grandparents."

So Livia's grandparents, dead many years now, would have likely come here in their time. That made her feel better, not as lost.

A maid appeared, and bobbed a curtsy, then another, until a staff of about twenty appeared. Not as much as a house like this would need, were it fully occupied, but more than enough to care for one woman. Then a plump woman glided out of a door at the back of the hall. She was dressed better than the others, her hoop wider, her gown satin rather than practical wool.

She could not be Adrian's mother. This lady was not a beauty, and would never have been one. Her gray-threaded brown hair was pulled back into a tight knot at the back of her head and her lace cap was adorned with but a modest frill of lace. The ruffle framed a face that was more comfortable than beautiful, round, with a button nose, shrewd brown eyes and a thin, unsmiling mouth. She folded her hands before her and waited.

"Ah, Miss Conway." Adrian led Livia forward, and spoke loud enough for everyone to hear. "This is my wife, the Duchess of Preston. We will be staying here for a few days."

Footsteps echoed in the space as two small boys scampered forward. "And this," he said, indicating the boys, "is my son. The duchess has agreed to help me care for him. The other boy is his companion." He didn't bother indicating which boy was which. "I would like them fed and they need a change of clothes. A bath would not come amiss."

A maid came forward. At first Livia thought John would refuse to go with her, but when Mickey took his hand, he went with him. "I want to know where they are," she said.

The maid curtseyed.

"I'll show you," Adrian promised. "But I want to see your needs attended to first."

Finch stood by the doors, but he addressed the woman waiting for his attention first. "My dear, this is Miss Conway, a distant cousin and my mother's constant companion."

"She's heard of your arrival, your grace," the woman said in a gravelly tone, low for a woman. "She's agitated. Wants to know who is here and did they come to see her."

"We did. But I would see her tomorrow, when we have rested."

Miss Conway sighed. "She'll make a fuss."

The words appeared more ominous than Livia had thought, because Adrian closed his eyes briefly and echoed Miss Conway's sigh. "I see." He turned to Livia and took both her hands. "Would you mind meeting my mother now? Are you too tired for this?"

"Won't she think it impertinent of me to visit her in all my dirt?" Livia longed for a bath and her bed, not to mention a decent meal, but she would not let Adrian down. What dowager duchess received a person straight off a long journey? True, she was not particularly grubby, thanks to Finch, but she felt it.

Adrian removed her cloak with his own hands, and then her hat, handing them both to a maid. "She will not object, or denigrate you, I swear it."

The heaviness in his tone made her look up from removing her gloves. But she could find nothing to say when she became aware of the bleak expression on his face. This mattered to him. And she was no nearer knowing why.

She had to go with him and trust him to know best, because she certainly didn't.

Consequently, when he held his arm at an angle, she placed her hand on it in the proper manner. The grand staircase leading up from the center of the hall proved more than adequate to take both of them.

They said nothing, all but oblivious to the chatter going on in the hall as they left. Finch was making herself busy instructing the maid on the distribution of the luggage and ordering a hot meal for her mistress. Adrian had traveled without a valet. Only Loomis, who strode into the hall as if he owned it, was there for him.

And her. Without a doubt Livia would always stand by his side.

He took her up another flight of stairs, and turned left, along a corridor decorated tastefully but in an old-fashioned way, that of a generation earlier. Heavier, darker furniture, and paintings that were covered with a thin layer of yellowing varnish. She would examine them later. This was her domain now, and she needed to take charge of it.

Adrian said nothing until they neared a door at the end, where they paused and waited for Miss Conway. "My mother has been ill for some time. I want you to see her as she is and understand. You are brave, Livia. I know you can face this."

Livia swallowed, but nodded her agreement. The dowager had contracted the pox. Rumors abounded about what the illness had done to her, but nobody had seen her since she'd fallen ill. The disease could render people blind, deaf and hideously disfigured. Either that or left its victim relatively untouched. The threatened tantrum Miss Conway had talked about indicated petulance, but the dowager had been notorious for that in her time.

"Very well." She tightened her grip on him before she released him and pasted a smile on her face. "Lead on."

Miss Conway tapped on the door but did not wait for a summons. She led the way into a pleasant room, with a sofa and a set of shelves holding books. It was empty but for a footman, who sprang up and bowed to them. He did not leave as Miss Conway opened an inner door.

The room inside was warm and welcoming. Comfortable, modern furniture was laid out here, but more sparsely. A fire blazed in the grate, and a woman sat next to it, a tea dish in her hand.

She was lovely. Breathtakingly so. Livia sank into a curtsy.

"Mama, this is my bride, Livia, the new Duchess of Preston. She is the daughter of the Marquess of Strenshall. Livia, my mother, the Duchess of Preston."

The woman sighed. "Conway says I'm a dowager." She spoke slowly, in a musical voice that charmed as the words dropped into the space between them.

She watched Livia dip and rise. Deeper than she should have, the curtsy she should give a queen, but this woman seemed to silently demand it.

"Pretty," the duchess observed.

"Thank you, your grace." Livia refused to seek help from the duke, who stood silently by his mother's side. He had bowed but said nothing.

The duchess nodded and turned her attention to Miss Conway. "May I have more tea?"

Livia blinked. The lack of manners astounded her.

Nobody else seemed to think anything amiss. Nodding, the companion stepped forward and poured a thin liquid from the teapot standing on a side table. The tea set was not as delicate or fashionable as Livia would have expected. Rather, it was pottery instead of porcelain, the thick stuff generally used in kitchens.

The duchess did not appear to notice, but took the dish, the brew an unhealthy pale color, and took a sip. No steam rose from the surface. On the whole, Livia was glad she had not been offered any. No refreshments accompanied the tea, no bread and butter, or dainty cakes and biscuits. Nothing.

This was strange. Perhaps the duchess preferred her tea unaccompanied. But in kitchen pottery?

The dowager wore a silk gown without a hoop. Ladies always wore hoops unless, like Livia, they were wearing riding clothes for traveling. She put her dish back in its saucer with great care, as if it were Meissen.

The duchess looked up at Livia. She had not yet asked her to sit. Her eyes were empty. "Who are you?" Before Livia could answer, she went on. "I feel sure I must know you. Did I see you at the Duchess of Mountsorrel's last week? You're very pretty, in a common kind of way." Glancing away, she noticed her tea and picked it up. "Dear me, this will not do."

Without warning, she tossed the dish at Conway, who dodged neatly to one side. The dish smashed against the wall. Now Livia understood why they were using cheap pottery. The sound made her start, but she held her ground, watching the woman carefully. Shock raked her as the dowager babbled on, darting from one topic to another.

"My husband will be home soon, will he not? With another whore, I'll be bound. They think I don't know, but they don't know anything about it. Not the servants, anyhow. I'll creep into bed with them later. Scare the woman half to death. Then I'll…" She lost interest, turned her head and met her son's eyes. "Oh, now you're a handsome one. I feel sure I know you. It will come to me later. But you will do."

Livia had never heard Adrian sigh so deeply. "Come," he murmured to Livia. "She will work herself into a frenzy soon. Let Miss Conway take care of her."

Numbly, numb realization striking her to the core, Livia let Adrian lead her out of the pretty set of rooms. They did not bid the dowager farewell.

Adrian took her to the top of the house, to a long gallery, ranked with portraits on both walls, interspersed with windows on one side. He sat her down. Livia tried not to shiver, but she wasn't cold. She took his hands, strong and capable, but trembling. "She's mad, isn't she?"

"Yes." He spoke quietly. "Her brain is eaten away." The bitter words horrified Livia, but she kept silent. She had to hear this, whatever it was, and Adrian was finding difficulty in telling her. He wouldn't look at her, but stared at their joined hands. Adrian closed his eyes and sucked in a deep breath. "I'm sorry. I've never told anyone this before. People either knew or they didn't." He got to his feet. "Come. I need to show you something."

Guessing that he needed time, she stood and went with him, slowly walking down the line of portraits. People dressed in clothes of ages gone by stared haughtily down at her. Whatever came of today her portrait would appear here, beside Adrian's. A housekeeper might lead visitors down the serried row, telling them, "After the first week of their marriage, the duke and duchess lived entirely separate lives."

She shuddered. That would not happen to them.

He stopped in front of a portrait of a man. He wore the full-bottomed wig men favored at the turn of the century, and robes of crimson and ermine. Coronation robes, which put the painting about thirty years old. "This is the last duke," Adrian murmured.

The painter had captured an excellent likeness. A man in the prime of life, with velvety brown eyes and olive skin. He gazed down his long nose at her, his haughtiness frozen in time.

She had seen someone like him before.

Gasping, she turned to Adrian, then back to the portrait. "How can that be?" Because except for the outdated clothes, she could be looking at her husband.

"Because he is not my grandfather. He's my father."

* * * *

Adrian caught Livia when she reeled. He should have waited to tell her. The shock of meeting his mother had been too much for her. On top of the journey through the freezing countryside, he'd given her the shock of her life.

Swinging her into his arms, he carried her downstairs and into his suite of rooms. He blessed whoever had lit the fire and left a tray of tea things by the window. Nobody was in evidence. He laid her gently on the bed, grateful that he didn't have to handle a hooped skirt. He came down next to her, lying on his side. Perhaps he'd better go. But when he went to roll out of bed, she grasped his arm. "No, stay. Tell me."

"Are you sure? You know it all now." She could work it out if she wanted to. "You can leave whenever you want to."

"Don't say that! Tell me the rest, Adrian, please!"

How could he leave her so confused? He owed her the full story, sordid though it was. "The contract between my parents was arranged before the last duke, the man I knew as my grandfather, knew that his son had the pox. He'd caught it in Rome, on the Grand Tour. But before the wedding he went and confessed to the duke, who insisted he go ahead with the ceremony. The duke wanted an heir, and he was determined to have one. The pox can be passed on to the children, so he refused to allow his son near his new wife. Instead, he took her."

His mouth settled into a grim line. His grandfather had been a hard, unforgiving man. "He made her pregnant. After I was born, the duke no longer cared what my mother did. He had the heir of his body."

He chose his words carefully, keeping his story as impartial as he could, but for all that, Livia's eyes filled with dawning horror.

Relentlessly he continued with his story. "My mother and—her husband went to London. That was when she caught the illness from him. Before that, the duke had refused to let him touch her. My mother adored her husband, especially his kindness after my grandfather had used her. I do not know who did the seducing, but she returned here with the chancres and the rash, and forced the duke to take care of her. She recovered, and her husband did not. But the disease lies dormant in some people, and that is what happened here. All those years it must have been eating away at her."

Tears filled Livia's heavenly blue eyes, making wet trails down either side of her face. "Oh, how terrible! What about his wife?"

"My grandmother? She died young. I never knew her." From all accounts she was a gentle soul. She'd never have survived this horror. "I didn't know my true parentage until I was nine years old, and the duke heard some visiting children taunting me about being the son of a blackamoor. After that how could I reveal the true story? Legally I was the child of incest, illegitimate, since my grandfather did not marry my mother. He put the fear of God—or the devil—into me. I always said nothing, but I never acknowledged the story of the blackamoor as a lie. It's far better than the truth."

"What happened to the page?"

A reluctant smile curved his lips. "My mother adored him. She kept him until he grew too big to be a page, then asked him what he wanted. He worked as footman for a while, then left. He has a chandler's shop at London docks, a wife and a brood of children. None of them my siblings. Although I wish they were."

"Yes." Her grip on his arm was like the clutch of death. "Adrian, none of this is your fault. Poor boy, to have suffered so much! And you were a scandal from birth."

"I feel guilty every time I take the Eucharist." That confession just slipped out. He'd never admitted that to a soul before.

"Do not!" She would make a bruise. He would cherish it. "It's not wrong, Adrian. You are not wrong. You have borne so much."

She made him sound like a martyr. With a harsh laugh, he waved his free arm around, indicating the large room with its brocade hangings and luxurious furnishings. "I have suffered in comfort. Many more people are worse off. But my only living parent is a woman who does not know my name half the time, and on the occasions she does recognize me, I distress her."

"That is not your fault. Or hers."

No, it was not. But she was hardly an innocent. "Having her so ill makes it easier for me to leave her here."

He bit his lip. He'd never told this to anyone before. Who would he tell? "When I was little, she coddled me, used me to bait my father. Now I know why she was so bitter. He had given her the illness that would kill her. Eventually. She'd always had wild changes of mood. Now she's completely unpredictable."

"That's why her rooms are so bare," Livia said.

He nodded. "She breaks things. I know people call me heartless for abandoning her, but what else can I do? She doesn't know me, takes no comfort in my presence." God, he'd never been so open. Confession hurt. He swung off the bed and strode to the door. "I should leave you to rest."

"Adrian, don't go."

Her forlorn tones made him return to her, cup her face in his hands as he always loved to do. The touch of her silky skin soothed him, the magic of her presence calmed him. She reached up, touched his cheek. "Adrian, I'm so sorry about your childhood. You've overcome so much. And yet you are you, not some warped, twisted person. Still the man I love—"

He could bear it no more. Instead of letting her finish, he brought his mouth down to hers and kissed her. Her lips clung to his as if she would never let him go. He didn't want to go. But how could she bear him near her, now she knew all the sordid secrets about him?

"You must not," he told her when their lips separated. "You cannot. I'm not worthy of you—" But he couldn't push her away.

"You're more than worthy," she assured him. "You're my husband and I love you."

Tears pricked at his eyes. He couldn't remember the last time he shed them, but if any situation deserved it, this was the time. He swallowed. "You shouldn't."

"I do," she insisted, banding her arms around him.

"You know I love you. Adore you. That's why you must not say these things."

"I knew no such thing until you told me just now. A normal husband would reject me, send me away for what I've done. You've never even shown repulsion. Adrian, I took a lover. I bore a child."

A smile curved his lips. "But I have done much the same. I don't have a child, but believe me, my love, I took more than one mistress. I was prepared to marry a woman who would go and find her own amusements after she's done her duty." He kissed her forehead. "I confess, I cannot bear the idea of you doing that. You have far too much power over me, but I would not have it any other way."

"Adrian, don't go. Ever. Make love to me."

How could he resist that request from the woman he loved, respected, adored more than anyone else on earth?

Considering they both wore so many clothes, the task of getting undressed should have taken much longer than it did. He could hardly recall it. But he did not want to take her that way. He wanted nothing between them. They had dropped every barrier, revealed all their truths. This act of lovemaking needed to be achieved naked. Skin to skin.

He blessed the servant who had thought to light a fire in here when they arrived. They could lie on top of the covers and gaze at each other while he kissed her, and told her the final truth. "I love you, Livia. Now and for always."

Her laughter rang around the room as she tugged him down to kiss her. "Then prove it," she said breathlessly when they came up for air.

Thoroughly. He would leave her in no doubt of his adoration. He worshiped every inch of her body, lavishing kisses and caresses on every curve, every delicious fold. The textures of her fascinated him—the way her nipples crinkled when he touched them and became rosy red when he took them into his mouth and sucked. The soft, wet flesh between her thighs, and how wet it became when he slid a finger inside her and teased her with his mouth. He craved the taste of her, the rising scent of her arousal, mingling with his as finally, he joined their bodies.

Adrian pushed himself up on his hands, so he could gaze at her, and the place where they became one. "This is mine."

Boldly, she touched herself and him, making him smile. His Livia was becoming adventurous in love. "And this is mine," she said. "Only mine."

"Only yours," he repeated, and proceeded to prove it.

Epilogue

Three years later

Sitting at her desk, Livia looked up, startled, as a whirlwind burst through the study door. Her son was proving a complete handful. He'd walked early, talked early and now he was escaping his nurse at regular intervals. Far too easily for Livia's liking. But at least he came to her. "Mama, John says I must learn my catechism. But why?"

Patient, careful John had turned out to be most unlike any Shaw she had ever known before. Even her oldest brother, Marcus, the staidest of them all, had his wild side. But John loved nothing more than his books and learning. She was already seeking a place at Oxford for him, when he felt ready. He would most likely become a bishop in the fullness of time.

"Because we all have to," she told Matthew now, pushing back her chair and taking his hands. She really didn't feel like going into long explanations today. Matthew would probably blithely ignore every one, in any case. "Where is Pennethorne?"

"I don't know. Looking after Susanna, I suppose."

Her husband strolled in. As usual, her heart rate went up. It happened every time he was in her vicinity, especially when he met her eyes and gave her the intimate smile that had charmed her from the first. "I knew he'd be here. You should leave your mama alone, Matthew, when she is trying to write letters."

Livia had decided to catch up on the correspondence she'd been shamelessly abandoning recently. With her siblings spread all over the country, she had a lot to catch up with. "Viola is expecting again," she said, nudging the top letter in the pile she was replying to.

"How many is that? Four?"

"This will be her fifth. And her last, Marcus says."

Adrian winked at her. "Perhaps we should give him some lessons." He meant in controlling the baby-making. At the rate they made love, they should have more than two children. And she had been relieved not to have twins. Marcus had not avoided that fate. Perhaps, considering the news she had to impart to her husband, she might not, either.

He handed their son over to his nurse, who appeared at the door, profuse apologies on her lips. Then Adrian closed the door and leaned against it. "Alone again. But not for long. We may have more visitors in a short while."

"Oh, who?"

"The Bennings." Their neighbors, the squire and his wife. As different to the Creaseys as anyone could imagine. Kind, thoughtful, well-informed and good company, they often had them over to dinner and a convivial chat afterward.

Once Livia had seen the house in Oxfordshire, she'd known where she wanted to spend the bulk of her married life. Unpretentious, though large enough to entertain when they had to, this house suited her in every way. After Adrian's mother had died, they'd moved the treasures here, and sold the rest, leaving the house for the orphans they were caring for there.

Turning evil memories into good ones, they'd set up an orphanage. Society thought they were mad, turning such a lovely mansion into a place for children to despoil, but the people who really mattered, her family, were won over by the plan and enthusiastically turned their hands to help. Rescuing Mickey had proved a turning point for them both.

"Our three are lively today. They'll appreciate having the Benning children to play with. Until then, it's just the two of us."

She loved that he always included John in that number. Mickey had refused indignantly, declaring he'd had parents. But in their hearts, he was another of theirs. He would probably not accompany John to Oxford, though. Mickey's intelligence was of a decidedly practical nature.

"Actually, we're not alone." Getting up from her chair, she crossed the room to join him.

He met her halfway, taking her into his arms as naturally as breathing. "How so?"

He knew. She could see it in his eyes. But they spent every night together, so how could he not? "I believe, despite our efforts with sponges, that we have another child on the way."

His lips broadened in a smile. "I thought as much when you sent your morning chocolate back untouched." Adrian missed nothing where Livia was concerned. "And I am glad. Except that I fear for you."

"Only because I make so much noise when I give birth." By rights he shouldn't be anywhere near the birthing-chamber, but the last time he'd scandalized the midwife by rushing in when she'd screamed, and stayed there until Susanna had been born.

"You don't. I do." He gave her a tender kiss. "Thank you."

"What for?" She had hardly been an unwilling participant in their enthusiastic and adventurous lovemaking.

"For saving my life. For giving me life," he said.

References and/or Bibliography

I've been studying the eighteenth century for a long time. I do have a long list of books that I read, which I keep meaning to put on my website. I keep reading. My most recent discoveries are Dan Cruickshank's "The Secret History of Georgian London" and Mark Morton's "The Lover's Tongue – A Merry Romp Through the Language of Love and Sex," both of which I heartily recommend.

Reading the accounts in these books, I wonder why I bother making anything up at all! The realities of the era were so amazing that if I wrote some of them as fiction, people wouldn't believe me.

Meet the Author

Lynne Connolly was born in Leicester, England, and lived in her family's cobbler's shop with her parents and sister. She loves all periods of history, but her favorites are the Tudor and Georgian eras. She loves doing research and creating a credible story with people who lived in past ages. In addition to her Emperors of London series and The Shaws series, she writes several historical, contemporary and paranormal romance series. Visit her on the web at lynneconnolly.com, read her blog at lynneconnolly.blogspot.co.uk, find her on Facebook, and follow her on Twitter @lynneconnolly.